SYNTHERS & BEASTS

JUDY LIU

CONTENTS

To Mom and Dad, who always made sure my sister and I had home-cooked meals no matter how busy you were or how tight the money was.

AUTHOR'S NOTE

Where do I start? This story was inspired by so many things. At the base, it's my parents. From a young age, I was a very sickly child. I remember them taking me to numerous doctor visits, regular asthma and allergy specialist visits, and eventually an operation where the nice anesthesiologist let me choose what flavor I wanted in my sleeping gas (I chose strawberry).

One thing that stood out to me were the visits to the Traditional Chinese Medicine ("TCM") clinic where they prescribed various herbs. I remember the tasty and sweet bird's nest soup, some bitter liquids, and some soups with cooked worms in them (I found out later these worms are called 'cordyceps' and are basically the worm that was infected by the cordyceps fungus...). To this day, my parents still cook with some ingredients that are important in TCM like ginger, red dates, goji berries, and lotus seeds.

TCM aims to treat root cause rather than symptoms and focuses on a body's balance of various things that I don't understand, but I thought it'd be interesting to view it as colors for a new magic system in this book.

I had a lot of fun reading into TCM and incorporating its influences into this book, but I will preface that I'm not a doctor nor a licensed TCM practitioner so nothing in this book is medical advice. If you're curious or interested, please consult a professional.

As for some of the research, in addition to visiting some TCM clinics in person, I also read a translated work of a TCM keystone work, the *Huangdi Neijing*, also called *The Yellow Emperor's Classic of Medicine*.

At the end of the day, I wanted to bring a bit of that into a fantasy apothecary story, and how else to wrap it all up in a nice bow than with eastern mythical creatures we don't see as often in western literature? Other than the serpentine dragons of the East and phoenixes, there are serpents with human heads, cow-like creatures with human heads and nine eyes, dragons with turtle shells, fox spirits, sheep-like creatures with eyes on their backs. Too many to list!

I hope you enjoy this journey of self-discovery and acceptance and learning how to slow down in this world that keeps pushing us to move faster and faster.

PROLOGUE

"Tell me. What do you see?" Grandma Wen asked as Halla squinted at the neighbor's extended tongue.

"It's... a little pale," Halla observed. Grandma nodded but stayed silent. "And it seems to have a coating of yellow."

"What do the colors of the tongue coating typically mean?" Grandma Wen quizzed.

Halla furrowed her brows as she recalled her learnings. "There should be a thin white coating. A *thick* white coating could mean a buildup of liquids or something else. A yellow coating could mean too much heat is in the body."

"That's right. Now, what does the paleness indicate to you?"

"Maybe a lack of Qi?"

Grandma Wen closed her eyes and nodded before addressing the neighbor who'd since closed her mouth. "How have your energy levels been?"

"I've been quite tired, but I chalked it up to raising my kids," Neighbor Qianton responded.

Halla reached an index finger toward the neighbor's hand, but Grandma Wen slapped it away.

"And how have you been providing yourself sustenance?" Grandma Wen continued, unfazed by Halla's attempt to prod the neighbor. Halla shot Grandma a glance, nursing her stinging hand, but said nothing.

"Well, I do eat, of course," the neighbor responded defensively.

"Yes, but tell us of your diet," Grandma encouraged with patience.

The neighbor put a hand to her chin as if recalling her latest meal was a difficult task. "I had some fried chicken the other night. I often grab fast food since I'm so busy. Occasionally, I'll have a banana."

Grandma Wen looked at Halla expectantly. Now that Halla was eight years old, Grandma had been letting Halla get more involved with patient diagnoses.

Halla dutifully obliged. "From your description of your regular diet, you may be inducing inflammation of the body. That coupled with lack of Qi may explain your chronic fatigue," she said to the neighbor.

She shot another look at Grandma, lifting a hand toward the patient once more. The older woman subtly shook her head, and Halla retracted her hand with a pout.

"I'll prescribe some anti-inflammatory herbal balls and have our runner bring them to your house by the evening." Grandma stood in dismissal and proceeded to the inner garden of their house.

"This way, please." Halla led the neighbor to the front foyer—a foyer so large it was called the Hall of Central Harmony, which regularly hosted their guests. She itched to use *Synesthology* by touching the neighbor, but remembering her grandmother's earlier stern expression, kept her small hands clasped tightly together to prevent herself from being tempted.

After depositing the neighbor at the front with her mother to handle payments, Halla made her way to the inner garden where Grandma waited, ready to debrief. The inner garden was the heart of the Nuan estate, an expansive, open-air square courtyard enclosed by walkways and doors that led into the building. Because of the layout, almost every room on the estate had a door leading to the central courtyard or at least a window to look into it.

She found Grandma Wen sitting on a stone bench next to the small man-made river that ran through the courtyard. Halla instinctively squatted at the herb garden next to the small stream and started foraging. This was something she liked to do to keep herself occupied, and she'd always found it relaxing.

Grandma Wen and Halla sat quietly for several moments, Halla picking herbs, and Grandma, eyes closed, listening to the bubbling murmurs of the water.

"Grandma?" Halla finally broke the serene silence.

"Hmmm?" Grandma kept her eyes closed.

Halla kept her focus on the herb garden. "Why did you not let me touch the neighbor?"

"That's not just our neighbor, dear. That is a patient," Grandma corrected.

"Okay..." Halla drew out the word. "Why did you not let me touch our patient?"

"Why did you want to touch the patient, Halla?"

"To see the colors!" she chirped, perking up from her herb gathering and looking up at her grandmother.

Grandma Wen shook her head, and Halla frowned. "But you touch the patients and use your Synesthology all the time! Why can't I?"

"We don't do it to see the colors, Halla. We do this to diagnose our patients, which you still need to learn. Without understanding our art of traditional medicinal practices, you will not understand the colors you synth. Does that make sense?"

Halla's little face scrunched at the explanation. "That doesn't sound fun."

"We don't do this for fun, dear Halla," Grandma chided.

Halla had only recently started developing her synthing skills, and she didn't quite understand why she had to go through her grandmother's medical training with it yet. For her, it was simply fun seeing colors every time she touched someone and yelling them out before dashing off.

Grandma Wen sighed at Halla's silence and held out both hands. "Here, take my hands, and tell me what you see."

A glimmer shone in Halla's eyes as she eagerly took Grandma Wen's hands in her own. Immediately, a bright spring green overtook her vision, and she gasped, eyes darting around looking for more.

"Close your eyes first," Grandma instructed. "It makes it easier to focus." Halla did as she was told. "You're seeing an expanse of color, right?"

Halla nodded.

"Excellent," Grandma noted. "Now, focus on your stomach. Feel the energy there."

Halla's brows knit in concentration as the color she perceived in her mind transitioned from green to apricot orange and the field of vision narrowed until it was a ball of orange. "Whoa," she whispered. "I can control it."

"That's right. What you saw earlier when you first made contact with me is my body's base color. Once you focused on yourself, it became your own color because you're now sensing yourself."

Halla nodded in understanding, eyes still closed as she focused on the bright orange ball. She was trying to keep it still, but it kept breaking form to look more like an amoeba.

"Now, extend that energy from your stomach up your body, through your arms, and out to your fingertips. Good. From your fingertips, stretch that energy beyond them, and push it into me. Focus on the contact between our hands and traversing that, have it run through my body."

As Halla did as instructed, instead of a ball or formless color, she saw the color morph slowly into the shape of her grandmother in a sitting position. The color transformed into that first green she'd seen and molded into hands first, then arms, then Grandma's body and head, as if mapping her grandmother's body sitting on the bench. Halla gasped in awe.

"You see it, right?"

Halla opened her eyes and found her grandmother smiling warmly. She nodded frenetically.

Grandma Wen laughed. "You really are a natural, dearest. Okay. Close your eyes, and do it again."

As Halla practiced, Grandma Wen explained how this mapping of the body with their Synesthology was something advanced sensors in the medical field did back in the day.

"Doctor Wen!" A boy a little older than Halla ran into the courtyard. "I'm here to deliver medicine!" he announced with an air of self-importance Halla felt young boys held for no particular reason.

"Ah, yes. Halla, take the runner to the apothecary. The parcels with names will be on the left counter. Check with your mother whether she's prepared Neighbor Qianton's parcels. Otherwise, the runner will have to come back later." Grandma Wen released Halla's hands.

"Yes, Grandma!" Halla piped, though a little disappointed at her lesson being cut short.

She brought the boy to the apothecary in another wing of the home. It was one of her favorite places on their estate with the strings of drying persimmons hanging from the wooden ceiling beams and drawers filled with various scents. Stacks of flattened, square-shaped parcels lay on the counter with twine holding them closed; her mother had already finished packing the herb parcels and left them for delivery. Halla grabbed them for the runner. As she passed off the parcels, her hands brushed the boy's, and he immediately retracted his own. The packages tumbled to the floor.

"What are you doing!?" Halla demanded.

But the boy grabbed where their hands had touched as if he had been poisoned, eyes wide. That's when Halla noticed he was wearing thin, skin-colored gloves.

"I... I didn't want to synth," the boy stammered.

Halla cocked her head. *Why would someone not want to see the colors?* "Why not? The colors are fun."

He shook his head quickly. "No, it's not fun. It's blinding. I don't like it. That's why I got gloves." He stooped to grab the packages and then scampered out of the room.

Halla looked down at her own ungloved hands before running back to the courtyard.

"Grandma! Did you know the runner boy is also a synther?" she asked.

The older woman looked at her and sighed. "Yes, Tao is a synther."

"Why does he wear gloves, then?" Halla plopped herself at Grandma Wen's feet.

"Because he cannot control his abilities."

"But," Halla cocked her head, "can't he learn like I am?"

A flash of sadness seemed to pass behind the older woman's eyes. "His family isn't used to synthing. Both his parents wear gloves. They wouldn't know how to teach him. I heard when his abilities first manifested, he screamed and clawed at his eyes every time he touched something organic, as if he were being burned."

"Could we help him, Grandma?" Halla tugged on her grandmother's pants.

"I wouldn't teach him our knowledge, but I did offer to teach him how to control the synthing like I did with your mother." Grandma Wen closed her eyes. "They refused. Said it'll be easier with gloves." Halla pouted, but before she could dwell on it further, Grandma Wen took her hands, reigniting that flash of green. "Don't worry about it, dear one. Let's continue our practice."

Halla perked up at the thought of seeing colors, the boy immediately forgotten. After Halla's fifth try mapping Grandma's body, she noticed a small blob of earthen red among the green in Grandma Wen's chest.

Grandma nodded in approval when Halla brought it up to her. "You'll have to learn more about the body and organs so you know where that is, but that is my lungs. I've started developing a cough and have some dampness there."

Halla opened her eyes. "I haven't heard you cough all day, Grandma!"

The older woman's eyes twinkled. "I simply haven't coughed around you, Halla. And that's why our family's skills are so important. You won't be able to be with every patient every hour of the day. You can't observe them all the time. Our synthing and knowledge provides a window into their bodies."

Halla's eyes widened. "Did I just diagnose you with my synthing?"

Grandma gave her a wide grin. "You did. Your first case with Synesthology!" Halla jumped in celebration, but before she could continue chanting her successes, Grandma raised a hand. "This diagnosis is not fully complete, Halla. You need to prescribe me something to address this."

Ah, that's right. Halla settled back into the grass and cleared her throat. "For dampness," she recited from memory, "we must strengthen the spleen. To eliminate the dampness and restore harmony to the body, one can incorporate roasted root vegetables like sweet potatoes with warming foods like ginger or onions into one's diet."

"Starting with diet is good. A good diet is crucial to maintaining balance within the body." Grandma Wen nodded to herself. "Speaking of diet," Grandma gave a big smile, "I have your favorite poached autumn pear dessert inside after a hard morning's work."

Halla hopped excitedly. "Really?"

She could practically taste the poached steamed pear, jujubes, and goji berries with rock sugar. It made for a traditional light and refreshing dessert. This was a home remedy for coughs, moistening the lungs and soothing dry throats, but in the Nuan household, it was also a treat.

"We will end your first synthing lesson here." Grandma patted Halla's hand, each pat resulting in a splash of green across Halla's vision. "Continue reading and memorizing the books I gave you. Did you have any other questions about this case or Neighbor Qianton's case?"

Halla thought for a moment before turning back to her grandmother. "About Neighbor Qianton, why do you have our patients tell you things you already know?"

"What do you mean, dearest?"

"Well, you already knew what the neighbor's diet consisted of, right? Just by touch, and you had taken her pulse earlier. Why did you ask her to tell you what she's been eating when you already knew?"

Grandma turned her head toward the stream as a distant look fell over her eyes. "One of the earliest practitioners in our lineage openly used her skills for the good of her community, only to be reported for black arts usage and subsequently used as a scapegoat for a politician's wrongdoing."

When Grandma broke her gaze from the stream and looked at Halla, she saw the young girl was gaping at her, aghast. "That doesn't happen anymore these days, of course. Synesthology and synthers are widely seen and accepted now that it's commonplace. Not many manifested it back then." Grandma laughed before her countenance darkened again. "Since then, we hold that story close to our hearts as a lesson in general, and it would do you good to learn from it as well."

Halla didn't quite understand what there was to learn from this story other than how she'd never want to live in the past, especially as a synther. "What else is there to learn from this story if people openly accept our skills and abilities now? We aren't the only ones in the world with the arts."

Grandma *tsk*ed at her. "Our family is not the only one, of course. But our line is one of the highest regarded medicinal arts synthing houses. Do not downplay what runs in your veins." Halla looked away, chastised. "Plus," Grandma heaved a sigh, "people often don't want to hear from others. If I had used my Synesthology and immediately told Neighbor Qianton that she's been eating too many fried foods causing inflammation, with her personality, you know she'd get defensive first, saying something like, 'How would you know? I haven't eaten it *that* often!' Then it's a game of 'he said, she said'. Sometimes, it's easier to have the person admit it themselves first."

Halla nodded, not quite understanding but thinking it sounded like her arguments with her mother.

"One day, you will carry this knowledge to help our people, my dear Halla."

Halla paused and looked up at Grandma's round face, the fun of seeing colors suddenly overtaken by this looming mass of knowledge awaiting her. "But what of Mother and Brother? We all have this knowledge. And what about our abilities? Can't we all use it to diagnose people?"

"Bah." Grandma waved a hand. "Sure, we're all in this family business. But your mother has always had more of a knack for finances, your father is useless in this area and clumsy, and your brother (bless his hardworking heart) has inherited your father's clumsiness. Clumsiness does not make for a good practitioner, despite having the synther art. Furthermore, without knowledge, our ability is useless. You wouldn't have known what that red color in me was if you didn't know how the human body is made, nor what recommendations to give me if you did not memorize those medical books I gave you."

Halla felt a weight settle on her shoulders, and the thought of seeing colors didn't seem as fun as it had a few moments ago. "So, it's all down to me?"

Grandma held Halla's gaze with clear brown eyes. "Yes, Halla. You're the only one in the family with the capacity to carry all I know. Our family knowledge of traditional medicine is unmatched in addition to our abilities, and no modern medicine can hold its light to what we know. What we know is holistic, an interaction with the world and environment. We're not just cold observation and isolation, nor are we machines. We are a product of the conjunction of how everything interacts and why. We look at the tongue, yes, but the tongue is a window into the body's internals. The pulse tells us more than heartbeat—it tells us the health of the person, whether they could be with child, how they may be emotionally, if they're lying." Her tone took on an edge at that last word before reverting back to her usual pleasant tone. "We look at herbs and understand their properties and grow them ourselves. This knowledge is valuable. It cannot be lost."

Halla started twisting two blades of grass together. "Why not open a school, Grandma?"

Grandma Wen shot her a stern look. "This knowledge is not for outsiders."

In a quieter voice, Halla asked, "What if I can't hold it all? Who can I ask questions to when you're gone?"

In a flow of movement abnormal for someone of Grandma's age, Grandma kneeled beside Halla, cupping Halla's face with her leathery-warm hands, the scent of dried chrysanthemums that always clung to her filling the space. "Oh, Halla. You can hold it all. Because you must."

CHAPTER 1

Halla stared at the golden font on the top of her flagship store with a pounding heart: The Green Thumb.

This was it. This was opening day.

Her flagship store was a sparkling white building with large windows on both sides of an automatically sliding door—exactly the way she'd always pictured. Slats jutted out of the top of the building like multiple massive fins breaking the ocean surface. Since the weather was sunny today, Halla set the rooftop to sunlight mode, the roof breaking into long segments and turning sideways to open the ceiling and let in natural lighting, like blinds of a window. Fresh air flowed through as a gentle breeze.

> "NUAN FAMILY PRODIGY OPENS PRACTICE"

The newspapers had been filled with such headlines and lauded praises of modernity, speed, efficiency, and accuracy of diagnoses for Halla. Halla had successfully married the traditional and the modern techniques and mindsets of medicine at the young age of twenty-two. Not only that, she'd standardized it and created a business to make it more accessible, and the public was enamored by her and this great feat. Halla felt a swell of pride whenever she saw these articles, but there was one person whose opinion mattered the most.

Today was the day Halla could finally show her family what she had been working toward for the past eight years. She had moved out of the Nuan estate to attend a traditional medicine vocational school in the capital all those years ago and had always attributed her passion for medicine to her grandmother. Halla shuddered, remembering the rage that had flowed the night her and her grandmother had argued about her decision to leave. Halla hadn't wanted to take over the family business in the countryside. She'd wanted the city and modern amenities, so she carved her own path, despite her grandmother's disapproval.

Now, as Halla waited for her family to arrive at her new shop, she couldn't help but tug at her sleeve, worrying about what Grandma might think.

The telltale quick steps of the family *ranyi* pulling the Nuan carriage—and a few gasps from pedestrians—made Halla's heart speed. Most people used cars to get around these days, so it wasn't common to see pulled carts on the road, much less one pulled by a ranyi. From a distance, Halla saw sunlight glint off silver-green scales as it trotted on its six-taloned feet, an ornate wooden carriage in tow with her mother holding the reins. She waved, and Halla smiled.

A squeak sounded next to her, and Halla turned to find her mousy employee, Cerul, half-hiding behind her.

"What is that?" Cerul stared at the glimmering creature. "A legged snake?"

Halla chuckled. "That's a fish actually, just with a snake's head. A ranyi, to be precise."

"So, your entire family is here?" Cerul's tone held an edge that Halla chalked up to one being starstruck. The Nuan family was well-known in the medicinal field, especially as one of the few families left that actively synthed in the occupation. Halla was the first Nuan to step out of the family business and start her own without relying on synthing.

"Just my grandmother and mother," Halla said.

Cerul's hand slowly came up to her heart as the fanged beast came into full view. "Ranyis still exist? I thought they were just myths."

"Well," Halla put a hand to her chin in thought, "I don't think the ones my family has are pure ranyi. The ones we raise are descendents of original ranyi that we've domesticated to an extent."

"Your family *raises* these beasts?"

Halla shot her an exasperated look, tired of explaining everything when there were more important matters on her mind.

"Even though they're fish, does the snake head allow them to breathe on land? Do they have lungs?" Cerul continued peppering her with questions that she ignored.

"Halla!" her mother greeted over the sounds of their grunting ranyi and carriage-on-cobblestone.

Halla's mother was dressed smartly in cream trousers and a long, loose top that flowed to her ankles. Her hair, cut to her ears in a fashionable short style, had subtle brown highlights that turned a slight red in direct light. Her natural-black hair gave off a green sheen as was common for those in the Nuan bloodline.

Cerul nudged Halla. "You didn't mention your mom is so... modern and chic."

She stared at Mrs. Nuan's dazzling visage, eyes stopping at the dangling kingfisher feather earrings that matched the cerulean blue of Mrs. Nuan's top.

Halla rolled her eyes. "Just because my family practices traditional medicine doesn't mean they live in the Ceramic Age."

Cerul leaned forward, trying to catch a better glimpse of the Nuan family from behind Halla, nearly pressing her body flush against Halla's in the process.

"And can you please give me some space?" Halla demanded. *Just because you work for me doesn't mean we get all chummy.*

As Cerul backed away apologetically, Halla's mother climbed down from the carriage and pulled Halla into a hug. "It's so good to see you!"

Halla mumbled similar sentiments but suddenly felt her hands go clammy. This was her day to show them why she left the estate. Her day to show them the path she carved for herself. Her day to show Grandma what she'd built to continue the family legacy in her own way. Although she was happy to see her bubbling mother, she couldn't stop thinking about the other woman inside the carriage—the one whose opinion mattered the most.

"Let me fetch your grandmother," her mother noted as she headed back to the carriage.

Halla called her parking attendant. "Tomas, could you put up my family's carriage?"

The man looked at her and then stared at the ranyi now tugging petulantly at its reins with its large fanged head, flanked with pectoral fins where the head met the rest of its six-foot-long body.

"You're telling *me* to valet park this *live* thing?" he asked incredulously.

"Yeah." She waved off his concerns. "Just get him to park the carriage next to the cars, and then stable him. Give him enough room for two parking spots, and bring three buckets of water for him. It's like leading a horse. He won't bite."

She headed toward the carriage to greet her grandmother as she dismissed him. Tomas mumbled something about having never dealt with horses, and that he drove cars for a reason, before lifting himself onto the carriage and situating himself. The ranyi was having fun pulling the reins away from Tomas. Halla stifled a laugh; she remembered that the ranyis were always particular, but she hadn't recalled any being so mischievous.

Mrs. Nuan had opened the carriage door and pulled a set of stairs down. Halla stood next to the carriage but refrained from looking inside. She didn't know if she was ready to meet the matriarch's eyes yet.

"Have we arrived?" a familiar but weathered voice called out. How long had it been since Halla had spoken with her grandmother?

"Yes, Mother. This is Halla's store." Mrs. Nuan prompted Halla to speak up with a quick nod. Halla opened her mouth but found it dry.

Before she could gather her voice in greeting, her grandmother stuck her head out. "Halla, dearest!"

Grandma Wen descended the steps, and before Halla knew it, she was embraced by the smaller matronly woman. Grandma was dressed in a similar fashion to Mrs. Nuan but in a pale green, and she matched it with a jade pendant around her neck. She released Halla and held her at arm's length, surveying her.

"Grandma! Are you synthing me?" Halla wrenched her hands back.

She didn't need her grandmother nagging her about whether she was taking care of herself or getting enough sleep. Especially not on opening day. Halla knew her colors wouldn't be in balance—a combination of stress, never enough time, and a few too many meals from the local convenience store. It was something Grandma, with her superior synthing abilities, would be able to see in an instant.

"Halla," Grandma chided. "I can't just look at my granddaughter? Besides, there's no synthing through your shirt."

Halla looked away in embarrassment. In the rush of everything, she hadn't been paying such close attention.

"Of course, you'd know this if you didn't move to the capital and instead, took more of my lessons," Grandma Wen threw in lightly, but it was like a punch to Halla's stomach.

Halla closed her eyes and took a breath. *It's because I left the estate and went to proper school that I now have this store and have made a name for myself. Not just off of our family name.*

"Grandma," she put her arm around the older woman's back, "come inside. I have some hot tea for you both while I take you on a tour of The Green Thumb."

"Hey, Halla?" a voice called from behind her.

She turned and found three of her parking attendants trying to get the reins back from the ranyi.

"Do you have any tips for us?" Tomas called as he jumped, trying to grab the reins from the ranyi's mouth. He'd gotten off the carriage and was now standing next to the beast. The creature stood as tall as a standard horse and was stretching its neck even higher so the attendants couldn't reach its head.

"Here." Halla's mother ran back toward the group and slapped the scaled creature lightly on its side. "Mogi, you behave, or we won't take you out again." At that, the creature lowered his large head, giving Tomas a slitted glare as if annoyed he got him in trouble and opened his mouth for them to grab the reins. "There." Mrs. Nuan handed the reins to Tomas and ran back to Halla and Grandma for the grand tour.

Upon entering through the sliding doors, they were met with the expanse of the store with sparkling floors and spacious aisles, customers already milling about. Halla noticed Grandma Wen's frown immediately. Memories of their last argument—about what was "best" for Halla—surfaced, but Halla pushed them down.

"As you can see, we pride ourselves in the perfect marriage of tradition and modernity and aim to bring nature into the store while you peruse." Halla indicated the open, slatted ceiling with a hand. "We have air filters crafted and imbued by medical synthers built into the ceiling to filter the air and reduce indoor air pollution, as well as state-of-the-art viewing orbs created by imbuers to deter theft. On our shelves, we have many traditional concoctions that we've successfully condensed into pills or other forms that enable us to quickly mass-produce at affordable prices to the general public. Everything is packaged and boxed in the back."

Halla glanced nervously at her family but could read nothing from their gazes other than Grandma's frown, so she continued. "This in-house process with our proprietary recipes and machines allows us to also quickly change recipes when needed or add bespoke alterations for certain patients."

Mrs. Nuan nodded approvingly, scanning the new store while sipping the chrysanthemum tea an employee had brought. Grandma Wen, however, stayed silent.

Halla pointed to the far left corner with a counter. "Additionally, we have hired practitioners, and patients can check in over there before being taken to our examination rooms in the back. Up front," Halla directed their attention to the corner to their right next to the main doors, "is the waiting area. People can either peruse our goods or wait here for their appointment."

The waiting corner was fitted with a long breakfast bar table that ran the length of the window so customers who sat there could look outside to the streets. It also had a few plush chairs arranged like a small living room.

"Very well-designed," Halla's mother praised as they moved forward.

As Halla took them through the store, Grandma Wen frowned and *tsked* while examining the ingredients lists on the merchandise. She was juxtaposed by Halla's mother who skipped and gushed over everything, practically rubbing her face in affection on the Inventory Assistant 3000 Halla had recently purchased.

After showing them the storefront, Halla brought them to the back kitchen, where the goods were prepared and packed, and through one of the examination rooms. She'd wanted to show them more, but with each passing second of Grandma's silence and disapproving looks, Halla found herself wanting them out of her store sooner. Halla finished their tour within an hour, faster than the allotted three she gave herself. She settled her mother and grandmother at the front waiting area.

"Would you like any more tea?"

"No, honey, I'm good." Her mother beamed. "What you've built is fantastic."

"Bah!" Grandma Wen said.

The other two women both turned to her in shock at the small outburst. Halla felt her patience fraying.

"If you have something to say, just say it," Halla said. The matriarch turned to her.

"Don't speak to your grandmother like that," Mrs. Nuan interjected. "I'm sure your grandmother didn't mean anything by it. It was just a long ride over, right?"

Mrs. Nuan shot Grandma Wen a meaningful glance, but the older lady didn't acknowledge it, continuing with her inscrutable look at Halla.

"I think Grandma did mean it, Mom. I mean, have you not seen how she's been acting? I'm over this passive-aggressiveness, Grandma. Just tell me what's on your mind. Let's get it out."

An employee bringing a tray of fresh tea overheard the tone and immediately turned back to the kitchen.

Grandma Wen leaned back in her chair and crossed her legs, judgment written all over her face. "Have you been synthing, Halla?"

"What?"

"How do you diagnose your patients, Halla?"

A pit formed in Halla's stomach. "With observations driven by knowledge of traditional medicine, of course. The standard taught in traditional medical schools."

Grandma waved one hand. "Sure. Things anyone can learn as long as they get into these schools."

Halla furrowed her brows. "Exactly. As long as they *can get into* the school. I didn't just go to any school, Grandma. I went to the Lianou Academy of Traditional Medicine. You know that's the top school in the territories." She had studied and worked hard to get top grades for acceptance.

"It's still a school anyone can go to," Grandma said dismissively. "But our family knowledge? That's something you can't get anywhere else. As sensors, we're able to pinpoint maladies or imbalances of the body by seeing colors that don't belong."

"Yeah, yeah." Now it was Halla's turn to wave off Grandma Wen. "The body is comprised of a base color with complimentary colors throughout the body in various areas when in balance, which means the body is healthy. Any other colors indicate imbalance," Halla recited from memory. "I know our 'family knowledge' is priceless or whatnot, but I did learn from you before I left, didn't I?"

"We never completed your education. If the skill is cultivated, some can extend that to sensing whether a person's mentality is balanced or picking up fleeting nuances. Without training, however, you would simply see the colors and not know the meaning behind them. "

"I did train with you, and I do know the meanings. I completed the rest of my education on my own. There's no need to sense-map when I have modern and traditional medicine," Halla retorted hotly. "And look where I am now." She opened her arms. "I have a flagship store, hired employees, a sturdy clientele base, and I'm projected to see more patients in a week than you ever had in a month."

Halla's mother gasped as the matriarch shook her head, lines forming between her brows in disappointment. "You know nothing, Halla. You were supposed to inherit all of our knowledge. Instead, you left prematurely, and anytime you came back, you refused to take synthing lessons from me."

"I don't need synthing," Halla said forcefully. "No one sense synths anymore anyway."

Synesthology was rather ubiquitous, the ability found in one-in-every-four, with sense synthing being the most common of the Synesthology Triangle. For the majority of the synther populace, Synesthology abilities were an additional *thing* to live with, and seeing a splash of color suddenly was part of the norm. In fact, over the last few decades, the number of professional medicinal sensors was dwindling as technology improved and people opted for machine-driven diagnoses. Some sensors wore gloves in their day-to-day lives to avoid contact and the inconvenience of colors. Something Grandma seemed unwilling to acknowledge.

"You taught me how to control my synthing and the basics," Halla continued. "I went to school, and I'm a doctor. I can still use basic synthing, but I don't need it for my job." She shook her head. "What do you mean that I 'refused' lessons from you?"

"There is so much more to synthing. Anytime I tried speaking with you when you visited, you told all of us you were busy and shut yourself in your room, Halla. If we tried more, you'd get upset, telling us you didn't have time for chatting and that you're under extreme pressure and trying to do well in school." Grandma sighed deeply. "I know many think the crafters and imbuers are more valuable since sensors are the most common of the Synesthology Triangle, but the refinement and cultivation of our abilities take time and training. There is so much more you can do with our abilities."

That gave Halla pause. She remembered studying all the time because she had to prove leaving home was the right decision by having good grades, but did Grandma actually try teaching her? She thought she'd learned everything she needed from Grandma. Was there really more she could be doing with synthing that her education couldn't cover? She couldn't quite believe that. Her store's popularity was evidence of that. She turned to her mother who gave her a raised brow and shrug.

Halla turned back to her grandmother. "Even if that's true, I was working toward this dream. I had reasons."

Grandma arched her brow. "And you couldn't spend more time at home to learn our family knowledge? Learn how to use what you were born with?"

"What do you want me to say?" Halla blurted. "That I should have stayed home? No. It was because of my decisions and my work that I've created this. I'm a doctor. Isn't that what you've always wanted, Grandma? I'm like you and our ancestors before. Why can't you just be proud of me?" At this point, her voice was loud enough that a few nearby customers cast them nervous glances.

Halla's rage boiled. She hadn't known exactly what to expect at her family's arrival, but this wasn't it. She'd hoped that Grandma would at least feign happiness, or even interest. Halla should have known better.

"You are not like us, Halla. You do not synth medically at all. In fact, you shirk synthing. You were born with a natural talent your mother and brother weren't blessed with."

"Wow, thanks, Mom," Mrs. Nuan muttered under her breath.

"Yet, instead of embracing it," Grandma continued, "you ignore it and leave. And now you say you're just like our Nuan practitioners? You do not practice the way we do. You've tossed your talents and lineage, and you use our name to push your personal ideals while disregarding the very thing that matters. Your lack of knowledge of synthing could put you at risk."

"At risk of what?" Halla challenged.

Grandma Wen pursed her lips before responding. "There's a lot you don't know, and a lot of dangers with other synthing families—"

"Synesthology is dying, Grandma. These families aren't around, and if they are, they are dwindling," Halla interrupted.

She couldn't believe Grandma was being so dramatic, trying to scare her into taking synthing more seriously. Pressure mounted at Halla's temples, and she clenched her fists.

"Why are you so dissatisfied with me?" she managed through gritted teeth. "After all the work I put in to be self-sufficient, to pursue medicine, to make you proud?"

Grandma simply shook her head, and the silence was infuriating.

"You know what? You can—"

"Will you look at the time!" Mrs. Nuan suddenly exclaimed and stood. "Halla, we must be on our way back. Please do remember to visit!"

She moved to help collect Grandma and led her toward the door. Halla followed them out, her anger simmering just below the surface.

Upon their exit, Tomas exhaled in relief and ran off to fetch Mogi and the carriage. With how fast he brought them out, Halla suspected he didn't bother to untether the ranyi from the carriage. Or he'd had so much difficulty managing the ranyi he'd ended up leaving everything hooked up.

As Mrs. Nuan helped Grandma Wen up the stairs and into the carriage, the older woman looked over her shoulder at Halla. Halla was expecting another disapproving frown, but instead, as the sun's rays hit Grandma Wen's face, she thought she caught a glistening streak down the matriarch's cheek. But then Grandma ducked inside, closing the door with finality.

Halla's chest tightened. It was her business's opening day, and *that* was the attitude her grandmother was going to have? Halla had given up years of her life to this venture. Grandma could have *at least* pretended to be proud.

"Sweetheart?" her mother addressed her. "Your store is lovely. I know Grandma can be… difficult. But she has your best interests at heart. I think she had a lot of expectations since you took to synthing so naturally, and probably because I wasn't very good at it ever." Mrs. Nuan's lips thinned at the memory. "She had to come to terms that maybe it wasn't meant for me, but when you were born and showed an affinity for it, she had a renewed hope. You were her joy. You still are her joy. She just has a hard time accepting that maybe you weren't meant to carry the knowledge, too. Give her time."

Halla thought about how fun synthing was when she'd first discovered it, but how that was quickly overwritten by the pressure to stuff everything her grandmother had to teach into her head.

"That doesn't give her an excuse to be rude," Halla muttered. "And I'm open to carrying the knowledge. I was just too busy. I really wanted to do my own thing. Not be shadowed by our family name."

"I know, Halla." Her mother cradled Halla's head in both her hands and looked into her eyes. "Even if Grandma won't say it, know that I am proud of you. I'm so proud of what you've created for yourself." She kissed Halla's forehead as Halla smiled gratefully at her.

Mrs. Nuan bounded toward the helm of the carriage and took the reins. "Don't be a stranger, Halla. Come visit for the holidays soon, and remember: It's fine to not want to carry the family knowledge. At the end of the day, Synesthology is commonplace anyway. A lot of people don't like their synthing abilities. You wouldn't be missing much." She turned her attention to the restless ranyi. "Mogi, let's go home!"

Halla waved after the departing carriage, considering her mother's last words. She appreciated that her mother acknowledged the work she put into herself, but the last part about Synesthology didn't quite sit right with her. Halla had always enjoyed synthing. She remembered the joy of seeing the colors when she was younger. As Grandma's lessons got more boring with all the synthing practice, Halla had grown to dread them. After moving out at fourteen to attend the best traditional medicine school in the city, she simply hadn't seen the need to further cultivate the skill as she got older and focused on her studies. If she was able to diagnose patients with her traditional medicine knowledge, why would she need synthing? Especially, as her mother had said, when synthing was so commonplace? But did that mean she didn't like synthing?

Halla looked down at her hands. It's true she hadn't tried sense-mapping a person's body in a long time. When she had asked her teachers about it in class long ago, they told her it was an outdated method of diagnosis and not to waste her time when doctors and hospitals had the medical machines and devices, like the MRI machine, for that. "Just focus on our traditional practices because patients who come to us are looking for this," one teacher had said. "Basic sensing is helpful, sure. But there's no need to hone that skill when we have machines that can show us every detail inside the body." A few other students had snickered at the time, and Halla retracted her raised hand in embarrassment at her silly question.

Halla missed synthing, but she found no need for it in her daily life, having tamped down that curiosity after attending school in the capital. She thought of her youth, practicing with her grandmother, and felt the anger build again.

"Grandma can get off her soapbox and stop projecting her dreams onto me. Instead of being proud, she gives harsh words all the time about how I should have never left. I don't need that energy," she muttered to herself as she spun to head back inside.

Despite her mother's requests, Halla did not return home for the holidays a few weeks later. Business was booming, and she was still angry at Grandma Wen. Nothing she did ever seemed to please Grandma, so what was the point of going back? Halla preferred to protect her peace. She called her parents to wish them a happy spring festival, but she didn't ask to speak to Grandma.

The phone shook in Halla's hands. She was numb, a ringing in her ears as she processed what she'd just heard. It'd been three months since her family visited The Green Thumb, and she'd spoken to her family during the last holiday, so she had thought this would be a usual check-in call.

She was very wrong.

Halla didn't know what to think as her mother relayed the news, sobbing. Grandma had always seemed healthy, especially with her medical knowledge and abilities. How was it possible for her to suddenly pass like that? Halla thought of Grandma's clear, brown eyes and warm, leathery hands—hands that smelled of sunsoaked chrysanthemums. Hands that taught her the feel of herbs between her fingers. Hands that taught her how to boil teas and that heated metal could be hot. Hands that taught her how to synth and feel colors. Hands that held hers while strolling through the grassy courtyard when she would lead Grandma to the various plants or bugs she discovered.

"There's no way." Halla sat down to steady herself. "How did we not know? There's no way she's gone," she muttered, putting the phone down.

Could I have caught whatever this was if I synthed her? Why didn't I try when I saw her? I could have done it even in passing if I held her hand. She looked up at the ceiling.

She knew exactly what Grandma would be saying if she were witnessing this moment from the heavens. "See? Now, all this family knowledge is completely lost! You should have never left. Bah." But then she thought of those warm days in the apothecary, feeling the satisfying crunch of grinding herbs under her pestle as Grandma talked with neighbors.

Halla squeezed her eyes shut, her jumbled emotions morphing. How could she leave like that? How could she simply leave after the way their last interaction went? How could she leave without giving Halla a chance to make up with her? How could Halla have let this happen? Her body shuddered involuntarily. She didn't know who she was more angry with: her grandmother or herself. She remembered the glistening streak on Grandma's face as she entered the carriage that last day Halla saw her, realization dawning.

"You knew," she said quietly at first. "You knew! Why didn't you tell anyone?" Halla clutched the armrests of the chair as the heaving sobs came. She thought of all the words left unsaid between them. "How could you leave before passing all your knowledge like you always said?" she whispered between tears into the silence. "How could you?"

CHAPTER 2

It had been two years since Grandma Wen passed. Whenever a whiff of dried chrysanthemums hit Halla or she thought of synthing, she felt a pang in her chest. Halla paid her annual respects, but she avoided thinking of Grandma. Besides, she had enough on her mind with her business.

Over the last few years, word had spread of her quality ingredients and acute sense for maladies and ailings. With The Green Thumb's numbers, Halla's investors had pushed for expansion, so this year, Halla had opened her second location and took a step back from treating patients to focus more on the business. Instead of running her fingers along drawers upon drawers of dried ingredients as she'd done since she was four years old, she was now running her fingers across a keyboard, crunching numbers and employee salaries. Her investors advised her to hire another accountant for the second store or someone for human resources, but Halla liked to oversee everything, especially when it was first starting.

There was a knock at Halla's open door, and Cerul, now a practitioner, poked her head in. "A man's asking to see you."

Without taking her eyes off her laptop, Halla responded, "You know I don't take patients anymore."

Cerul's eyes shifted nervously. "Yeah... he's quite insistent."

"You can handle it, Cerul."

"He says he has to see you."

Halla closed her eyes for a moment. She thought of all the tasks she still had to complete today: the budget for quarter four, inventory in the kitchens, potential brand collaborations. All things she couldn't do if she was taking clients, which shouldn't have been a problem since that was no longer Halla's job.

She shot Cerul an exasperated look. "Why did I hire you if you can't help me handle difficult customers?"

Cerul opened her mouth to retort when Brandus, a practitioner Halla hired a year ago, stopped in the doorway.

"You're the one who's supposed to help us if we encounter difficult customers, Boss." Emphasis on 'boss'.

Halla threw up her hands. She tolerated Brandus' quippy remarks because he was particularly good at acupuncture, and he usually wasn't wrong with his diagnoses and prescriptions. Deep down, she also appreciated his bluntness, but she would never admit that.

"All right. I'm going. Tell me at least one of you asked who he is." She was met with blank stares.

A surge of irritation sparked within her and was about to let loose when Brandus snatched Cerul's arm and sped away. "Not our problem! Thanks, Boss!"

With nowhere to vent, Halla stalked out of her office and through the door leading to the expanse of her store. The Green Thumb was doing well, with a healthy number of customers perusing the aisles. There were older mothers looking through a list to find the best concoction for their expecting daughters, women looking for youth-retention products, men pretending to casually browse while actually looking for hair loss remedies, and young girls squealing at some of her packaging. Packaging was everything these days.

The man in question was not hard to miss. He was immaculately dressed in a dark suit and bowler hat, and he wore shades inside. Who wore shades inside? Her flagship store had open air slots to bring in the sun, but it definitely did not warrant sunglasses. He sat atop a barstool in the waiting corner of the shop, stoic and unmoving.

As she walked toward him, a few within the store pointed at her.

"It's her! The celebrity apothecary!"

Halla had learned to ignore them, but she secretly enjoyed being identified in such a way. It made her feel important, like all that work she'd put in actually mattered... at least to someone.

The man saw her approach and stood, removing his sunglasses. Halla was surprised at his full height. He was probably taller than anyone in the shop, standing at well over six feet. *At least he has some manners.*

"Ah, Miss Nuan. Thank you for seeing me." He took off his bowler hat and dipped his head.

"Please, call me Halla." She was not partial to being associated with her family name. She was *not* her grandmother. Her chest tightened at the thought before she pushed it away. "What is it I can help you with that my fellow practitioners could not?" She couldn't help the annoyance that seeped into her tone.

"As you wish, Halla." He smiled in a way that didn't meet his eyes. "I have a sensitive matter to discuss with you. Might we take this somewhere more private?"

Do I have a choice? "What is this about?"

He maintained his lifeless smile. "I'm afraid I can't say in public. Please, Halla. I promise this will be worth your time."

She didn't like being made to do things in her own domain, but she was curious so she turned and indicated for him to follow her to one of her conference rooms, where she usually met investors or business partners.

Once she shut the glass door, she turned back to him.

"How may I assist you, Mr. ...?"

"Thrum. I work for the Urquart family."

A muffled gasp sounded from the closed door. Both Halla and Mr. Thrum swiveled to find Cerul and Brandus, hands over mouths and wide-eyed, peeking through the glass. Halla rolled her eyes and stood to frost the glass door and enable soundproofing.

"Excuse my employees, Mr. Thrum. You can rest assured that I'll speak with them afterward, and that they will keep this quiet. Now, when you say the

Urquart family—as in *Lord* Urquart? The founding family of the Urquart territory?" Halla asked.

Mr. Thrum settled back into his seat. "The very one. His son is very ill. We've gone to various doctors and have been told the same thing: He only has a few more months to live. Lord Urquart and his wife have just about lost hope when we heard of you and your apothecary."

Halla straightened, intrigued. "Oh?"

She loved a good puzzle, and she'd heard of the Urquart son, but mostly that he was confined to the family estate due to poor health. She didn't know that he was near death. *I'd keep that under wraps, too, if I were in the family. It would show weakness to other governing territories.*

Her mind was already whizzing with what this mystery case could be. "Bring him. What are his symptoms?"

Thrum shook his head. "The young lord has been sick for years, and we seldom bring him out. If we do, it must be done with the utmost care as he's very weak."

Halla frowned. "Then how could I diagnose him? Should I come to the estate?"

Thrum shook his head more fervently. "The family is very private. We *can* bring him, but due to the sensitive nature and the care that must be put in, they sent me to inquire. We need to be assured that you will keep the matter confidential. You'll need to sign an NDA."

A non-disclosure agreement? "You offend my expertise. As a practicing apothecary, of course we keep all of our patient records confidential."

Thrum was unfazed. "In our area and with the family's standing, it never hurts to be additionally... cautious."

Halla's brows knit together. *If this man wanted to talk shop, then let's talk shop,* she thought before responding. "Signing an NDA is no issue as long as there are caveats for the essential people of my business like my investors, legal counsel, and accountant. Might we discuss payment then?"

Thrum waved her question away. "That won't be a problem. You name it, and it's yours. Fifty percent initially and the final fifty percent upon full cure. We have it all stipulated in our contract." He produced a leather briefcase from who-knows-where and pulled out a folder. He slid it across the sleek glass table to Halla. "You have twenty-four hours to review the contract. I'll be back tomorrow to hear your answer."

She put a hand on the folder and narrowed her eyes. "This feels quite rushed, Mr. Thrum."

"Time is of the essence for Young Lord Urquart," he said smoothly.

I'm sure he could wait a little longer than twenty-four hours, though. "Very well. I'll send these to my lawyer to review."

"Excellent." Thrum stood to leave and extended a hand. "I look forward to, what I hope, is the answer we want to hear."

Halla flashed him a saccharine smile as she deftly placed an index finger on his wrist to feel his pulse within the handshake, something any traditional practitioner could do. She frowned at what she felt but schooled her expression immediately, hoping Thrum didn't catch the change. "That answer will be dependent on your contract, seeing as you appear unwilling to negotiate and have put me on a tight timeline."

Thrum paid her no heed and turned to leave, briefcase in hand—a briefcase she was *sure* Thrum was not carrying when he entered her shop. The whole situation felt odd: with Thrum, how he presented the Urquart case, his magic briefcase, how fast it was proceeding, and the fact his pulse felt... *industrial? Too perfect?* It had been a while since she synthed, but Halla had tried after searching his pulse and saw no colors—something even the most basic synthers would be able to do. His pulse was steady and smelled mechanical, but she wasn't sure what that meant either. She'd never encountered a pulse like his before. The closest thing she could think of was the medical dolls at the Academy, but Thrum was very much alive.

Halla's mind screamed at her to not take the case, but she was intrigued. An illness no one had been able to identify was like an itch she had to scratch, and she thought of the exponential business it could bring if she successfully brought the heir back to full health. *Imagine the headlines for that. Even Grandma would have had to be impressed.*

Another pang. But she was curious about one more thing. "Mr. Thrum?"

He turned at the door and looked back.

"Why me?"

He raised his brows. "We heard that your diagnoses have no wrong. And that you prescribe the swiftest cure. Surely, that's not all a marketing ploy."

Halla narrowed her eyes in defiance, her grandmother's constant chiding ringing in her ears. "You think I'd spin up lies to feed the media? All of those anecdotes are true, and those are patients who willingly went to the media to talk about it."

"Well, if you are as good as they say, then perhaps we have hope just yet. And that's why we came to you. I trust you won't disappoint us."

Halla clenched her jaw. How dare he question her expertise? She didn't do all those years of schooling, claw through the most intense clinics and apothecaries with late nights, and forego holidays with family for this kind of treatment.

"I *am* as good as they say. And I will successfully diagnose Young Lord Urquart, should the contract be sufficient."

Thrum gave his first true smile, and it sent shivers down Halla's back. "Very well."

CHAPTER 3

After Halla's legal counsel noted the contract was airtight, and Halla determined a fair price, she signed it. Thrum returned to the shop the next day, as he promised, to retrieve it.

Revealing a row of straight white teeth, Thrum told Halla the family was pleased and would bring Young Lord Urquart in three days. "I will be your point of contact. There will be no emails nor other written means. Any letters will be burned upon receipt, other than prescriptions our Young Lord receives from you."

Within an hour of his departure, Halla's phone gave a light *ping*. She sucked in a breath as she checked her phone. The Green Thumb's bank account was 725,000 *feiqian* richer, enough to buy a massive plot of land or three small houses.

Wow... they're the real deal. No questions asked about my listed price. And this is just half upfront! Halla considered her acquired case of rich-family's-son-impeded-by-mysterious-illness with a newfound intrigue. As she stared at the number, her phone rang. "Justine" flashed across the screen—The Green Thumb's accountant.

"Oh, no," Halla groaned. In the haste of the contract, she'd forgotten to mention the incoming funds. Reluctantly, Halla answered. "Hey, Justine."

"Don't 'Hey, Justine' me!" she screeched from the other end. Halla flinched. "What is this, Halla? What is this number in the account? Who's this from?"

"Well, I received an interesting proposition, and it's a great opportunity—"

"Are you engaged in drugs? And you know what I mean, Halla!" Justine interrupted. "I'm not talking about our good, legal drugs. Are you engaged in illicit drugs? Weird businesses? I've never seen an amount like this!"

"Justine, please," Halla said in a calming tone reserved for her more difficult customers. "I already ran this through Ernest."

"And that's already the first red flag. I'm telling you. Even though the man's a lawyer, as long as money is involved, I question his morals."

"Justine!" Halla rolled her eyes. Her accountant and lawyer always had a standing grievance against one another. "He reviewed a contract. I'm treating an important patient. This is their payment."

"And just who could this be, huh?" Justine challenged.

"The Urquarts." Halla was met with silence. "Justine?"

"Yes, I'm here," she snapped. "You're sure it's the Urquarts?"

Like she could forget. "Yes. They're bringing the patient in three days. In the morning before we open. You can come by if you want to confirm it yourself."

"Great Doa, Halla. You can't just agree to this without consulting me. I'm your accountant, for goodness sake."

"I ran it by our lawyer! This is just like any other business transaction, if a higher sum," Halla responded defensively. It was Halla's business after all, she could manage it however she wanted.

"Ernest doesn't know anything," Justine said. "The Urquarts are not 'just like any other' customer, and 725,000 feiqian most definitely is not 'just like any other transaction'," Justine huffed.

Halla did flinch, then. Justine *was* right. The Urquarts had the ability to change The Green Thumb's clientele for the better. And as Halla's accountant, Justine was only doing her job.

"All right, Justine, I'm sorry. I'm sorry I didn't tell you about this beforehand, and sorry for scaring you."

Justine sighed. "Was it really that hard to apologize, Halla? Or just text me about it?"

"It all happened so fast!" Halla retorted. "They gave me a total of one day to review the contract and sign."

Justine said nothing for a moment, then breathed, "All right, well, no harm done, I suppose. Just do your job. This is a great client to have."

Halla rolled her eyes. "You don't have to tell me that. Anyway, thanks for keeping an eye on everything, Justine. Talk to you later."

"And I'll be giving Ernest a piece of my mind. I bet he was ecstatic he knew about this before me, that wily—" She hung up the line.

The morning of the Urquarts' first visit, the roads were slick and a slight haze hung in the air from a storm the previous night. Halla arrived at The Green Thumb at 5:30 AM, three hours before opening, and had Cerul come in to help prepare materials, just in case. Halla didn't know what to expect and wanted to be prepared. Brandus complained too much in general, so Halla hadn't bothered asking him to come.

The sky was still gray with clouds—contrary to the excitement Halla was feeling about the case—when a dark vehicle pulled up to the shop's back entrance. Thrum was the first to exit the vehicle, followed by a woman dressed in a blue satin blouse with a white collar and a matching mid-length skirt with low heels.

"Is that them?" Cerul squeaked in Halla's ear.

She nodded. "Yup. Time to see what this is all about." She turned her head slightly toward Cerul. "Watch the front of the shop while I diagnose the son. If I need any assistance, I'll call you."

Cerul made a small noise of acknowledgement but lingered before heading back inside.

The woman led a small, pale ten-year-old boy dressed in a cream collared shirt and knee-length shorts toward Halla. For how sickly they made him out to be, Halla was surprised how relatively well he looked. She hoped she could glean more from examining his tongue later. Thrum's tall form followed at the rear. The boy stumbled slightly while walking, resulting in the woman grabbing him around the shoulders to keep him upright. The two whispered an exchange. The young boy nodded and tried to shrug his mother off, but he suddenly looked fatigued.

Halla extended a hand, palm-up, as was customary for greeting children, when he approached. "Hi. I'm Halla. What's your name?"

He looked to his mother for approval before placing his right hand on Halla's, their palms resting against each other. "Rexford Urquart. Nice to meet you."

Halla straightened and glanced at his mother. "You must be Mrs. Urquart. It's my honor to make your acquaintance and to have you here at my humble shop."

Mrs. Urquart smiled warmly. "Your store is anything but humble. It's quite magnanimous." She placed both hands on Rexford's shoulders. "We are grateful you've accepted our son as a patient. My husband wished to be here, but he's often occupied with state matters."

"Father never comes to my appointments, anyway," the boy grumbled.

"Rex!" Mrs. Urquart exclaimed. "You know your father is busy. Now, please. We are in the presence of others."

Halla didn't miss Rexford's eye roll.

"Yes, Mother."

Halla watched the interaction with curiosity. Eager to ease the tension, Halla motioned for the trio to follow her inside, leading them to one of their numerous examination rooms.

"To best treat Rexford, I'll need to know which doctors and practitioners he has seen, as well as what they've prescribed. I'd also like their records or observations of his state and how he reacted to the different prescriptions," Halla listed as she guided them through The Green Thumb.

"Of course," Mrs. Urquart responded demurely. "Thrum, please make sure Dr. Halla receives the records she asks for. Coordinate with our previous doctors."

"Certainly," Thrum's voice sounded from behind.

"With a family of your standing, I assume you have a family doctor?" Halla continued.

"Indeed. Dr. Kurand has been with us for years and has monitored Rexford's health since birth. He's the one who's been keeping the illness at bay, until three years ago, that is, when Rexford had an episode. His health" Mrs. Urquart paused for a moment, sniffing— "has been in decline since. That's when we started seeking other professionals and specialists."

And the family doctor is still employed? Halla thought. *He must have worked miracles for many years before, or they truly view him as family.* Out loud, she asked, "Can you describe this episode? What did Dr. Kurand say of it?"

"Rexford said it was a sudden chest pain, and I was there. It was..." She paused again. When Halla looked back, she saw Thrum had produced a handkerchief for the elegant woman, and she was wiping a few glistening marks off her face. *Gosh. Even in distress, she's elegant.* "I'm sorry. It was just... such a difficult moment," Mrs. Urquart finally finished. "It was so hard seeing how much pain Rex was in."

Rexford reached for his mother's free hand. "I'm okay now, Mother."

Mrs. Urquart smiled back tenderly. "Yes, my dear. Because you are so strong." She looked back at Halla who'd stopped walking as they'd reached the examination room.

Halla stared at the open door. She'd requested Cerul to prepare a room for them and indicate the room by keeping the door open. For some Doa-forsaken reason, out of all the rooms they had, Cerul had decided to prep Examination Room 8—a room Halla had kept closed for years.

"Is something the matter?" Mrs. Urquart asked.

Halla started. "Nothing," she responded quickly.

She didn't want to enter the room; there was a reason she'd kept it closed. But for their first visit from an esteemed guest, she didn't want to seem shaken or indicate anything wasn't going as she'd planned. She took a deep breath and shoved away the tightening at her chest, with a mental fortitude that really just meant she ignored the pain, and gestured for the family to enter the room.

Halla had almost forgotten what they were talking about until Mrs. Urquart continued. "He's always been ill, but that time, Rexford was clutching his chest and couldn't respond or move. Fortunately, Dr. Kurand was on the grounds and administered what was needed. He said it wasn't a heart attack, but he wasn't sure what else it could be. Scans show that his arteries aren't blocked, and his heart seemed to be functioning just fine. But Rex has been so sickly since."

From that description, Halla ruled out a heart attack—though she'd still request they do a full blood work-up at a hospital. Could it be some sort of musculoskeletal issue? "Thank you for that background. His medical records should shed more light on this. For now, let me examine him. You may enter the room with him, but I ask that Mr. Thrum stay at the door." Halla stole a glance at him.

Thrum quirked a brow at her while Mrs. Urquart was about to retort, but he started first. "Not a problem, Halla. Mrs. Urquart, I'll be right outside." With that, and with a sense of triumph, Halla entered the room with the mother and son and shut the door.

Examination Room 8 was different from the nine others within The Green Thumb. All other examination rooms were basic white-walled rooms with a comfortable bed against the wall, a computer, sink, three chairs, and some drawers of basic herbs. This examination room had dark wooden paneling along the bottom half of the walls with two screened windows of intricate lattices along the back, opening into an interior garden. Patients who sat on the cushioned bed next to the windows were able to breathe fresh air while listening to the sounds of running water. The room used warmer lighting and was furnished with dark wooden stools, though it also had a sink and computer as well as drawers and jars of herbs like the others.

Halla had dedicated this room to Grandma Wen. It was reminiscent of the house back at the Nuan estate, but Halla had never gotten to show her grandmother; Grandma Wen had been so cold at her last and only visit. Halla felt her throat close as she took in the room that she'd avoided for years.

"Dr. Halla?" Rexford asked with concerned eyes, a hand lightly brushing Halla's. At that, she felt a tinge of warm nostalgia hit at the tip of the pain—a pang of familiarity she hadn't realized she'd missed. The wooden screens, the garden within view, the stools, the warm hands.

She blinked rapidly and smiled. "You can settle yourself onto the bed."

Rexford positioned himself on the patient bed and looked at his mother expectantly. Mrs. Urquart nodded.

"Before we proceed, Dr. Nuan, there's something we must tell you," Mrs. Urquart settled into a wooden chair, cushioned with a square green silken pillow.

"Sure. I'll need all the information I can get to best aid your son." Halla took a seat at the chair next to the bed and situated an armrest so that it sat at Rexford's arm level.

Before settling his arm, however, Rexford put both his hands on a pendant around his neck and pressed. Particles dissolved from the crown of Rexford's head and created a shimmer effect from the top to the base of his neck where the pendant sat.

Halla's eyes widened as the haze of particles surrounding the boy's head cleared.

"Yeah, I'm a girl," Rexford stated matter-of-factly.

CHAPTER 4

Sitting in front of Halla was a young, tan girl with shoulder-length, wavy, brown hair. Her eyes were now a shade of gold rather than blue. Halla took a step back and jerked her chin at the pendant.

"What is that? Who are you all?" The necklace must have been an imbued synth tool, created by a crafting and imbuing synther, but Halla had never seen a synth tool made to change one's appearance. Why would anyone need that?

Mrs. Urquart remained seated. "This is Rexford. From birth, we've hidden her true identity for her protection. What you see today is her true form, and we ask you to keep this to yourself. The pendant is one of many tools our family uses."

So that's *why they asked me to sign an NDA. No one's ever seen the Urquart heir like this. Every account, every person knows Rexford as a son.* Halla eyed the pendant again. *I guess I shouldn't be surprised the Urquart family likely has all the resources to hire skilled crafting and imbuing synthers to create items. Very unique items...*

"I understand the desire for privacy, but you are already a very public family. Why hide Rexford's true identity all these years? Is she to live behind that mask her entire life?" She caught Rexford shooting her a glance.

"I find your question inappropriate, Dr. Halla," Mrs. Urquart stated sternly. Halla looked away in embarrassment; it *had* been a personal question, but if Rexford has enemies, Halla would like to be aware of it. Mrs. Urquart sighed. "It's for her protection. A son strengthens our claim on the territory. As you know, the Cru Territory have pushed harder at our borders in recent years, and they're openly and shamelessly attempting to recruit the Doan monks for their martial prowess." Her expression darkened briefly before she exhaled. "Thank Doa that the temples are committed to peace and spiritual guidance, but I don't want the Crus knowing much about my daughter in case they get any ideas to send someone into our territory to take her and wed her for access to us. Rexford doesn't need to hide all the time. She only dons the pendant at formal events where we present the family."

"That's basically everyday, Mother," Rexford finally spoke. "Our family is on all the time. Not even our staff know who I really am."

"The less people who know, the less likely the Crus will figure it out. It has to be done, Rex."

"No, it doesn't. Do you know how hard this is for me? Do you know what it's like? On top of my illness?" Rexford demanded, gradually raising her voice with each question.

Halla swivelled her head between mother and daughter. This outburst was very different from the earlier calm poise the heir held when she had on her disguise. "Are you saying no one knows except for you two. And now... me?" The enormity of this secret dawned on Halla.

Mrs. Urquart turned to Halla. "No. My husband knows. And Dr. Kurand and Thrum know. Maybe three previous doctors we've been to. We didn't disclose it to the others, nor did they figure it out. You would be the ninth person in this entire nation to know."

Well, that doesn't make me feel any better. Halla took a seat again to process.

"This should not affect your diagnosis—"

"It would, Mrs. Urquart," Halla cut her off. "Respectfully," she added when she remembered who she was in the presence of. "Yes, we all have bodies with the same functions. But men and women have different dispositions and reactions to certain drugs, different ailments sometimes. I would have known Rexford is a girl once I took her pulse even if you didn't take off her disguise."

Mrs. Urquart nodded. "Of course. A practitioner of your stature would be able to determine that. That's why it won't affect your diagnosis. You would have known her true nature anyway."

"Sure." Halla threw up her hands in annoyance. "What I'm saying, though, is that my prescriptions may be indicative that I'm treating a woman, depending on what is ailing Rexford. If anyone got their hands on my prescriptions, they may be able to deduce what I'm treating, and if it's an ailment or symptom that more commonly or only affects women, that could endanger your secret."

"Then we will be careful with the prescriptions. Only Dr. Kurand will handle administration of your drugs. I won't have any other staff see it. I appreciate your concern, Dr. Halla, but we've been hiding this for ten years. We know how to be discreet and protect my daughter. I do not need to hear more of it from you. We hired you to heal my daughter, not tell me how to keep her identity a secret, and I suggest you start your examination."

Halla clenched her jaw at Mrs. Urquart's tone. *I don't care who you are. You are making my job more difficult. You know nothing of medicine, and now I have to worry about a secret identity, as well?*

Halla felt like she'd somehow been tricked into taking this case, but she took a deep breath. She hated being blindsided, but she kept her mouth shut and settled back in front of the bed and armrest. "As you wish, Mrs. Urquart." She turned to the girl. "Rexford, place your arm on the armrest for me to take your pulse. I will start and conduct the Four Examinations on you."

Halla asked multiple questions about how Rexford felt in general, where discomfort was sensed, and what other doctors had tried in the past while she took Rexford's pulse, pressed various pressure points on Rexford's body, and examined her tongue. Rexford reported constant fatigue and being out of breath over the smallest amount of exertion. She had seemingly random bouts of abdominal pain and joint pain, often after meals.

Strangely, all physical observations reflected Rexford to be in good health. Her heartbeat was strong and healthy. Her breathing wasn't labored and sounded clear. Her breath did not carry the stink of illness, and her tongue was a healthy pink with just the right amount of coating on it. If it weren't for the family paying Halla a large sum, she would have thought this was a prank.

It had been a while, but Halla's last resort was to synth. Halla had never had to fully rely on her Synesthology to diagnose a patient. The extent of her synthing ability was being able to control when to actively synth and to sense whether someone was lying or sense their emotions. She seldom used her skills to check the physicality of a patient because her medical schooling and knowledge were always sufficient, but this was something Grandma Wen was known for during her prime. Halla felt a quick pang of regret but shoved it down.

Halla asked Rexford to lie supine on the bed and then sat next to her. She took the girl's small hand, closed her eyes, and tried to recall Grandma Wen's teachings.

"*Closing your eyes makes it easier to focus, Halla,*" she heard Grandma's clear voice. "*Now feel the energy within your stomach and extend it to your fingertips and beyond. Find any colors that don't belong.*"

Halla took a deep breath and dipped into the energy at her core, extending it out to Rexford. When she made contact, she inhaled sharply between her teeth. A cacophony of loud colors overwhelmed her, slamming into the back of her closed eyelids. She pulled back instinctively.

"What's wrong?" Mrs. Urquart shuffled her chair closer.

"Nothing," Halla hastily responded. *I will figure this out.*

Back in Grandma Wen's prime, she was known for her acute synthing. There were tales of her finding a hairline fracture within a child who had fallen into a ditch or catching a clogged artery within a minister thereby preventing a potential heart attack. Halla could do this. Grandma had taught her, right? She had to do this.

She re-placed her hand on Rexford and tried again. Once more, she was hit with a flood of various colors so strong that Halla couldn't tell what Rexford's base color was. At this rate, she couldn't identify what issues were assaulting the heir. Halla only knew something was very, very wrong.

Halla spent an hour reading Rexford's body. After adjusting to the state of Rexford's energy, Halla was able to decipher some patterns. *It looks like some swelling at her lymph nodes. Let's address that first and see how her body reacts.*

"Thank you for your patience, Rexford. Mrs. Urquart," she addressed them both and had Rexford sit back up. "Your illness is indeed a strange one. Everything on the outside tells me you're healthy, but when I examine you, I see a webbing of ailments. It will take me time to detangle this."

Mrs. Urquart's eyes glistened as she took Halla's hand. "Thank you, Doctor. Your excellent reputation precedes you. You're a skilled sensor indeed. Numerous doctors and other sensors have dismissed us. Do you know what could be wrong with Rex?"

Halla tried to pull her hand back but found Mrs. Urquart's grip ironclad. She, however, took the opportunity to sense and confirm Mrs. Urquart's genuine relief and appreciation. *At least, she's a mother who cares.*

"Like I said, it's a webbing. I believe the lymph nodes are swollen. The lymphatic system is important for helping the body fight diseases. With that down, it could lead to many other issues, so I'm hoping by addressing her lymph nodes, it can help improve her condition from there. I'll prepare Rexford some calendula and linba fang to take back. Please follow the instructions for consumption. I also recommend regular massages to clear her system. I'll provide a diagram, and I can give a demonstration at our next appointment."

"Will this heal me?" Rexford asked as she got off the bed and re-enabled the disguise pendant.

Halla turned to her male form and answered bluntly, "It won't. But it's a start."

Rexford nodded with the gravity of someone much older than her true age and headed out the door with her mother.

Mrs. Urquart and Rexford waited in their vehicle in the back alley with Thrum while Halla fetched the prescription packages. The streets were just coming alive with sounds of people milling about. Fortunately, calendula and linba fang were common herbal prescriptions, so she had them on hand, but—given Rexford's complex ailments—she would likely have to make bespoke concoctions later on.

Halla waved them off as the vehicle drove away with the sun rising, and for the first time in ten years, Halla found herself wishing she could go home and consult Grandma Wen.

CHAPTER 5

"Transferred?" the word echoed in Herb's mind as he stared at his superior. "And to the Green Division? Captain, you can't do that!"

The Green Division dealt with menial paperwork for clear-cut cases. In other words, Herb knew he was being demoted.

"I can, and I will, Inspector Mooran. In fact, this is coming from higher up. You are to follow these orders," the woman, adorned in an emerald green uniform with three gold armbands, responded sternly.

"Please. Captain Ray, there must be something you can do."

The captain heaved a sigh. "Herbert. Let me level with you." She brought her elbows to the desktop, head resting on interlocked hands. "It's out of my control. You are lowering our case closure rates, and my boss saw the numbers. You hyperfixate on details that don't matter. Myself and many of your peers have given you that feedback. I've been getting a lot of complaints about it and fronting it for you, but we can't deny this fact. There's only so much I can do."

Herb looked to the spackled ceiling like it might tell him how to change her mind. But the room only stared back in isolated detachment, just like everything else in this department.

"You can't deny that I'm thorough," Herb retorted as his gaze swung back to Captain Ray. "You know I have the best documented cases. Some of the older cases only have a few lines in them, and you know I graduated top of my class."

"Your pedigree is impressive, yes, and your attention to detail is applaudable. But in practice, in the real world, we need numbers. You're unfortunately not hitting them, Herbert."

Of course he wasn't hitting them. The cases were full of holes, missing details, and definite signs of hurried paperwork. It took ages to wade through the lack of information to gain a starting place at all. *Management is always concerned with numbers. They never look at anything else.* Herb was tired of how disconnected and surface-level his management was.

"Don't give me that lip service," Herb said. "That's spittlebork."

"Herb," Captain Ray cautioned. "I am your friend, but I'm also your superior. Watch your tone."

At that, Herb dipped his head, admonished, but clenched his fists. This wasn't the way to treat a friend. He'd felt that over the years; Ray had distanced herself from him.

"Fine. Order received," he muttered.

"Excellent." Captain Ray gave a pleasant smile. "Oh, and this is effective immediately."

Herb stared at her for a moment, dumbfounded. "What?"

Ten minutes later, Herbert was in the middle of the cubicle that had been his workspace for five years, packing his belongings. He wasn't even given a grace period.

He had scored perfectly on the Inspector Certification Examinations, something only achieved by one in every ten thousand test takers. The last perfect score was achieved twenty years ago by a legendary inspector—one who had since been promoted into the bureaucracy and worked there for as long as Herb could remember. Herb's excellent scores landed him his position in the Onyx Division. Those in the inspector force had high hopes for him when he joined five years ago. Some had even thought he may go on to be the next division captain. Yet, here he was. Relegated to the Green Division, and publicly humiliated to boot.

Herbert emptied his drawers into a cardboard box and sealed it. He tried not to look at the rows of cubicles on either side of the aisle as he made the walk of shame to the Green Division.

The whispers immediately picked up.

"Detective Mooran? He's just been fired, huh?" a woman noted under her breath to a neighboring inspector.

"Finally. He really wasn't an efficient worker."

"Not fired. Demoted, I heard. Should have just let him go, though."

"I was wondering when it'd happen."

"Inspector Mooran? More like Inspector *Moron*." This comment was followed with some snickers.

The inspector occupation was a female-dominated field, with government scientific research having determined decades ago that women were typically better suited to decision-making, rational actions, and disciplined enforcement. Studies had shown that the general populace was more at ease with women as enforcers. As such, the government held initiatives to bring more women into the field. Although men were not discouraged from pursuing this line of work, it had become increasingly rare to find men in any of the policing divisions or occupations. Herbert was one of three men who worked in the Onyx Division. Before he was demoted, that was.

Herb reported directly to the Green Division just three floors below his previous desk. He clutched his box to his chest as he presented himself to his new captain.

A dark-toned woman with thick-rimmed glasses and red hair tied in a tight bun swiveled in her chair to face him. Her emerald uniform was adorned with two gold armbands.

"Ah, you must be Inspector Mooran. I've heard of your situation. There's no need to brief me. I'm impressed with your scores and your cases, but let me establish right now that I have no need for people who spend months on one case. Do you understand? This is the Green now, kid. Our cases are simpler. In-and-out."

Herb gulped. "Yes, ma'am. I understand."

He hadn't expected the Green Division's captain to be so stern, though he supposed she likely had to be this way to be taken seriously by captains of other divisions—given the Green was at the bottom of the social ranking ladder.

"The name's Asma. Seeing as you score well and have some status, you'll report directly to me. That desk," she nodded in the direction of an empty seat beyond her glass wall, "is yours. I've had a gopher put some cases there for you already. Get started."

Great. Here starts my paper-pushing era. Herb turned away and rolled his eyes, heading to his new desk pressed against the wall. He noted the Green had no cubicles—just open-concept desks in a row. *Another kind of demotion,* he thought as he set his box in his new space.

He glanced at the inspector to the right of his desk and the one sitting across from him, both diligently stamping paperwork and dropping it into a stack. No one spoke to each other, despite the open concept, unlike the chatty atmosphere of the Onyx. Herb hoped this would at least make for a better working relationship with his new deskmates than what he'd experienced in the Onyx.

CHAPTER 6

It had been four months of treatment, and Halla was slowly but surely eliminating the additional, rampant colors within Rexford's body. Although Halla wasn't partial to children, she'd grown quite fond of Rexford. The heir was mature for her age, and yet when a genuine smile popped up, Halla found it rewarding, like she was getting a peek at the real child.

Halla saw Rexford every two weeks, and the process had become a regular one. Cerul came in early to watch the shopfront. Halla greeted Rexford and a guardian (either Mrs. Urquart, Thrum, or both), Rexford deactivated the pendant, Halla sat and examined Rexford's physical countenance and pulse, and finally, she examined Rexford with her sense synthing before prescribing more herb packets. It was frustrating, not knowing exactly what was wrong with Rexford to warrant so many colors in her body, but Halla was satisfied that the treating of symptoms one at a time was working.

She'd found it difficult to chat with the young girl with Mrs. Urquart's hovering. But when Thrum alone accompanied Rexford, Halla had him wait outside. During these appointments, she found Rexford spoke more openly. Rexford maintained a certain composure, as expected of the Urquart family, but she spoke more of her fatigue.

"I don't blame you for being tired. As you know, something is very wrong with your health, Rexford," Halla responded one morning, one hand on Rexford's pulse.

"No, no. That's not what I'm talking about." Rexford waved her free hand as if batting away Halla's comment before hacking out a string of coughs. "I'm tired of all these appointments." She wiped her mouth with a handkerchief Halla offered. "Tired of all the secrecy. Of keeping this pendant on. Of being stuck at home. And I'm not talking about your appointments specifically. I'm tired of the last three years of medical talk and probing." The girl heaved a sigh.

"Your parents love you very much," Halla said absently as she synthed Rexford. "That's why they're blazing through doctors to find the one that can help you. And keeping you home is for your own protection, is it not? I see news about the Cru Territory getting more bold, and they're known for sending skilled mercenaries into territories to assassinate or kidnap. That's what they did to the Tripa Territory thirty years ago. That happened a few years before I was born, but I know it shook all of the ruling families on the landmass. Your parents keep you at home so they can keep you safe from something like that and from pushing yourself too hard. And so Dr. Kurand can monitor your health."

Rexford's face fell, and she turned to look at the blank wall. "This is all I know. I'm tired of hearing I'm too weak. That I can't do this or can't do that. If what's ailing me can't be fixed," she paused and continued in a quieter voice, "I'd rather go live my life. See the world. Make the most of it. I don't want to be shackled by this."

Halla stopped focusing on Rexford's colors and looked at the girl, alarmed. "Hey. Don't say that. You've been improving. Don't lose hope yet."

Rexford's face broke into a bitter smile. "That's what they all say."

"Well," Halla settled herself more comfortably into her seat as she tried to think of how to pivot the conversation, "I've helped you live beyond the few months other doctors projected you had, right? That's good. What would be the first thing you want to do when you're healed?"

Hopefully, that will keep her mind occupied.

She shot a glance at Rexford and saw a real smile creeping at the corners of the young child's lips. "I want to try food from a random hole-in-the-wall restaurant. The ones I see people featuring on television as a 'hidden gem.' "

Halla raised her brows. "The first thing you'd want to do is try a restaurant? Don't you have private chefs?"

"We do, but they make the blandest food for me. Dr. Kurand's orders," the girl mourned. "It's not just that. I want to sit in that environment. See all sorts of people come in, see what they order, hear people chatting, feel that energy."

Halla put a hand on Rex's shoulders. She knew a thing or two about wanting to see the world when she was younger. That was a part of why Halla had left the Nuan estate to study in the capital.

"You and me," she said to Rex. "Once you're healed, that's the first place I'll take you."

The small girl smiled up at her.

Over the past month, Halla had been able to isolate lymphatic, kidney, and stomach issues and treat those symptoms for Rexford. The family and Rexford reported she'd stopped vomiting three times a day (a previously regular occurrence), and seemed to have built more strength, now able to take longer walks. The results were better than anything they'd ever seen, but Halla was determined to go further.

She prepared twenty-eight parcels tied with twine of jujubes, yub shrooms, apricot kernels, lotus seeds, and deer antler. She also grabbed three vials of her dried bee venom salve. Halla handed these to Thrum as he and Rexford exited the back door.

"Each parcel is a serving. Rexford is to have two servings a day: morning and evening. The salve is to be used on her main pressure points each evening."

Thrum nodded and ducked into the car. Rexford, back in her boy form, rolled down her window.

"Halla?" she called.

"Hmm?"

"Thank you, again. I haven't felt so lively and light in a very long time."

Halla warmed at the sentiment. "Of course, Rexford. This is my job."

"I know." The boy smiled sadly at her. Halla found it disconcerting to speak with Rexford's male form, as Rexford seemed more solemn or adult-like with that face, as if it were a mask.

"Rex, I will do my best for you." *For Grandma*. For some reason, the months of sitting in Examination Room 8, chatting with Rex, Halla had found it easier and easier to think of Grandma. Synthing was the last thing she had of her grandmother's. She had to keep it alive.

"Halla. Halla, do you hear me." She opened her eyes to the familiar voice, and Grandma's clear brown eyes stared down at her. She was lying in Grandma's lap back at the Nuan estate in the courtyard. She pushed herself up, sitting next to the senior lady.

"What's going on? Grandma? What are we doing here?" She rubbed her eyes, noting a strange, blue haze hung within the family courtyard.

"My dear." Grandma Wen cupped Halla's face within her hands. Strangely, the hands smelled of fresh cut grass rather than the usual dried chrysanthemum, but it had been so long since Halla had experienced this, her heart suddenly tugged as she stared into her grandmother's eyes. "I didn't get to teach you everything I know. I never taught you how to fully use your synthing abilities." Tears pooled Grandma Wen's eyes.

"That's okay," Halla soothed, all the tension of their previous arguments gone with the wind. "You didn't have to. I'm carrying the family legacy, and I do a great job with the other basic skills you taught me, in addition to what I learned at school." Seeing her grandmother again made her chest ache with grief. "Grandma, I have so much I want to tell you."

She placed her hands on top of Grandma's, still cradling her face, but then Grandma Wen's expression darkened and her usually clear eyes turned an opaque white, as if storm clouds covered them.

Halla startled and tried to back away, but the creature with Grandma's hands held firmly to her face.

"You know nothing! You learned nothing. You went to learn from strangers who had nothing to offer," said the form resembling her grandmother, tone pitching deep. "And now look at you. What are you doing?" The form finally let go of Halla's face and stood, growing to over seven feet. Halla immediately scooted backward. "Sitting in your shiny store counting pennies? Looking at a number on your screen? Grasping at colors you don't understand?"

The creature's volume rose as the voices of ten men tumbled from its mouth at once.

"I'm a sensor," Halla stammered. "I can see the colors. I'm healing patients. I'm helping Rex."

"You see nothing," the creature spat as it drifted toward her. "You've relegated yourself to cold, isolated observations like modern medicine. You are missing pieces of the whole. You *know* nothing."

Halla had wanted to make up with her grandmother, but these unfounded statements brought nothing but rage as she balled her fists around clumps of grass, her self-doubt boiling into a familiar anger. Besides, this creature was not Grandma Wen.

"You don't know me. You don't know how hard I've worked to live up to the family. To carry our name!" she screamed. "You never understood!"

The figure cackled and swooped down until its face was mere centimeters away from Halla's. It whispered, "You never sought to understand. Look around you. It's all dead."

Halla looked down at the grass balled in her hands and realized the blades were yellow and dry. Around the hazy courtyard, the fruit were trees barren, the stream dried, and the plants withered.

"What did you do?" she yelled as she turned back to the figure, somehow now ten feet away.

"You did this, Halla. You refused to learn, and the family legacy and knowledge is dead. You did this to us."

"No!" Halla roared and stood. "I'm synthing! I'm keeping this alive!"

"Oh?" The figure cracked a smile with her grandmother's face. "You reject this?"

It cocked its head unnaturally before suddenly stooping and crawling with supernatural speed toward Halla.

"Great Doa," Halla managed to gasp, her earlier courage doused, and turned to run, but it was too late. The creature grabbed Halla's leg, pulling her down and crawling on top, breathing in her face.

"Come home, Halla." It unhinged its jaw, opening wider than Halla's face, and leaned in to clamp shut.

"No!" Halla screamed as she struggled to free herself.

She opened her eyes and found herself in a pool of her own sweat in her room in the city. She sat up, her heart beating erratically.

"Just a nightmare," she muttered to herself as she ran a hand down her face and threw her legs over the bed.

Halla needed a glass of cold water. Grandma had always said cold water wasn't good for one's stomach, but she didn't care right now. *I haven't dreamt of Grandma in years, and* that's *what my brain comes up with?* Regardless, she didn't see herself sleeping much more tonight, so she brought her water to her study and settled in with a book.

She tried reading herself to sleep but found her mind wandering back to the dream. Gooseflesh ran down her arms. *What did she mean 'I see nothing'? That everything's dead? I'm thriving, am I not?*

Her family had believed in meanings behind dreams and had sometimes hired dream-readers to help interpret them. When Halla was a child, and Grandfather was still present, he had many-a-story about how his dreams saved his life. And so Halla found herself particularly disturbed with this dream that consisted of a creepy version of her grandmother, a barren family estate garden, and being told she'd basically killed them all. Could it be connected to Rexford? Related to the fact that she couldn't properly synth-diagnose someone who needed it? Or was there something more to Rexford's case?

She shook her head to clear it and went back to reading. She'd think more about her dream some other time.

CHAPTER 7

It was 5:30 AM on Wednesday, the usual time for Rexford's appointment. Halla stood outside with Cerul, waiting for the familiar dark vehicle to make its appearance. It didn't come.

Halla checked her watch. The Urquarts were never late.

Cerul rubbed her hands together, fidgeting and humming quietly, and it was getting on Halla's nerves.

"Can you stop that?"

Cerul squeaked in surprise at the break in silence in the cool morning air. "Sorry, Halla. Where are they?"

"I don't know," Halla snapped and massaged her temples. She didn't need someone telling her what she already knew, what she was already worried about. "It's fine." She took a deep breath, saying it more for herself than to Cerul. "They're only running a little late. We still have plenty of time before opening shop."

Cerul made an incoherent grumble before asking, "Could we give them a call?"

In normal circumstances, that would be the next move, but the family had stipulated Thrum was Halla's only point of contact, and he never left a means to communicate. Over the last five months, he would show up in person with a note or verbal message. Otherwise, they all knew the appointments were every other Wednesday at 5:30 AM.

"No," Halla answered shortly.

Cerul waited for an additional explanation, but when she was met with nothing else, she rambled, "Why can't we call them? How about texting? How could we have been treating the Urquart son without any means of communication?" She chewed at her fingernails. "Don't we usually take down patient information which, of course, includes a phone number or contact information? What if something happened to them? What if we actually missed a message about a change in sche—"

"Cerul!" Halla exclaimed as she faced her employee. Cerul startled at the force of Halla's voice. "Please. This is *not* helping. At all."

Cerul stayed silent, wide-eyed. Under the pressure of running The Green Thumb, especially with the new second location, Halla had occasional outbursts at work, but Cerul seemed to butt into her business, like how she had prepared Examination Room 8 for Rex's first appointment. Halla still had to talk to her about that but had put it off because once she got over the initial pain, she started to find comfort in the room again. But this meant the mousy employee had taken the brunt of Halla's temper usually. Sometimes, Halla's guilt nearly had her addressing her behavior, but Cerul was paid well enough to be able to handle it.

Halla took a deep breath. "Let's wait and see. It's only ten minutes past." Cerul opened her mouth again before Halla sliced a hand in the air. "In silence. Please. Let us wait in silence."

Halla wasn't sure how much more of Cerul she could take before falling into an anxious spiral herself. *Yes, silence would be nice right now.* If Cerul wasn't her only professional with valuable knowledge of plant toxicity for herbal remedies, Halla probably would have let Cerul go by now.

The two women waited, cool air blowing through their coats for another hour, but the Urquarts did not show. The neighboring stores were just coming to life as their shop owners finally arrived to prepare to open.

At this point, Halla was sure something had gone terribly wrong or the Urquarts somehow rescheduled without her knowing. "Cerul, prepare for opening. I'll wait a little longer, but I don't think they're coming."

Cerul nodded and ducked inside, wordlessly, to Halla's relief.

What happened? Are they going to show up another day? Or did we agree to skip this visit, and I forgot? I didn't pack her enough herbal packets to last until next visit, though.

Arms wrapped around her body for warmth, she turned to head in when a car pulled up. She stopped.

The car parked before the back door, but no one came out. Instead, the driver-side window rolled down to reveal Thrum and his stoic face. This time, he did not grace her with one of his emotionless smiles; his face, although usually stern, teetered on grave.

"Mr. Thrum," Halla greeted as she approached the car. "Is Rex not coming today?"

The man shook his head. "The young lord is gravely ill," he announced.

Halla's stomach lurched.

"What do you mean?" she demanded. "How would she—I mean, he," Halla corrected herself since they were on public streets, "be ill? Yes, he's *been* ill, but he was on the mend. What happened?"

"His health has taken a turn, Dr. Nuan. We were not able to wake the young lord today no matter how much we shook him, so we called for Dr. Kurand. He has announced the young lord to be in a coma."

Halla staggered back. "He's comatose?" she whispered. How was this possible? Halla was positive Rex had been stable when they left. "Do we know what triggered it?"

What about the street-side restaurant she'd promised Rex?

Thrum suddenly looked uncomfortable, avoiding eye contact. "I believe my services are being called. I must return. I was sent by Mrs. Urquart to inform you not to expect us for a while." He turned to face the road and started rolling up his window.

"Wait!" Halla exclaimed, holding onto the glass. "Please. Let me help diagnose him. Let me help figure this out."

At that, Thrum frowned and snapped his head back to Halla. "I think you've helped enough. That's all I'm allowed to say right now. Goodbye, Dr. Nuan."

At that, he drove away, leaving Halla standing in the middle of the road, confused and concerned.

What could it possibly be? Halla thought to herself as she sat behind the counter of her shop an hour later. Rexford's ailment was still a mystery, but Halla had thought she'd gotten most of it under control. Rexford had been on the mend. How could she suddenly go into a coma?

Halla stood with renewed determination. She was going to check the list of prescriptions she'd made for Rex over the last five months to see if she could glean any information from those. To her knowledge, she was the only practitioner or doctor treating Rexford.

She paused. Dr. Kurand was the Urquart family doctor, and she wondered if he'd been prescribing anything additional to her parcels. She wasn't privy to that information, however. *Is there any way I can get in contact with Dr. Kurand without Thrum to help me communicate?* Halla went to the back of the shop and logged into her computer, eyes running through the list of herbs she'd given Rex.

Nothing stood out.

"Maybe it was a relapse," Halla murmured to herself. "Her illness was already so strange, so it shouldn't be surprising if it has unknown trajectories or triggers." She locked her computer and returned to the front of the shop, pacing among her shiny aisles. "Perhaps I prescribed too many cooling ingredients to address the heat." Mindlessly, Halla had picked up a duster and started cleaning. "Maybe I missed striking that balance. Too much cooling could induce other ailments."

She continued muttering to herself for another hour before she found she had nothing more to dust. She was replacing the duster when she saw Cerul and Brandus speaking in hushed tones behind the counter. Halla rolled her eyes as she approached them, ready to tell them to go back to work lest she dock their pay.

"Are you both so idle because you finished everything you could be doing?"

Cerul looked back at Halla with shock, but Brandus confidently piped up, "Yes, we've finished with our patients for the first half of the day."

"Right. Because all you both do here as practitioners is see patients," Halla replied, a hand on her hip.

Brandus looked a bit unsure at that, and Cerul explained, "She means that we could be filling prescriptions or prepping ingredient concoctions or drying them."

She gave Halla a quick glance.

At least she's sharp sometimes.

"Oh!" Brandus collected himself. "Right. We can go do that right now, Boss."

As the two of them passed Halla, Brandus turned back around with a glint of curiosity.

"Actually, Boss, we do have a question." He pulled Cerul closer, but it looked like the smaller woman wanted nothing more than to slink away and hide. Halla raised a brow at them. Brandus took that as permission granted. "What was the big deal with the Urquart family? Who was it? What happened this morning? Why didn't they come?"

Halla shot Cerul a dirty look for having told Brandus that much, and she slunk away from the glare as if it burned. If Brandus hadn't been holding her arm in a steadfast grip, Halla was sure Cerul would have simply melted into the floor.

"Brandus, I appreciate the candor. I, too, would like to be transparent with you. Unfortunately, I have signed an NDA, so I cannot say much more other than we cannot speak of this, and it's nothing of concern for you."

Brandus' frown deepened with each word, but he nodded.

"Thanks, Boss. Cerul and I will go on now."

Halla watched them leave, but she made a mental note to speak with Cerul about keeping her mouth shut. She should have had Cerul sign that NDA with her.

The next day, Halla arrived at her shop early just in case Thrum stopped by again, but she found the streets empty. She opened the shop and had the usual early morning crowd.

Halla was just checking the schedules and productivity of her employees (calculated by a formula from her Board of Investors which looked at number of patients per month multiplied by price of prescribed medication and herbs plus any additional projects or training the employee did) when she heard a light rap on her open door.

"Yes?" she answered without looking up.

"Halla," Brandus greeted.

"Brandus." She closed her eyes. "I will not tell you more about that Urquart matter. You know I can't, and no amount of asking will change that."

"Right, uh, Boss." Something within his tone alarmed her, so she looked up and saw his furrowed brows.

"What is it, Brandus?"

"There's a person asking for you."

Halla stood immediately in eagerness. "Mr. Thrum?"

Brandus shook his head. "No, it's not that tall man. It's a woman." He paused.

"Excuse me?"

"Really official-looking woman." *Who could it be?* Halla shook her head. "All right. Well, we don't want to keep her waiting. She didn't tell you what this was about?"

Brandus shook his head as she approached. As he led her out of the back office, he spoke in a lower tone. "Boss, you know you sometimes take yourself too seriously, right?"

"What do you mean?" Halla tensed.

"I know you run this company and whatnot. You have employees to manage. But take it easy. You just always seem... uptight. Like the meniscus. You're like the water tension doming at the top of a cup that's about to burst at the slightest touch."

Halla glanced at him as they continued walking. "Okay… that's a very specific example."

"I'm just painting a picture, Boss." He shrugged.

"Brandus, I appreciate the concern, but I'm fine. I'm used to this. I know we're the same age, but there's a lot more responsibility riding on me, and I have to be accountable for all of it." She thought for a moment. *It would be nice if I could forget some of these responsibilities sometimes, but that's not my life.*

"Boss." Brandus stopped in his tracks and turned to face her, placing his hands on her shoulders. "Have you taken a vacation since I started working for you?"

"No."

"Have you taken a vacation since opening The Green Thumb?"

"No," Halla answered, more tentatively.

"Have you taken any days off… ever?"

Halla looked away. "No."

Brandus exhaled. "Maybe you need to take some time off. Unwind a bit."

Halla looked back up at him. "Who would run this if I take time off? Who would meet with the Board of Investors? Check everything?"

Brandus laughed. "Boss. We can function a few days or a week without you. And I'm sure the investors could always wait until you're back."

"You don't know them," she grumbled, and Brandus laughed but let the matter drop.

Halla wasn't going to immediately change her ways, but the conversation had her reflecting on her life approach and remembering how young she was. With everything she was focusing on doing, she often forgot she was actually in her young twenties—just like Brandus and Cerul. This was a time when most people were enjoying their lives with friends, taking trips or attending concerts, or searching for a life partner. Not running a business, paving the way for approachable traditional medicine, presenting to investors, or attempting to diagnose mystery illnesses.

She followed Brandus, mind occupied, when they finally made it to the waiting area at the corner of her store. A woman in an emerald uniform stood before them. She was tall, lean, and well-built. Her brown hair was cut short at ear-length, shaved shorter at the sides with a longer top and a wavy fringe down her forehead that fell right above her eyes. Halla paused, stunned, and saw Brandus shoot her a smirk before stepping away. She collected herself and extended a hand in greeting.

"Hi, I'm Halla. I heard you're looking for me?"

The uniformed woman spared her no smile. She grasped Halla's hand firmly. "Indeed. I'm Inspector Dine. I'm investigating a case." She glanced around at the busy shop. "Can we speak privately somewhere?"

Deja vu, Halla thought while considering her first encounter with Thrum. *But investigating a case?*

"Sure." Halla led Inspector Dine to her office and closed the door. "How may I help you, Inspector?"

She settled into her seat as she waved a hand for the inspector to sit across from her. The woman observed Halla's office with calculated efficiency, as if making mental notes, before focusing on Halla. She remained standing. Halla squirmed under the scrutiny. *I wasn't prepared for an interrogation...*

After an uncomfortable moment, Inspector Dine broke the silence. "I'm investigating a poisoning."

"A poisoning?" Halla released the tension that had been building at her shoulders. It was common for inspectors to consult her with toxicology from time to time. "Of course."

Inspector Dine continued. "The poisoning of the Urquart heir. Where were you the night of Tri-summer 5th?"

Halla blinked, having to remind herself not to let her mouth drop open. "I was probably closing The Green Thumb and heading home," Halla stammered.

"What was your relationship with the Urquart heir?"

"I was—" Halla stopped herself. "I'm afraid I can't say, Inspector."

Inspector Dine raised a brow. "Why's that?"

"I signed an NDA." Halla's palms started to sweat.

"Interesting," the inspector noted. "So, you were involved with the Urquarts in some way."

Halla shook her head. "I can't say. I'm sorry, Inspector."

"That's fine." Dine nodded perfunctorily. "We will figure it out. I've actually already spoken with the Urquart family, so I know you were treating their son."

Halla's eyes widened. *So much for signing and respecting an NDA,* she thought before collecting herself. "Great. Yes, I've been treating their son, and we've seen some success."

The uniformed woman stared back at her silently.

"Hold on," Halla said. "Am I a suspect? Of this poisoning?"

"I think we're done here," the inspector responded, turning to leave. "Make sure you don't leave the city over the next few weeks. We'll be in contact."

"How am I a suspect?" Halla stood, following Dine out. "Is there evidence that points to me? I was here at the shop. You can check our cameras."

"Poisonings don't require someone to be immediately present, Ms. Nuan. Have a good day." Dine exited the back offices and made for the shop exit. Halla stilled, dumbfounded.

I need to contact the family somehow. Explain everything. What makes the inspectors think it's me? But she didn't know how to reach out to the family without Thrum. The Urquart estate address was not public knowledge, and she was sure it'd be heavily guarded even if she somehow figured out where they lived. Still, she had to do something. She hadn't poisoned anyone. She couldn't let this investigation affect her business or her reputation.

She suddenly remembered Justine mentioning her partner worked in the inspector force and dug out her phone, retreating back to her office.

Justine immediately picked up. "Don't tell me you've picked up some other client who's about to send us billions of feiqian? Actually, that would be great news."

Halla ignored that. "Clarke is an inspector, right?"

"Yeah, she is. Why?" her friend asked.

"You remember how the Urquart heir didn't show up the other day, and slenderman incarnate told me he's comatose?"

"Yeah?"

"An inspector just came to The Green Thumb about the heir. They said he'd been poisoned!"

"Great Doa," Justine breathed. "So, they're asking you for help?"

"That's the thing," Halla whispered. "I think I'm a suspect."

"What!?" her friend screeched. "That makes no sense. The Urquarts are basically a cash cow; why would we do that? Unless it was accidental, but you don't make mistakes like that."

Halla nodded in agreement. "Exactly! They must have other suspects. I was wondering if Clarke could glean anything from the file or whatever they have at the inspector offices."

"I'll give her a call and see if she's heard anything. Even if she has, I'll see how much she can actually share." The line clicked as Justine hung up.

It felt like both minutes and hours of Halla pacing her office before the phone rang.

"That was fast," she commented as she picked up Justine's call.

"Yeah, because this Urquart case is the talk of all the divisions there. Clarke told me she was going to tell me at home, but since I called, she managed to step out." Justine took a breath. "It's bad, Halla."

Halla's stomach sank. "Am I a suspect?"

"You're not the only one, but you are the top suspect. Clarke says that she heard there's incriminating evidence mounting. Her division isn't investigating it, but it's so high-profile that people are talking. A lot of things are pointing at you, and it sounded like the inspectors investigating want to close the case to curry favor from the Urquarts."

Halla's mind was in a haze. "How is that possible? What evidence?"

Justine's voice dropped to a whisper. "They found remnants of the poison within the packages you prescribed the Urquart heir!" "What?" That seemed to be the only word Halla could muster at this point.

"I told Clarke that's impossible, but she said that's what she heard. I'll see if she hears more. I know Ernest isn't this kind of lawyer, but maybe he can help.

It's the least he can do for being so annoying. There's no way they're throwing my friend in jail for this," Justine huffed before ending the call once more.

Halla sat at her desk in shock. They found poison within her prescription parcels? What kind of poison? Some herbs, while medicinal and helpful, could also be poisonous in certain doses. They had to consider that, at least. But Halla had written those prescriptions herself. And she was quite positive none of the herbs she prescribed fell within that category. Did someone else manage the parcels between her packing them and Rex receiving them?

"You know what," Halla finally said to herself. "I trust the system. There is no way they'd put an innocent person behind bars. They'll investigate and find it wasn't me."

She nodded to herself. Although she'd said it out loud, she wasn't sure if she truly believed it. Her mind wandered back to her earlier nightmare, wondering if it was an omen.

"*Come home, Halla,*" the dream creature called.

There was something about this situation that her dream must have been trying to tell her. Perhaps it was time to go back home and reconnect with what she had lost.

CHAPTER 8

"Mooran," a commanding voice called over the desks.

Herb looked up to see Captain Asma motioning him to her office. He gulped and rose, smoothing his uniform. He'd been keeping his head down, stamping cases closed. He didn't want to be demoted again.

"You called for me?" Herb stood at the captain's door.

She peered at him from over thick-rimmed glasses, pursing her lips, before swiveling her chair to face the back, grabbing a file.

"Yes, close the door behind you," Asma requested as she turned once more.

He did as he was told and sat.

"You'll take this case." She slapped the blue folder onto the table.

He raised his brows before picking up the folder and examining its contents. One word immediately stood out to him: Urquart. His stomach flipped in excitement as he glanced back up at Asma. Why would she have given him such a high-profile case? Was there a catch?

"Captain," he addressed her. "This seems like a sensitive case. Am I to partner with anyone?"

She shook her head. "It's your case, unless you want any help. Have you read the details?"

Herb took another glance at the documents, flipping through them quickly. "I'm surprised a case of this caliber is coming to our department. No offense, Captain."

Asma waved a hand dismissively. "None taken. Indeed, usually the Onyx Division would take this. However, they already had an inspector review it. It's pretty straightforward, so it was reassigned to us."

Herb nodded thoughtfully. It made sense that a case involving the Urquarts would go directly to the Onyx. If they found it wasn't worth their time, they delegated. Any win was the entire department's win anyway.

"What do you glean from the information, Inspector Mooran?" Asma interrupted his thoughts.

"Well..." Herb looked back at the papers, scanning through the information. "The heir was clearly poisoned. They had screened the kitchens and his food and found nothing during the silver spoon test. That's when they turned to his medication," he summarized. "Traces of aconite in the prescriptions..."

It was common knowledge that aconite was an accessible poison as it could be used for medicinal purposes. When prepared improperly, it could be poisonous. But reactions to aconite were usually acute and quick. This didn't necessarily explain the heir's coma.

"Perhaps there could be other poisons," Herb said out loud.

"Indeed," Captain Asma nodded.

"Then they investigated where that prescription came from. The practitioner's background check is clean, and the store has a pristine reputation. But they did find some aconite that was thrown out, prepared incorrectly..." Herb paused. *How convenient.* "The issue is that the family refuses to allow inspectors close to the heir. But without examining his stomach contents, we don't know exactly what poisoned him. And we can't examine his stomach contents unless we force the heir to throw up or cut him open, both of which are impossible while he's still alive."

Why, though? Sure, it was a tumultuous time between the territories, and the ruling families should be cautious, but their son was arguably in more danger in a mysterious coma right now. It was imperative to allow them to examine the heir to potentially identify the poison. Could the Urquart family be hiding something? An even bigger secret?

"Perhaps a blood test, then?" Asma suggested.

Herb nodded slowly. "Yes. That would be another way to see if it's in the bloodstream. They have a family doctor, don't they?"

"Indeed. Dr. Kurand. Been with them for years."

"The family should trust their own doctor. Perhaps we request he take a blood sample for us."

"They've also searched The Green Thumb's inventory and premises." Asma pulled another file out. "The warrant came in, and they just completed the search this morning." She handed the folder to Herb.

He accepted it and opened the file, eyes widening. "They found a bag of Thunder God Vine and multiple herbal drugs derived from Aristolochiaceae Juss, plus a stack of feiqian from the Cru Family?" he asked incredulously.

Either The Green Thumb was magnanimously careless or someone had intentionally stacked evidence against it.

"That's right. The Crus have been on our border for years. This could be a way for them to sow chaos within our governing family to bring weakness to our system."

"And Thunder God Vine has been banned in our territory, with the only place to source it being from the Cru territory."

Captain Asma nodded. "It's pretty clear. Everything points at that practitioner: Halla Nuan."

Herb frowned. The Nuan family was well-connected, and this could make the case more complicated. It also rang alarm bells that the evidence pointed so perfectly at a Nuan. "Does this not seem much too convenient to you, Captain? The Nuan family is well-known. Why would she do anything this risky for money?"

The captain shrugged. "I heard maybe she was disowned. Perhaps her business isn't doing too well behind-the-scenes. They *did* just open a second location."

"I don't know," Herb murmured. "Is that motivation enough? Have the Onyx not found all this evidence suspicious? We still don't know what exactly poisoned the heir. Has anyone questioned Ms. Halla Nuan?"

"She claims she knows nothing, and that she was treating the heir. The heir does have a rough medical history. As for the Onyx Division..." She frowned. "No one has flagged it. There seems to be pressure from higher up to resolve the case."

"So, the Crus found out Halla Nuan was treating the heir and hired her to poison him?" Herb said flatly.

"So it seems," Asma mused. "It's all lined up quite well, wouldn't you say?"

Herb stared back at her, surprised at what she was implying, despite him reaching the same conclusion. But this was the Green Division, where cases were closed. Were they to look the other way?

"You've been doing well. Keeping up numbers," Asma continued. "I see you're a reasonable man, and I know you're a good inspector, so I'm giving this case to you to close out."

This case was different from the others Herb had been closing. All the other cases that came in were indeed straightforward, although lacking in details. But this one? Herb didn't want to simply close it. His head was buzzing with questions, and he was itching to dig into it. But could he afford to? And why was the Onyx so keen to close it that they'd ignore these clearly suspicious clues? Then again, he remembered being constantly criticized for his attention to detail and jumping into details he supposedly didn't need to when he was at the Onyx.

He met Asma's gaze. "You said my numbers have been good?"

She nodded. "I'm satisfied so long as you keep your average up."

The average? "Are you saying," he drawled tentatively, "that as long as I'm closing other cases, I can thoroughly look into this? I just have to keep my average closed numbers up?"

Captain Asma gave a sly smile as she leaned back into her chair. "I'm merely saying keep up the good numbers. And that I'm assigning this case to you to close. There will be some scrutiny on it given its high profile, but as long as your numbers are doing fine, we can manage. Do keep me posted." She turned her chair to face her computer, dismissing Herb.

He stood, dumbfounded. Was Captain Asma giving him permission to properly investigate the Urquart case? If so, why? Given her speech about closing cases his first day, Herb couldn't help but wonder if this was a ploy to get rid of him. Dangle a ripe case in front of him that he wouldn't be able to resist investigating. Or was there more to Captain Asma?

Her words echoed in his mind again. "As long as your numbers are doing fine, we can manage."

Herb smiled. He hadn't expected much of the Green Division since no one wanted to land there, but he was starting to like its captain more and more. She was giving him a chance to prove himself, and he was not going to let it go to waste.

CHAPTER 9

I *need to leave.*

Halla was lying face down on her lush carpet made to mimic the grass of soft meadows. But none of this luxury could erase the fact that she was now suspected of poisoning Rexford. The heir of their territory's founding family.

"No." She propped herself up. "I'm not running from the inspectors," she said to herself. "Why am I even considering running? I have nothing to hide. If anything, running would make me look more suspicious."

She nodded as if trying to convince herself but not before imagining herself on the news, being filmed running from inspectors armed with Apprehenders—those synth-imbued tools were the main weapon of choice for inspectors on serious cases. The glowing chest mounts were like massive spiders that could either shoot ropes to capture the person-of-interest or electric bolts to incapacitate.

With an image of her writhing on the ground from an electric bolt, Halla ran a hand down her face. *I should have never promised I would cure the Urquart's beloved son. I should have never gotten involved.* The deal seemed to be a deal of a lifetime with high yield, monetarily and reputationally. She'd forgotten that high-yield opportunities also usually held the highest risk. Grandma Wen's story of their ancestor being framed before Synesthology commonly manifested surfaced in Halla's mind. *I should have kept my head down, like Grandma always said, and not taken this case.*

Investigator Dine had come the other day with a warrant to search The Green Thumb. To Halla's shock, they had found a bag of Thunder God Vine stashed in one of the inventory rooms and multiple herbal drugs from a plant Halla didn't use for her medicine. Thunder God Vine was illegal, and there was no way Halla would source that and jeopardize her business. It was incredibly effective for treating arthritis and some inflammation, but the potential side effects made the herb too much of a health risk to use commonly.

While Halla vehemently denied stocking that herb and those drugs, another officer had found a stack of cash in an envelope with the wax seal of the Cru family. Halla had stared at the bundle and the wax seal, speechless, while Inspector Dine grinned satisfactorily. Halla didn't engage much in politics, but she knew the Cru family was the ruling family of the territory next door and had been pushing the border, waiting for it to weaken. She had no idea how that bundle of cash came to be at her shop. She had spluttered how she'd never seen it before, much less communicated with the Cru family, but that likely made her seem more suspicious.

Fortunately for her, those vital pieces of evidence were found in public backrooms and not her personal office, which was always locked. As such, Inspector Dine refrained from arresting Halla on the spot, given they still needed to establish if everything did indeed belong to Halla. Before leaving, Dine told her not to leave town, again. But with evidence piling up that Halla could not explain, leaving town was looking increasingly tempting.

The Green Thumb shut down the day of the search. Halla and her accountant, Justine, had wanted to conduct their own investigation of their employees, but Inspector Dine assured them that they were interviewing everyone. When Halla tried reaching out to Cerul and Brandus, the only response she received was, "Sorry, Boss. We were advised to minimize contact with you," from Brandus.

No response from Cerul. Halla thought her mousy practitioner was probably scared witless from everything that had happened.

As Halla wallowed in despair at her situation, her phone rang. She slammed her hand over it and raised it sluggishly.

"Hello?"

"Halla! Any updates?" It was Justine.

"You're not supposed to be talking to me," Halla said morosely.

"I know. But is some inspector person going to stop me from talking to my friend? No!" Justine exclaimed. "I know it wasn't you. There's no way you poisoned the Urquart son. You'd never poison anyone. And you're much too careful to have done it by accident. And the Crus' dirty money and those illegal herbs? That's not possible. You're smart enough to not leave massive clues around even if this were intentional."

"Justine!" Halla protested at the thought it could have been intentional. "It's at my shop, though." She sniffled. "I'm responsible for my shop."

"Well, you can't control what everyone does. I bet it was one of the newer employees. What's his name again? I'll ask Clarke if she can run a background check." Papers rustled on the other end. "Nattie! I never liked him. We didn't have issues until he came on. I suggest the inspectors investigate him," Justine huffed through the phone.

"We can't accuse my employees, Justine. And I've always liked Nattie. Inspector Dine assured me that she's interviewing everyone, and I don't know if we can use your partner's job as a way to run personal background checks."

"What does Inspector Dine know?" Justine angrily said. "If you ask me, I feel like she's out to get you. I feel like she has already made up her mind. Some kind of inspector, she is!"

She smiled sadly. "Thanks, Justine. I appreciate it. You've not only been the most efficient accountant I've ever had, but you're also a true friend."

"Now, now. Let's not talk as if your life is ending. Clarke will keep us posted about anything else she hears. Probably not the details, but I've asked her very nicely if anything massive develops to give me a vague update." Justine sounded proud of herself, but Halla wasn't sure how a 'vague' update would help.

There was a heavy pause as the two women considered the increasingly dire situation.

Justine broke the silence first. "We'll get through this. How about I come over this evening? I'll bring some beverages and snacks, and we can watch some trash television and forget about this for the evening. What do you say?"

As much as that sounded like a wonderful idea, Halla knew she wouldn't be able to get this matter off her mind. "Thanks, Justine. Maybe some other night. I'm not really feeling it today."

"You sure?" Justine asked. "I'll get that shikuwasa orange drink you like!"

Halla paused again. She really did love that drink, but she shook her head. "Not today. Thank you, Justine. Really."

"All right. I'll still get you the drink, but I'll leave it at the door so you can enjoy it. Don't spiral too much, okay?"

Halla was definitely spiraling an hour after the call ended. She wondered whether she should pack her bags and flee to Cru territory. But if Inspector Dine found out, she'd probably take that as admittance of Halla working with the Cru family. Halla could try fleeing to the Tripa or Armand territories, but those were much farther and required multi-day trips. Despite understanding herbs, Halla wasn't very good at camping or working outdoors.

She thought of her dream. *Or I hide back at the Nuan estate,* she thought before vetoing it immediately. *No. That would bring the inspectors to my family. I don't want them getting pulled into something.*

Halla flopped back onto her rug, facing the ceiling. She couldn't sit and do nothing. She'd worked much too hard to see it fall apart. "I'm going to go back to The Green Thumb," she said to herself. "Take a look around."

No one will be there anyway, since I had to shut it down. I'll do my own investigation.

CHAPTER 10

Herb shut the file in front of him, placing it on top of the stack on his desk.

"Finally finished with this stack," he said while stretching.

He checked the wall clock and noted he was finished before ending hour. That was a first. He usually got bogged down by details, finishing right on the dot. *I must be eager to get to the Urquart case.* He opened his desk drawer and took out the file, reviewing the contents again. There was only so much he could deduce from these notes. He'd worked with Inspector Dine previously in the Onyx Division. She was an efficient inspector, but would she take time to look at all the avenues if she found one that was promising? Too many clues did not line up, but there was no other glaring suspect. When there were no other suspects, and all the evidence pointed at only one, Herb got suspicious.

The best way to learn more is to go to the place in question. None of the other inspectors in the open-concept office paid him any attention as he rose. Captain Asma glanced up and gave him a slight nod from her office before continuing her work. He smiled to himself, placing the file into his briefcase, and headed out.

Herb had been to The Green Thumb once before. His nephew was having trouble sleeping a year ago, so he had come to The Green Thumb for their well-known over-the-counter tummy stickers. He had been amazed that a wad of crushed longan, four-river peppers, and mugwort attached to a round sticker applied to the belly button was so effective. He'd taken a few from the pack to try himself and found it helped with his bloating as well.

Standing in front of the store, it looked no different than it did a year ago. Other than being closed and no longer filled with customers, that was. He wondered if he could search the premises again with Dine's warrant and decided to poke around today and revisit that question tomorrow at the office. There was probably nothing to be found around the shop, but walking around and seeing it made Herb feel like he was doing something more useful than sitting at a desk.

He checked the trash area at the back where the previous team had found aconite. Today, it was pristine. *Probably because the store's been closed.* No matter how he looked at the store, Herb couldn't imagine it being a front for a political enemy. He figured he'd have to interview Halla Nuan sometime. He took the file out again to find her home address. It wasn't very far.

Herb turned to head in the direction of Halla's home when he saw movement out of the corner of his eye. He swiveled his head back to the store's large glass window and noticed a light in the backrooms had turned on, the glow coming through the doorway at the back wall of the shop.

Is someone here?

He walked around the building to the back door again and saw light pooling out from under the door. He tried the knob, and it was unlocked. *Do I knock? Tell them I'm on official business? Or do I let myself in and see if someone else is snooping around?* His hand was still on the door knob as he teetered between the two decisions. After a few seconds, he decided to proceed the proper way. Either the person opened the door or didn't. If they didn't, it would be suspicious, and maybe then, Herb would invite himself in to investigate.

He knocked. "Is anyone inside? This is Inspector Mooran," he announced. After a few moments, he heard steps approaching from inside.

"Another inspector?" a woman's voice called. "About my case?"

"Yes. I've been assigned to your case recently." He figured the woman must be Halla with her earlier question. "Do you have a moment to speak?"

The door opened a crack, and a woman with long wavy black hair peered at him. "What's this about?" she asked.

"Are you Halla Nuan?"

She seemed to hesitate a moment. "Yes, I am."

"I'm Inspector Mooran. I have your file, but I'd like to hear from you personally as well. I was going to stop by your home when I saw some movement inside the shop." He showed her his insignia badge.

Her eyes widened in alarm. "Why were you checking out my shop while no one's here? Actually, nevermind. Of course you would look around. Yes, come in. I'd stopped by because I couldn't clear my head." She opened the door wider, shaking his hand before inviting him in. As the light caught on her hair, Herb noticed it gave off a green sheen. *How strange. Is this due to Nuan family closeness to mythical creatures like rumors say?*

He followed her down the hallway and into a lit kitchen. One wall looked like a standard industrial kitchen, like one would find in a high-end restaurant: multiple stacked stainless steel ovens with state-of-the-art ranges, two large dehydrators, wall-mounted pot fillers, a sealed door to a freezer, and numerous pots and pans hanging on the walls and from the ceiling. The rest of the room was filled with large machines for batch roasting or packing. Herb was amazed at how clean and organized the room was. He imagined if it weren't for The Green Thumb having been closed for a few days, he probably would have seen machines on, roasting and packing. They exited the large room to another hallway.

"I thought Inspector Dine was handling my case," Halla said as they walked down the hallway.

"She was," he confirmed. "And the department decided to delegate to another division. That's when I was assigned to your case."

"So, you're continuing the investigation?"

"That's right." He paused, considering how much to share. "Frankly, there's a lot of information in the file that wasn't clear, so I wanted to look into it more." He wasn't sure why he decided to tell Halla that much but had felt it wouldn't do any harm.

"Really?" Her voice pitched higher.

Was she surprised? Hopeful? Or was she really the culprit and surprised she could get away with this?

The two of them arrived at her office, and Halla offered him a seat and some pre-brewed tea. He accepted the small, green-glazed cup, not intending to drink it, but he caught a whiff of it as he put it down.

"This is quite fragrant. What is it?"

Halla smiled as she inhaled deeply from her own cup. "It's our jujube goji tea. A blend of dried dates, goji berries, and dried chrysanthemum. We sell some, if you like it. Marketed as our 'Stress Tea'." She took a sip. "It's great for digestion and alleviates stress. I figured I needed some." She suddenly snapped her head back to Herb. "Not that I'm stressed about the investigation, of course. I have full confidence the poisoner will be caught." She glanced away.

She must know that she's the top suspect. "Thanks for the tea. Let's get to the matter at hand. Were you treating the Urquart heir?"

"I was." Halla sat straighter.

"How did you come to treat him?" *If she really was approached by the Cru family, she wouldn't say that. She'd make something up. But maybe she was approached by someone who works for the Crus; like an intermediary. Then she wouldn't know the connection.*

"One of their employees, Mr. Thrum, approached me. You can ask them."

Herb shook his head. "Unfortunately, although the Urquarts have promised to assist our investigation, their priority is identifying the poison within their son, which they've left to their own family doctor to determine. They want to catch the culprit, but I can't quite knock on their door out of the blue. I need to put in a request to speak with them, and I don't know when that would be."

The woman frowned. "How can there be a proper investigation if you can't question the Urquarts?"

"It definitely makes it a bit more complicated," Herb sighed. "But we work with what we have. Inspector Dine was able to interview them initially, so I have those files."

Halla opened her mouth but then stopped herself, crossing her arms.

"Was Mr. Thrum approaching you the first time you'd ever seen him?" Herb asked.

"It was!" she answered defiantly. "I'd never seen him before."

"And they paid you for treating their son?"

"Correct. I have my bank statements. You can ask my accountant, as well."

"What of the payment we found on your premises from the Crus?"

"Inspector Dine waving it in front of me was the first I'd ever seen it. I don't know where it came from."

"As for the aconite on your premises—"

"That's not mine," Halla interrupted. "That ingredient is too particular. I don't use it, and you can check my inventory stocklist. Nor do I use the Thunder God Vine and the other herbs they found. I have a large shop with multiple employees and large traffic. Anyone could have placed those things at my shop."

Herb looked at her thoughtfully, observing her firm voice and steady gaze as well as a whisper of anger behind those eyes.

"Do you have any cameras or viewing orbs in your shop?"

Halla looked away in embarrassment. "I have them in the shop as a deterrent for shoplifting or theft, but I don't have any in the backrooms. I've vetted my practitioners and put a lot of trust in them. Besides, our prescriptions and recipes are confidential. I can't have that getting out."

I guess you didn't vet them thoroughly enough if you don't know who planted illegal substances and cash in your own shop. He didn't let his judgment show, just nodding instead.

"If your shop reopens, I advise you to invest in some cameras or crafters to create viewing orbs for the back."

She looked at him. "*If* my shop reopens? Are you saying there's a chance it won't? I assumed once the investigation was over and I was cleared, that I'd be able to reopen."

"I think you know that the evidence is stacked against you, even though a lot of it doesn't fully pan out to me—"

"Exactly!" Halla exclaimed, interrupting again. "Some of the evidence doesn't make sense!"

Herb put his hand up to continue. "Even then, your shop has taken a huge reputational hit with this high-profile case. It will be hard to recover."

The more he talked with Halla, the more his gut told him it wasn't her, unless she was an incredible actor.

Halla looked away, crestfallen. "That's true," she muttered. "I've had to close my second location as well because no one has been going since the news articles came out."

"I'll get to the bottom of this, though." Herb found himself assuring her. "I'm known for keeping cases open for a long time because," he smiled, more to himself than to her, "I can't help but dig and examine every lead and potential. I get in trouble for it quite a bit. I love figuring things out, but sometimes, the job doesn't call for that."

He looked back at her and found her smiling softly at him.

"I get that, in a way," she said. "That urge is probably what got me in this mess in the first place. When I heard about the Urquart son, I wanted to figure out what his illness was. When I examined him and observed how complicated the state of his health was, I was more determined to dive into each color and identify it."

Herb perked at that. "You're a synther?"

She nodded, face taking a quizzical expression. "A sensor, in particular. You didn't know this from my family name?"

"Well, I know the Nuans are a medical family with extraordinary sensors. But there'd never been any mention of it in the articles about you. I thought maybe you just didn't receive the ability."

She looked away. "I did. But I wasn't trained thoroughly in it. I left home at a pretty young age, which was untraditional for our family. Honestly, Rexford was the first person I'd used synthing on in a long time."

Rexford? She must be pretty close to the heir if she's referring to him by first name. "Hold on. You treated the heir with a method you haven't trained in?"

"Well, don't look so aghast!" Halla said. "I didn't say I wasn't trained in it at all! I said I wasn't 'thoroughly' trained in synthing! There's a difference."

Not much... Herb internally rolled his eyes. He would never try a new investigative method or tool in a big case. It was much too unreliable.

"Do you practice Synesthology at your job?" Halla asked, likely trying to turn attention away from herself.

"No."

"I thought a lot of inspectors were sensors," she said unconvincingly. Everyone knew synthing skills weren't needed anymore.

Herb gave her a look. "Only a handful," he said. "We have lie-detection machines and polygraphs anyway. Synesthology is just a nice-to-have. A lot of the synthers we have don't really use it anyway since we wear gloves with our uniform."

"I noticed."

At that, Herb narrowed his eyes. Had she tried to synth him through his hands earlier? Perhaps the handshake? *I thought she said she wasn't well-practiced in the art.*

Halla shrugged. "It doesn't matter anyway. I guess, like in the medical field, synthers willing to use their abilities are becoming few and far between."

Herb wanted to get back on topic, not discuss Synesthology philosophy. Despite his intuition telling him Halla was innocent, he had to conduct his due diligence.

He opened his mouth to start his next line of questions when something crashed outside Halla's office.

Both he and Halla fell silent, staring at each other.

"Did you hear that?" she whispered.

"Of course, I heard that," he whispered back. He put a finger to his lips, signaling her to keep quiet. "The backroom kitchen?" he mouthed.

That was where the sound seemed to have come from. Halla nodded quickly.

Herb slowly stood from his chair, careful not to scoot furniture. He reached back to unsheath the black baton affixed to his belt. With his intention, the stick reacted and elongated into a six-foot staff. Halla stifled a gasp at the imbued synth tool. Herb had always been more taken to his studies and investigations, not fighting or physical enforcement. But all investigators received basic training. Investigations sometimes got them into sticky situations, and Herb hoped he didn't seem too nervous.

Without looking back at Halla, Herb headed to her office door to make his way toward the kitchen they had passed through earlier. Before placing both hands on his staff, he motioned to Halla to stay put and then exited her office.

CHAPTER 11

Maybe it's one of my practitioners, Halla thought. But that didn't seem likely given all her employees had been advised by the inspectors to minimize contact with her, resulting in them probably avoiding their previous workplace like a contagious disease.

She knew Inspector Mooran had signaled for her to stay in her office as he investigated, but this was *her* shop. She got up silently and peeked out her doorway. Inspector Mooran made his way down the hall, focused on where the crash came from, so she inched out fifteen feet behind him. He slipped into the kitchen. Since she was most familiar with her shop, Halla felt she could be of help spotting an intruder in that room full of equipment.

As she passed multiple doors, she noticed one was open. The door of Examination Room 8: the one that was inspired by the Nuan Estate and dedicated to Grandma Wen. Halla frowned and paused. She was sure the door had been shut when they'd gone through the hall earlier. She stepped through to close it when she noticed slight movement inside.

She jumped and flipped on the lights. Someone was huddled under the examination bed. Halla opened her mouth to scream when the figure put out a hand.

"Wait! Halla, it's me!" In Halla's state of alert, she hadn't recognized Rexford's male form.

"Rex! What're you doing here?" Halla whispered, rushing to Rex and putting her hands on the heir's shoulders. "Actually, *how* are you here? I thought you were in a coma."

She glanced back in the direction of the kitchen, wondering if Inspector Mooran had heard them, then placed her hand on Rex's. Although Rex's body was still a cacophony of colors, it was in the same general state as the last time she'd examined the heir. She breathed a sigh of relief.

"I was!" Rex whispered back. "Well, not really. I was just in a near-death state, but it was temporary!"

"What do you mean?" Halla's mind whirled at a thousand miles a minute. "Do your parents know you're here?"

Rex avoided Halla's eyes. "Not really..."

Halla stood and placed her hands on her hips. "You're going to have to answer with more than 'not really'. We need to tell them. In fact, there's an inspector here. We can announce to him you're fine."

She made it one step toward the door before Rex's arm whipped out and grabbed her ankle.

"No! We can't!" Rex said.

Halla clenched her fists. How could Rex not see how serious this was? "Why not?"

"I ran," Rex said, more quietly than her previous whispers.

Halla wasn't sure she'd heard correctly. "You what?" She kneeled next to Rex.

"I ran from home. I'm tired of being locked there like a bird in a cage."

"You ran from home?" Halla repeated, flabbergasted. "Why?"

"I'm dying, Halla. I hear all the whispers. I know. I want to see the world before I die rather than being hooked to machines or pendants," Rex said firmly.

"Halla?" Inspector Mooran called from afar.

Rex shot up and ran out the door.

"Wait!" Halla called.

She darted after Rex, running down the hall away from the kitchen. Rex was going to escape through the front of the shop.

"Hold on! Your body is still not stable! You have to be careful!" she called.

"Halt!" Inspector Mooran demanded behind her. Halla stopped in her tracks and turned to face him. He was at the doorway of the kitchen.

"Where are you going, Halla?"

She glanced over her shoulder after Rex. Clearly, Rex didn't want Inspector Mooran to know she was here, but she was also just a child who didn't know what was best for her. And Halla's life was on the line too—being a suspect of poisoning the heir who was apparently *not* in a coma.

"It's Rexford," she called back to Inspector Mooran. Her fingernails dug into the palms of her hands as she clenched.

"What?" he yelled, running toward her.

"Rexford is awake!" She glanced back in the direction Rex ran. Halla didn't want to lose her. "I have to go after her—I mean, him! I have to go, Inspector! Sorry!"

And then she left him, hoping Rex hadn't gotten too far.

"Where are you going?" he shouted.

"I don't know! I have to go after Rex!"

"Halla, you can't run from the inspectors! I can't help you if you do!"

"I'm not! I'm going after Rex!"

Why doesn't he get it? She didn't have time to explain when Rex had a head start. If Rex was running from home, she definitely would not last whatever journey this was without treatment.

Halla ran through the opening to her dark storefront just in time to see Rex running past the store window, outside already. The front door was cracked open.

"Great Doa." Halla cursed under her breath and ran after the small figure lest she lose her.

"Halla!" Inspector Mooran called.

Halla burst through the front door into the cool night air and didn't look back.

Ahming's Cooking

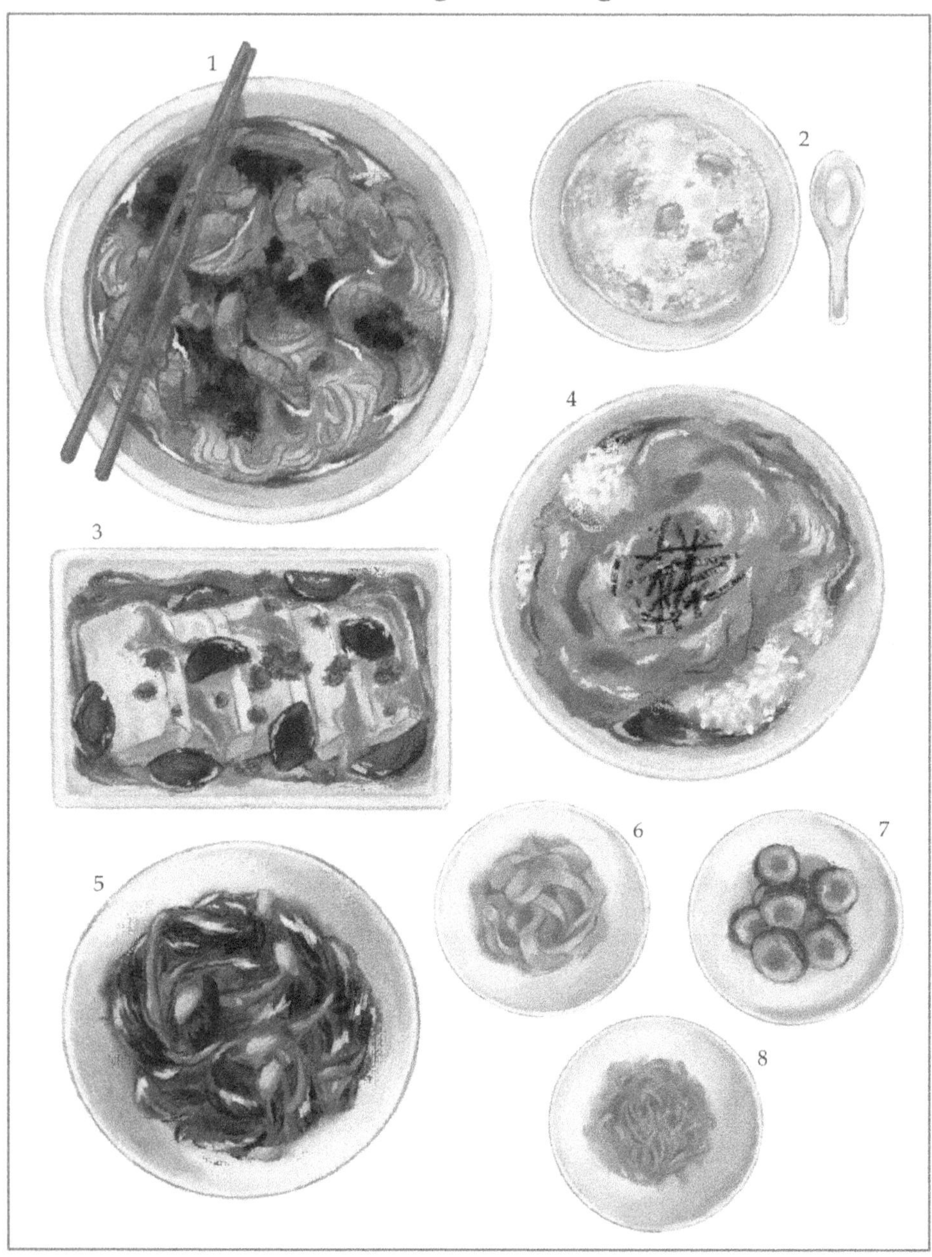

1. pork and pickled mustard greens noodle soup. — 2. sweet potato congee. — 3. century egg with silken tofu. — 4. scrambled eggs with soy sauce over rice. — 5. stir-fried yu choy. — 6. pickled red onion. 7. pickled cucumber. — 8. pickled yellow radish.

CHAPTER 12

Halla finally caught up to Rexford at a noodle shop. The girl—in boy form—stared at the shop display of wax imitation foods depicting heaping bowls of soup with thick noodles lifted by floating chopsticks. It was already dark outside but still early in the night. Halla walked to Rexford before resting her hands on her knees.

"Rex, you need to explain to me what's going on," she said between gasps. It had been a long time since she'd run that far or that fast.

"I've never had noodles like these," Rex said without taking her eyes off the display.

"What?"

"My parents always said it had too much sodium and wasn't good for me." Rex suddenly turned to Halla, startling her. "I'm going to have some today."

That's right. She'd wanted to try a proper restaurant. She straightened. "First, do you have money? And second, you can't enter the restaurant. Everyone knows who you are. Even if you weren't running from home and wanting to keep this all a secret, people would stare or record you."

Rexford smirked in her male form. "Not if I do this." She raised a hand to her pendant and deactivated it.

Halla watched Rexford's transformation to her true female form in shock. Halla had seen this transformation multiple times but always behind closed doors. To see the change occur in public felt like she was seeing something she shouldn't.

"Rex!" Halla exclaimed while moving to shield Rexford with her own body. She glanced over her shoulder. "You shouldn't be doing that here! Do you want people to know who you are?"

"Relax, Halla. No one was around. In my true form, no one knows who I am anyway. Time to finally live some life." Rexford pushed past Halla, opened the door to the noodle shop, and entered. Halla had no choice but to follow.

A savory aroma of pork broth and mushrooms hit Halla upon entering.

This would be an imbuing synther's worst nightmare. As a sensor, Halla saw colors through touch, but imbuers saw colors through smell. She briefly wondered what colors an imbuer would have seen with the scent of the simmering broths and meats wafting throughout the shop before finding a seat across from Rexford.

A waiter meandered over, providing utensils and water. "Are you ready to order?" he asked them.

"Order? How do I order?" Rexford asked.

The waiter gave her a confused look before looking to Halla for help.

"We tell him what food we want. They have a menu we choose from," Halla explained.

"Oh. It's not a set menu that they serve?"

Halla gave Rexford a deadpan expression, annoyed at the privilege and wealth Rexford's question copiously leaked. She reminded herself that Rexford likely grew up sheltered and ate only at the Urquart estate before explaining, "No. There are options."

"Oh." Rexford looked thoughtful.

"Are you going to order or not?" The waiter tapped his foot impatiently.

Halla shared in this impatience. She had to get to the bottom of this poisoning, and Rexford was sitting right in front of her. Did Rexford know anything more about the poisoning case? Then suddenly, another inspector showed up as if they're throwing her case around? Frankly, Halla liked Inspector Mooran better than Dine, but it didn't feel great that her case seemed to have transitioned hands without much thought.

"Yes, we'll order right now," Halla said tersely. She had questions and needed Rexford to stop thinking about food in order to ask them.

Halla turned to Rexford and snapped. "Which one in the display did you want?"

"All of them looked so good," Rexford said contemplatively.

Halla frowned. *How long will this girl take to order?*

"What's your most popular dish?" she asked the waiter.

"It's our pork and pickled greens noodle soup."

As Rexford's doctor, Halla knew Rexford didn't have food allergies. "Then we'll have two orders of that. Thanks."

The waiter scrawled something onto a sheet of paper and then yelled to the kitchen as he turned away. "Two PPG noodles!"

"Aye, two PPG noodles coming right up!" the kitchen staff responded in unison.

Halla turned her attention back to Rexford and found the girl staring at the kitchen with saucer-like eyes.

"It's so lively," Rexford said with wonder.

Halla looked at the young girl curiously, musing at how a girl her age had never been to, nor seen, the most common kind of shop. Then she remembered the arguments she'd heard Rexford and Mrs. Urquart having in front of her about Rexford being constantly monitored at home. She'd previously empathized with the small girl trapped at home, but today, she was confused and angry. What had Rex gotten her into?

"Rex," Halla addressed her. "Can you explain what in Doa is going on?"

Rexford met her eyes before looking away.

"Rex," Halla urged. "Whether you like it or not, I'm now involved in this. How are you not in a coma? Why does everyone *think* you're in a coma? And why were you at my shop this evening?"

"I'm sorry, Halla," Rex said to her lap, not meeting Halla's gaze.

"For what?"

"I... I stole from you."

"You what!?" A few customers shot their table a dirty look at Halla's outburst, so Halla collected herself. Pursing her lips, she tried to keep her cool. "What did you steal?"

"A few herbs," Rexford said quietly.

Halla raised her brows. "If you wanted some specific herbs, you could have asked me. I don't mind giving herbs as long as they're used responsibly."

"You wouldn't have given them to me," Rexford muttered.

"And why's that?" Halla crossed her arms.

"I took some thorn-apple."

Halla froze in shock. "Why would you want thorn-apple?" she asked, but she already had a feeling she knew the answer. Thorn-apple leaves could be used to treat asthma and had antispasmodic and sedative properties. If not properly prepared, however...

"I had to fake a coma," Rexford said.

Halla sucked in a breath, not sure if it was in relief or disbelief. On one hand, she could not believe Rexford would try such an insane plan. On the other hand, she was glad Rexford wasn't actually poisoned. By someone else, that was. She supposed Rexford had actually poisoned herself.

"I don't know what to say," Halla finally said.

"I did it responsibly!" Rexford said. "I not only had thorn-apple, but I also took some of the dried wax apple-pear which is the antidote! With the right mixture, I knew I'd wake up within a time limit."

"Doing it 'responsibly' is not the issue here!" Halla said. "What you did was incredibly dangerous! Even trained professionals do not do this. How did you even know how to make the draught or what thorn-apple does?"

Rexford shrugged. "A book."

"A book?" Halla echoed incredulously. "You read a book and decided to just *try it*?"

Was the girl incredibly irresponsible, or was she a genius?

"I read it carefully!" Rexford defended herself. "I tried making the draught multiple times with different dosages and tried on mice! From there, I calculated the difference in weight to get my dosage."

Halla couldn't believe her ears. "How could you treat your life like this? Anything could have gone wrong!"

Rexford suddenly frowned, anger blooming on her face. "I've been sick for years. My body's been prodded left and right. I've been told that my life is tenuous, and that it could extinguish at any moment. How is this any different from what I've been told?"

Halla threw her hands up in frustration. "That doesn't mean you can just throw away your life. Your parents have tried so hard to keep your health up. Dr. Kurand. Myself."

Rexford looked away. Her frown softened, but it was still present. "I didn't ask for that."

Halla looked away as well. There was a lot she, too, never asked for. Like Grandma's expectation that she inherit the family business long ago.

As the shock of what Rex had done began to wear off, more questions bubbled to the surface.

If Rex had stolen some thorn-apple and wax apple-pear, then how does that explain the Thunder God Vine, the aconite, drugs, and money that were found at The Green Thumb?

"Two pork and pickled greens noodle soup," the waiter announced while placing two large, steaming bowls onto their table.

Halla's mouth immediately watered. The light-colored soup seemed to glisten in richness under the light with slivers of pork and greens resting atop the mound of noodles underneath.

Rexford brought her face close to the bowl, inhaling the steam before digging in. She stuck her chopsticks in, pulling up the noodles, and slurped. Halla followed suit and found the noodles to be an excellent bouncy texture and the broth to be flavorful. They ate silently for the next few minutes, Halla casting curious glances at Rex the whole time, surrounded by sounds of quiet conversation among other customers and their own sounds of slurping and soup spoons clinking against the bowls.

"That was so good," Rexford sighed contentedly.

Halla agreed with a hum. "I didn't know about this shop. I don't think it's recognized on any gourmet lists."

"Gourmet lists?"

"A lot of restaurants and shops get rankings. Restaurants will be ranked by gourmet lists that will identify top twenty restaurants and give a star ranking. My apothecary shop, for example, is listed on the wellness lists and is given a five-star."

Rexford nodded thoughtfully. "I'd be curious to see what else is on these gourmet lists. I recall many of the chefs at our estate have worked at highly ranked restaurants. But my food was always boring and cooked separately." She pouted.

"Honestly, take those lists with a grain of salt. Some things could be skewed. People say some shops donate a lot of money to make their way onto them. To accept a spot on the lists, you have to pay a fee as well, so there probably are a few establishments who get nominated but don't pay to retain the spot. There are still plenty of restaurants that have delicious food and aren't on any list. Like this noodle shop," Halla found herself saying. She then wondered what that meant about The Green Thumb. Was it important to be on those lists? She immediately tossed that thought away. "Anyway, before the food came out, we were talking about how you faked your coma."

"Right..." Rexford said slowly, uneager to continue the discussion.

"Why did you do it?" Halla tried her best to keep her tone even.

She could understand Rexford's frustration at home, on one hand, and the want to be free, but on the other hand, she could not understand why Rexford put Halla's life's work on the line.

Rexford met Halla's eyes. "Halla, you've done more for me than any other doctor has. For once, I can stand for longer periods of time and run and not feel like fainting. I ran all the way here, for example." She puffed her chest proudly before slightly deflating. "I know my body still needs a lot of work, but I want to take advantage of this health you gave me. I had asked my parents if I could go out more or finally go on a school field trip, but they vehemently opposed it. That's when I realized it made no difference. No matter what, they'd want to keep me close.

"I know they think it's best and want to protect me from the Cru family or from overexerting, but I don't want to live my life in fear like this. So, I decided I'd fake a coma. With them expecting me to be unconscious in bed, they wouldn't monitor me as closely, and I would have more chances to sneak away. I'll go back home later, of course," Rex added quickly. "But this is my chance to live a little first."

Halla rubbed her temples with both hands. She couldn't blame Rexford's thought process, but she still felt it was incredibly childish. "Your parents don't know? Do you know how worried sick they were about the coma? And probably incredibly worried now that you're gone. You could have gotten more sick without treatment on your own. And now, the inspectors think I poisoned you!"

"I know," Rexford said quietly. "I didn't mean for it to blow back on you. Once I woke, I left my parents a note that I was alive and well, and that I'd come back soon. I left it in my room so they won't be too worried."

I feel like that doesn't assuage any worries. But at least she did *leave a note.* "Why did you come by The Green Thumb today?" she asked Rexford. "I can't imagine you'd be returning the herbs that you stole since you used them."

"I came by to leave you a note," Rex said. Halla quirked a brow. "I overheard that you'd been blamed for my coma. I never intended for that to happen! I thought they would just think something developed in my illness. So, I wanted to leave you a note explaining all of this and to apologize."

Halla crossed her arms. "I think an in-person account would be more helpful for me, but I suppose a note works for the most part. I, too, have no idea how this came to be, but they found poisonous substances among the prescription parcels I gave you, among other things, at The Green Thumb. Nothing matches up, but these substances shouldn't be here, and I have no idea where they came from. Your little *stunt*," Halla emphasized that last word, "has put me in a precarious situation."

"I'm sorry, Halla," Rexford said.

"But," Halla said, perking up, "maybe the notes you left will acquit me of any potential charges. Where is it?"

"I left it in that examination room at The Green Thumb."

Halla nodded, hoping Inspector Mooran found it. "Time to go back then?"

She was keen for Rexford to explain everything to the authorities and the Urquarts so that Halla could be out of this situation.

Rexford knit her brows. "No. I'm not ready yet. I just need a few days. A few days to experience things."

Halla clenched her jaw, frustration spiking. Why could this little girl not understand the trouble she put Halla in? She gave Rexford a once-over and determined she would not have the strength to pick up or drag Rexford back easily. She also knew how Rexford felt, to a degree, so she decided to try another route rather than directly opposing Rexford.

"Fine. Let's say you get these few days. Where would you go? What're you going to do?"

"I know they'd be able to track me if I used my parents' credit cards, so I brought some cash feiqian that we stash away. I have enough to last me a few days. I'll explore."

"Where will you go then? Where will you sleep at night?"

Rexford suddenly looked a bit unsure. "I'm unfamiliar with the city. Maybe I'll walk around, catch a ride here or there?"

Halla threw her a withering look. "You didn't plan this too thoroughly, did you, Rex?"

"I was a bit more concerned with making sure this coma draught worked, okay?" Rex retorted. "And I did a pretty good job with that. I'm sure I can figure out the rest."

Halla sighed. As Rexford's doctor, she couldn't let Rexford run around without medical supervision now that she was aware of the situation. Not on her conscience. But where could they go? Once the Urquarts found Rexford missing, would they think that she kidnapped the heir?

An idea formed in Halla's head, but she wasn't sure if it was the best idea. It would require her to leave the city. Exactly what Inspector Dine told her *not* to do. With nowhere to go, the safest place would be the Nuan estate. Close enough to town, but far enough that Rexford could live out her day or two of freedom before Halla dragged the girl back. Perhaps her family could help convince the girl to return sooner. She hadn't wanted to bring the problem to her family, but being at the Nuan estate would also provide the apothecary resources and herbs Halla needed to keep Rexford's health in check. Did she want to help the girl, though? Especially when she'd significantly complicated her life? Did Halla want to go home? She thought of her dream and ran a hand down her face before clearing her throat.

"If you don't have set plans, how about you come with me to the country-side?"

The girl's eyes widened. "I've always wanted to see the countryside! But isn't that too far?"

"Well..." Halla smiled at the girl's excitement and wonder, which reminded her of her own excitement when she'd decided to move to the capital many years ago. "If you're going to dream, at least dream big. Let's go out. My family's estate is out there, so we can visit them. I'd like to continue treating you during this journey of yours."

Rexford clasped her hands together. "That sounds amazing! I'd love to see what a country estate looks like! And is it true your family raises mystic beasts? And makes all sorts of mystic potions?"

Halla guffawed. "We're not deities, you know," she said between laughs. "It's 'mythical', not 'mystic' beasts. Yes, my family raises ranyi, but they're descendents of the original beasts. My family doesn't make 'mystic' potions, but my grandma's concoctions always worked wonders."

"I'd love to see some ranyi." Rexford's eyes widened. "And meet your grandmother, then! Maybe she can help me, too."

Halla's face fell. "She passed a few years ago."

"Oh, I'm so sorry," Rexford said, curbing her earlier excitement.

"It's fine," Halla responded, knowing full well it wasn't quite fine.

She had suggested her family's estate so that she could at least keep an eye on Rexford's health with the materials and herbs she needed. Hopefully, the country estate would also scratch that exploration itch Rexford had, and maybe she could learn more about synthing that could help Rexford.

"Sounds like a plan."

"Great. I'll call a cab." Rexford slurped the remainder of the soup.

Halla checked her watch. "At this hour? Nightfall is upon us. By the time we arrive, it may be near twilight."

Rexford shrugged. "My time is limited. I'd rather get to it. I have the cash anyway." She stood up, then looked back at Halla. "How do we call a cab?"

Halla groaned. She waved the waiter over for the bill. After fighting with Rexford over it, she prevailed and paid for Rexford's first "outside" meal. Apparently, this was a special occasion to be remembered. They both exited the warm shop into the brisk air, and Halla called the taxi line.

"Since this is a nighttime drive, there will be a price surge," she said to Rexford. The girl was bouncing with excitement.

"A full belly. Being out in my own skin. And now on the way to the countryside under the moonlight? We're just getting started!"

Halla rolled her eyes. She was babysitting a sheltered child who was supposed to have been comatose, supposedly poisoned by Halla. With Halla being a number one suspect and seen running from the last inspector, Halla was sure it didn't look good for her and wanted to clear her name. But she also couldn't find herself dragging Rexford back after all the effort and planning the girl had made for this sliver of freedom.

It didn't sound so different from the hard work Halla put into leaving the Nuan estate and building her own life to escape her family pressures. As the cab they requested approached with its bright headlights, she put a hand on the girl's shoulder, feeling a responsibility for Rexford.

Halla woke up the next morning to sun rays peeking in through latticed windows. It was her childhood bedroom. She and Rexford had arrived at the Nuan estate in the night and knocked on the massive wooden front doors. After some time (as it took people a few moments to walk from the inner chambers to the door), Halla's brother had inquired who they were. With wide eyes, he'd opened the doors to find his sister and a small girl. Halla had put a hand to his face, telling him she'd explain in the morning.

When Halla got like that, he didn't push. She'd led Rexford through the front door into the courtyard that was the center of the estate. With her exhaustion, she'd paid the courtyard no heed and brought Rexford to a guest bedroom, warning the small girl not to wander without her, before she shuffled to her own bedroom and slumped into bed.

Now, that was where she lay, a forearm across her face as she shielded herself from the sun. Her family had insisted on no curtains so they could rise with the morning light as nature intended.

"What am I doing here?" Halla murmured to herself. Her bedroom had remained the same even though she didn't often visit anymore, as if her parents had been waiting for her all this time. There was a knock at her door, and she sat up.

Her mother, Mrs. Nuan, floated into the room without waiting for permission. "Halla! What are you doing here? When Harley told me, I couldn't believe it! Why didn't you tell us you were coming? Why'd you come so late? Where's all your luggage?"

She settled herself on the edge of Halla's bed.

"I didn't give you early notice because I didn't even know I was coming, Mom. It was a very spontaneous decision." Halla rubbed the sleep out of her eyes.

"I have nothing but time, dear." Her mother waited patiently.

Halla took a deep breath and figured there was no time like the present. She started from the beginning, when Mr. Thrum approached her. She regaled every detail to her mother, leaving out the fact that Rexford was the Urquart heir. Instead, she glossed over it by saying Rexford was the daughter of a family business conglomerate. By the end, her mother had a hand clasped over her mouth.

"Halla, if I didn't know how serious you were in general, I would have thought you were pranking me! This all sounds so fantastic."

Halla gave her mother a flat stare. "If you mean 'fantastic' as in it's unbelievable, then yes, I agree. If you mean it in a positive connotation, then I strongly disagree. I'm suspected of a criminal act! A criminal act." Halla dragged out the last sentence to emphasize the gravitas of the situation.

"Of course I don't mean it in a positive way!" Mrs. Nuan put a hand to her heart, affronted. "Why don't we just talk to the inspectors?"

Halla groaned. "I *was* talking to them! But it doesn't look good for me. And now, I ran after Rex, and that inspector probably thinks I was running from *him*! Do you know how high the percentage is of innocents who are falsely convicted?"

"What is it?" Her mom looked genuinely curious.

"I don't know!" Halla threw up her hands. "I just know it's high. And I'm soon going to be a part of that percentage. I'll become a statistic students read about in books." She groaned in despair.

"Now, now, honey. A lot has been happening over a short period of time. Let's take some deep breaths. We can discuss more after we've eaten. As you know, Grandma's always said that one can't think without a proper meal." Mrs. Nuan patted Halla's legs through the covers. "I'll have Ahming prepare breakfast while you change, and I'll fetch the girl that was with you."

Halla nodded as her mother left the room. She undressed from her city clothes of a blouse and jeans and rummaged through the wardrobe. It had remained untouched as well, filled with the traditional clothing they wore on the estate and within the nearby village. She picked out a fit, pulling on trousers that transitioned from cream to a bright orange at the hem, and donning a long, loose top of honeysuckle orange. She tied her hair into a messy low bun and entered the central courtyard from her room, walking across to the wing of common areas, including the massive Hall of Central Harmony for entertaining guests, the kitchen, the Room of Inner Fulfillment where they dined, and other shared spaces.

When she entered the Room of Inner Fulfillment, the round table at the center of the room was already filled with steaming dishes. Taking it in, she'd forgotten how much she missed having hot breakfasts. It was something she grew up with, at Grandma Wen's insistence. In traditional medicine, it was said warm foods made it easier for the stomach and body to digest since the temperature was closer to body temperature. Despite Halla being a practitioner and opening an apothecary, she didn't follow this advice within her own schedule, usually opting for a quick cold cereal or yogurt before running out the door. It was a well known fact that doctors made the worst patients, oftentimes.

A pot of steaming congee with chunks of sweet potato sat in the middle of the table, surrounded by dishes of scrambled eggs slathered in soy sauce, tofu and preserved egg drenched in oyster sauce and scallions, stir-fried leafy greens, grilled whole mackerel, pork sung (meat dried to the form of a cotton-like texture), and various small, fermented vegetables. Ahming, a woman with a speckling of grays within her bun, brought in the last bowl of purple rice and sat, noticing Halla with a soft smile, and motioned for her to come in. Ahming had worked for the Nuan family for years, and Halla viewed her as an aunt who was there for her whenever her own mother was too busy. Halla greeted the woman with a hug.

Mrs. Nuan, Halla's brother—Harley, and Rexford were already seated. Rexford stared at the table hungrily.

At least she seems to have a good appetite. Halla reminded herself that she'd need to examine Rexford's condition later.

"Where's Dad?" Halla asked as she sat.

"He's traveling for work," Mrs. Nuan said.

Halla's father, Mr. Yong, was in the business of procurement. Procurement of mythical beasts. Many did not exist in their modern times, but descendents were in certain ecological pockets. Ever since Grandma Wen's passing, the Nuan's main income from treating patients had taken a hit, since no one else in the family other than Halla had inherited her talents. Mrs. Nuan could diagnose minor ailments and prescribe treatments for the flu, cold, upset stomach, or general pain, but anything else was beyond her as she couldn't synth as many colors as Grandma Wen or Halla could. As a result, Mr. Yong, who had married into the Nuan family from a ranching family, decided to expand and diversify the family business.

Many mythical beasts were sacred, but their descendents had diluted blood and weren't viewed as revered beings. Since the pure, mythical beasts no longer existed, people referred to such descendents by the name of the mythical beast ancestor anyway. These beasts no longer had the mysterious power or magic of ancient creatures. However, the mythical blood within the descendents had incredible properties in their consumption. For example, ranyi meat was known to chase off bad dreams. Meat from descendents of the Chi Long dragon were rumored to bring career promotions or temporary general luck.

Raising mythical beasts was no small feat, and they were usually acquired by seasonal hunters. But with the Nuan family's sprawling acres of land and their experience with ranyi, breeding and raising them was something the Nuan's could do. Mr. Yong aimed to be a mythical beast supplier to keep the family business running, selling premium meats as an additional source of income.

"Bi fang!" a crane called from outside the window.

"What's that?" Rexford asked. Halla also didn't recognize the green bird. Upon closer inspection, she noticed it only had one leg.

"That's a bi fang crane. Your father's latest achievement. He recently procured a pair," Halla's mother said.

Hearing the name, Halla recalled that the one-legged cranes were once known to be harbingers of inevitable fire disasters. The meat of the bi fang descendents, however, was known to bring great warmth to the body. There had been several accounts of bi fang consumption saving someone from hypothermia. Some hospitals stocked freeze-dried bi fang meat as a quick solution when needed. If they could afford it, hikers typically packed bi fang jerky to keep themselves warm in high altitudes.

"The sound a bi fang crane makes is 'bi fang'?" Rexford asked, tickled.

Mrs. Nuan smiled. "Indeed. It's name is an onomatopoeia of the sound it makes. It's quite fun."

"Actually, it's quite annoying hearing it call out its own name," Harley griped under his breath.

Rexford stared at the crane outside for a few more moments before resuming eating. Halla turned to her own bowl of steaming rice and dug into the meal, reaching for the numerous side dishes. She was famished after her long night.

Mrs. Nuan had updated Harley and Ahming of Halla's situation, so they ate in silence—much to Halla's relief—but she could see the questions burning in the looks her brother shot at her and Rexford. Rexford paid him no attention, trying every dish and taking two servings of the congee, mumbling between chews how delicious everything was to Ahming's delight.

"All right." Halla set her chopsticks down. "Out with it," she said while looking at her brother.

Everyone paused, Rexford with a piece of fish halfway to her mouth.

Harley stared at Halla before slowly setting down his bowl and crossing his arms. "You told Mom everything?" he asked.

Halla cocked her head. "Yes, I did."

Harley raised his brows. "Even who this is?" He jerked his head in Rexford's direction. Rexford still had the fish halfway to her mouth, eyes darting between Halla and Harley.

Halla narrowed her eyes. At her silence, Harley sighed and pulled out his phone, then slid it across the table. "Explain this."

A news article titled "Urquart Heir Missing: Kidnapped?" flashed across the screen.

Halla's stomach dropped.

"What is it?" her mother asked worriedly.

"It's nothing," Halla said quickly.

"Halla," her brother warned. "We can't help you if you don't tell us everything."

"I can't! I signed an NDA."

"An NDA?" her mother echoed, confused.

"An NDA?" Harley exclaimed, uncrossing his arms. "Halla. I don't care that you signed a nondisclosure agreement. This is your life we're talking about. And if I'm connecting the dots and this girl is who I think she is, this is a huge matter that transcends an NDA. These are serious allegations!"

The siblings stared at each other angrily.

Ahming broke the silence by gathering the empty dishes.

"What's going on? Halla, what are you not telling us?" Mrs. Nuan finally asked.

Halla broke eye contact with her brother, losing the silent match. She slid Harley's phone to her mother and waited for her reaction.

Her mother's eyes widened as they moved across the small screen. She finally looked up at Halla, then Harley, then Rexford. Halla wanted to shrink away. To Rexford's credit, she continued sitting up straight and eating her food, either not noticing the tenseness of the air or fully embracing it. *Must be her upbringing.*

"Harley," Mrs. Nuan finally addressed her son. "Are you saying this girl is the Urquart heir?"

Rexford looked up, and Harley nodded while continuing to stare at Halla. "That's exactly what I'm saying."

"How's that possible? The heir is a son, not a daughter."

"I don't know either, but here's an article about how Halla had been treating the heir and suddenly the heir disappeared. The next thing we know, Halla shows up with no explanation, nor luggage, with an unknown child." He crossed his arms again. "If this is true, this is extremely serious, and you've now brought this to our house, Halla. We deserve an explanation so we know what is to come."

Halla hung her head. She knew her brother was right. She had briefly debated whether bringing Rex to the Nuan estate was the right move. It would inevitably drag her family and the Nuan name into the situation if the inspectors made chase. They all stared at Halla expectantly.

"It's my fault."

Everyone swiveled their heads to Rexford. Rexford placed a hand onto her pendant and pressed.

CHAPTER 13

"**S**he what?" Captain Ray exclaimed, standing from her chair and slamming her hands onto her desk.

"Halla Nuan ran," Captain Asma reported, sitting calmly. Herb stood at attention behind her.

Captain Ray turned her gaze to Herb. "And you let her escape?" she asked incredulously.

He opened his mouth, but Asma spoke first. "He didn't 'let' her escape. In fact, it was unclear at that moment whether she was running from him or after something. At any rate, we cannot locate her anymore."

Captain Ray threw up her hands. "Why did Mooran even go that evening? He should have had backup." She paced behind her desk. "This is why he couldn't make it in the Onyx."

"Ray," he warned. "You can't seriously be doing this right now? How is that relevant?"

Captain Ray and Herbert had once been classmates and friends. However, she'd increasingly felt like a stranger to him as she rose through the ranks.

Captain Ray whipped her head toward Herb, ready to strike, but Captain Asma put up a hand.

"Inspector Mooran. Regardless of what may have been said, do remember that Captain Ray is your superior, and you will address her as such." Herb pursed his lips but kept silent. *Of course she'd take Ray's side.* "However," Asma continued. "As the head of the Onyx Division, I expect more of you, Captain Ray."

Ray turned her attention to Asma, eyes a mixture of confusion and furiousness. "Excuse me?"

"Although we're all aware Inspector Mooran was moved to my division for certain reasons, that doesn't make referencing them effective for this case. In fact, he's been quite efficient at closing cases in the Green."

Herb gawked at the Green Division's captain. Of all his years at work, he'd never heard anyone speak up to Captain Ray.

Captain Ray's face had turned a bright red, making her look like a tomato in her emerald uniform.

Without waiting for a response, Captain Asma motioned to Herb. "What's the status of locating Halla Nuan?"

"R-right." Herb gathered himself as Captain Ray seethed. "Halla is not at her residence, nor at The Green Thumb. No one's seen her in twenty-four hours."

"The Urquart heir is missing now," Captain Ray said, seeming to have collected herself. Asma nodded. Ray ran a hand down her face. "Asma, this was supposed to be an open-and-shut case. That's why I sent it to you. And then you assign it to Herbert?"

She pointed at him accusingly.

"Inspector Mooran was doing his job, Ray. I did not report this to you for you to vituperate *my* inspectors. I let you know, since the case came from you, but this is no longer your case nor of your concern. I came to let you know that the Green will handle this." Captain Asma stood.

"The Green?" Captain Ray scoffed. "You couldn't even handle a case I handed over on a silver platter."

"I think if you looked more closely, Ray, you'd see discrepancies within the case. You relinquished control to me when you handed it over."

"Are you calling my inspectors careless? Incompetent?" Captain Ray was livid, but Herb thought he saw a flash of a different emotion behind her eyes. Fear? Worry?

"I didn't say that," Asma responded calmly. "This case is more complicated than it initially seemed, and it's become increasingly so. If the Urquarts or senior officers ask you about it, tell them to come to me." Captain Asma turned briskly for the door. Herb followed her out and glanced back to find Ray glaring at him. He didn't linger.

Herb and Captain Asma debriefed in her office on the Green floor. She had a newspaper article flipped open to the latest headline "Urquart Heir Missing: Kidnapped?"

"This complicates things," she said as she read through her thick-rimmed glasses.

That's putting it quite simply. "I didn't see Halla with the Urquart heir the night I saw her. But she said the heir was actually awake, and she had to go after him."

"What does that mean?" Asma asked.

Herb shrugged. "I don't know. She rushed off before I could ask anything else, and then I lost her. The Urquart family reported their son missing. With the timing, Halla running and the heir's disappearance are likely related. The big question is *how* are they related?"

Captain Asma nodded and took off her glasses to rub her temples. "The article is likely some journalist creating a sensational title for their own promotion. We'll ignore it. I'll tell Public Affairs there's no truth to it, and they'll handle it. They've been calling me all morning."

"And the investigation?"

Captain Asma met Herb's eyes. "It's your case. You need to close it."

"I can't close it like this!"

The usually stern woman gave a smile. "I didn't ask you to close it this instant. But it's your responsibility. I know you have thoughts on this, Mooran. What're you thinking?"

Herb balked at the words. He hadn't been asked for his opinions on an investigation ever since the academy. He found himself increasingly wondering how someone like Asma was in a division like the Green rather than a higher one.

Captain Asma waited patiently.

"I need to find her," Herb finally said. Asma's smile widened, so he continued. "I'll get a list of her friends, family, and close associates and start from there. I *will* close this case."

"Excellent." Asma leaned back in her chair. "As for the missing heir, I'm sure the Onyx will take that case. Because of that, our cases may collide, and they may try to insist our search of Halla is their jurisdiction. Stand your ground, if so. Our jurisdiction is Halla Nuan, so we have every right to pursue her. Additionally, I'll dispense a Tracker to you."

Herb stared at her. "You'll give me a Tracker?"

Trackers were excellent tools used by inspectors, but because of the labor and cost of creating one, quantities were limited, and divisions were quite stingy in assigning them. The creation of a Tracker required two kinds of synthers: crafters and imbuers. The crafter created the vessel, and the imbuer embedded the magic within the vessel to take scents and match them. The tool could take samples from a surrounding, find the matching scent in its vicinity, and direct the user in the direction that the runner took. Herb was surprised Captain Asma would give him something so valuable, and he was sure he'd find Halla at a friend's house. She seemed harmless enough and very much a city-gal.

"You do know how to use one, correct?" Asma raised a brow.

"Well, yes. We learned at the academy. It's been a few years, but it's not difficult—that's not the main question! You think we'll need a Tracker? I don't think Halla has gone far. But the Onyx will probably need a Tracker to look for the heir."

Asma waved a hand. "We have plenty of Trackers. They won't miss one. It'll be good to have, just in case you need it, and before the Onyx try to block us and hoard them all. We have to be a step ahead of them." Herb nodded slowly, amazed at her foresight. "Pull together that list of known associates and family today. I'll give you my seal tag when you're done. After that, I do not expect to see you here. Report back via comms every twenty-four hours."

It was all happening so fast. "What about my stack of cases?"

"Your numbers will sustain you for the month, Mooran. You're quite an efficient worker when you put your mind to it, you know?" Her eyes twinkled with humor.

Herb huffed. "Well, I guess I'm quite an efficient worker when my job is on the line," he mumbled.

Asma laughed loudly. "Look, Mooran. I know you're good at what you do. But we work in a world of numbers. Treat this 'Halla case' as a reward for selling your soul briefly. Everything else, I'll handle. I will not have anyone in my division losing their job. The only people who leave my division are those who do so of their own volition or via a promotion."

The way she stood up for her team was so inspirational, Herb wanted to kiss the ground at her feet in the most reverential way. He'd never had a superior like her, and hearing how she stood up for him with Ray and her speech just now, he suddenly felt the tightness in his chest loosen, knowing this manager had his back. For the first time since school, he felt he could deep-dive into a case, following all the possible tracks to find the conclusion.

"I won't let you down," he said.

"Good," she nodded. "Now, be gone. There's work to be done."

CHAPTER 14

"**S**pittlebork!" Mrs. Nuan choked on her tea.

Ahming squawked in surprise at the same time from the kitchen doorway. Harley jumped in his seat but tried to play it off. Rexford sat at the head of the table wearing the face of a boy.

"Mom!" Halla exclaimed. "You curse?"

"Of course I do," Mrs. Nuan spluttered. "Especially after seeing that." She gestured at Rexford who was grinning impishly in her male form with her startling blue eyes.

"Great Doa. Isn't that the Urquart heir?" Ahming stammered, adjusting her glasses as if that would help her vision.

"That's what I've been saying!" Harley exclaimed. "But I've never seen a device that does a visual transformation." He eyed Rexford's pendant. "It was made through Synesthology?"

Rexford nodded. "My family had this pendant made to protect me. In public and throughout the house, I wear this mask. Only when I sleep, see Halla, or see our family doctor do I take it off."

"I wouldn't call that a 'mask', child," Mrs. Nuan said. "It's much more convincing than a mere mask."

"Protect you from what?" Ahming whispered from the corner, but only Halla heard her.

"If I put it on," Harley interjected, "would it also give me another face?"

"Harley! Why would you ever need a disguise?" Mrs. Nuan said.

"I'm just curious how it works!"

Rexford laughed. "This pendant was imbued with this particular face. We update it as I age, as well. I'm afraid if you tried it, the visuals would either be stretched in a disturbing way, or we'd see a child's face on an adult body."

"Equally disturbing." Halla stifled her laughter at the conjured image. Harley scowled.

Over the late morning hours, Rexford explained the situation from her side, including her stealing from Halla and dosing herself. The Nuan family absorbed the information in silence.

"Well," Mrs. Nuan finally said. "It sounds like we need to hire the young heir as a part of our apothecary given her extraordinary skills to create the draught and antidote successfully with no side-effects."

"What!?" Halla interjected. "*That's* what you got from this?" She threw up her hands. "Yes, that's impressive. But that's not the point right now. I brought her here to allow me to look after her, but we need Rex to agree to come back with me to explain everything to the authorities and her family to clear my name."

"No," Rexford snapped, now changed back into her true form. "I told you that I'm going to live my life for a few days. I worked and planned for this for months."

"That's irresponsible," Harley interjected. He gave Rexford a stern look. "I'm sure you're used to giving orders to people around your house, but we're not at your house. At the end of the day, your actions have consequences, and you've unfortunately spilled some of that consequence onto Halla. You cannot selfishly refuse to go back and doom her just because you want to live a little."

"Exactly what he said!" Halla felt like hugging her brother. They'd grown apart the last few years, but he'd always been a good older brother to her.

"No!" Rexford stood, pushing her chair back. "I'm not going back, and you can't make me!"

She ran out of the room. Halla made to follow her, but her mother stopped her in her tracks.

"Halla. Let her go. She needs some time."

"But, Mom—"

"I have something to speak with you about anyway. Ahming," Mrs. Nuan turned to the other woman, "can you please follow the heir and make sure she's doing okay?" Ahming nodded and shuffled away. "Harley, could you step out? I need to speak with Halla."

He raised a brow and shot Halla a questioning look, to which she responded with a clueless shrug.

"Of course, Mom." He stood, gave Mrs. Nuan a peck on the head, and left.

Mrs. Nuan patted the now-empty seat next to her. Halla obliged.

"It's been a while since you've been home, Halla."

"I know. I've been busy."

"I understand." Mrs. Nuan paused. "I'm glad you came, Halla. You know we're always here for you. I will protect you to my last breath."

"Mom!" Halla was shocked at the sudden, serious tone from her mother who was usually so light-hearted and whimsical. "I'm sure this isn't that bad."

Mrs. Nuan ignored her. "I was tasked with giving you something the next time you came home, Halla."

Halla sat straighter, a pang of guilt rending through her for not having come home sooner. "An item? What is it?"

"Before she left this world, Grandma Wen asked that I hand this to you."

"Grandma?" Halla's breath hitched.

"Because you never came home, I think there were some things left unsaid." Mrs. Nuan pulled out a folded, cream letter and handed it to Halla before standing to leave.

Halla stared at the letter. "You're not going to stay and read it with me?"

Mrs. Nuan shook her head. "I know your grandmother placed a lot of pressure on you. She viewed it as hope, you know. Whatever is in that letter is meant for you alone." Mrs. Nuan stopped at the door, turning to look back. "Your grandmother and myself said our goodbyes. I know she didn't get to say goodbye to you." And then she left.

Halla sat alone in the Room of Inner Fulfillment, her throat closing up. She had been avoiding the thought of Grandma, when she was alive and now in passing. Why did Grandma Wen have to be so harsh on her and the path she chose? Why could she not make Grandma Wen proud? Why did Grandma have to anger her so much that she didn't go home when Grandma was drawing her last breath? And now she held Grandma Wen's last words in her hands. She couldn't ignore this.

She found herself walking to the inner courtyard and sitting herself on Grandma's stone bench next to the small river. She looked around, absorbing the garden she grew up in for the first time in years. Glimpses of the garden being barren and dead from her dream flitted into her mind. She shuddered. *I'm glad that was just a dream.*

The wraith-like creature crawled into her mind, and Halla recalled the way it told her to come home. Was it for this letter? She looked down at the folded paper in her lap and took a deep breath.

> Dearest Halla, I wrote this because I'm not great at conveying my feelings. Writing has helped organize my thoughts. I want to start with, first, how I am greatly disappointed.

Halla rolled her eyes. *Of course she was.*

> I'm disappointed that our arts have been lost. I have failed. Generations before me have carried out their duty, but I was not able to do so. You hold so much within you, but I'm afraid my own fear of failing manifested into pushing you, instead of toward synthing, away from it. You weren't just a natural; you loved it. That's hard to find these days, my dear. I'm sorry I took away the joy of synthing.

When you went to school and your mother supported you
doing so, I panicked. School and academies will always be there,
but I wouldn't. My time was limited.

Once your Synesthology manifested, instead of spending my
limited time enjoying your brightness, I tried pushing knowledge onto you at an exacerbated pace. It's hard to admit my
mistakes because I still believe you had to take my knowledge,
and I likely would have done it again if I went back in time, but
knowing my last breath is drawing near, I've had time to reflect.
I know I've been hard on you, and I didn't want you coming
back to see me merely out of filial piety, so I didn't tell anyone
about my nearing time until it was too late to notify you.

There's so much I want to tell you. To hold you in my arms
again in our garden. But most importantly, I want you to know
that I'm proud of your accomplishments. You've done something I could have never imagined. I carried out my family duty,
but you broke that and chose a whole new path. I believe instead
of being close-minded, perhaps these two ideologies are more
harmonious than we initially thought. After all, as synthers, we
look for balance.

You are free to do as you choose with my blessing, my dear.
Should you discover that joy in synthing again, and I'm no
longer present, you can seek out your aunt, Sarai Leng, who
resides in Tanheli. Her synthing manifested at a later stage in
life, but she has deep medicinal knowledge and was able to learn

much from my sister. Ask your mother for my jade pendant, should you decide to pay Sarai a visit.

I love you, my dearest. I hope you can find harmony within your skills, and I'm excited to watch over your accomplishments from afar. Go forth, and make the Nuans proud.

Halla looked up from her grandmother's note. She blinked rapidly to clear her blurred vision, and the pooled tears fell. Her lips quivered as she tried to collect herself but failed.

She was hit with the scent of dried chrysanthemum as her tears made contact with the paper, taking her back to the sun-drenched apothecary where Grandma ground herbs. She felt sorrow for the words she could never give her grandmother in response, and she felt a lightness from the heartfelt sentiments left for her. She'd never sought to understand Grandma Wen, but with this note, she felt that she was starting to. She had heard that her mother's synthing limitations had tested Grandma Wen, but she never paused to consider the lasting impact of that and how that may have carried forward onto Halla.

Halla listened to the birds chirp and the stream bubble playfully as Grandma Wen used to on this very seat.

"Bi fang!" the one-legged crane croaked.

Halla jumped. The bi fang perched on a railing at the perimeter of the garden separating the courtyard from the surrounding walkway, which connected various rooms and halls.

"Where's your mate?" Halla called to the crane. "Didn't my father procure two of you?"

The crane stared back, blinking with its translucent nictitating membrane. At its silence, Halla glanced back at the letter in her hands and noticed new words had formed where her tears hit the paper. She gasped as she brought the letter closer. *I need more water.* She quickly dipped her fingers into the stream and carefully dripped onto the blank area of the letter at the bottom.

> As much as you currently deny your birthright, it flows within you. I support you, but I leave you with one warning: Remember the weight our name carries beyond just us.

Halla frowned. Grandma's last word was contrarian, supportive yet it told her she couldn't run from her birthright? What did Grandma mean by the weight of the Nuan name? And why was this warning hidden? Halla read Grandma's letter again, this time paying more attention to the details.

"How have I never heard of Aunt Sarai? She lives in Tanheli?"

Halla recalled from her geography classes that Tanheli was a town on the edge of an animated root forest. Textbooks had mentioned it due to the soil's prime conditions for growing various herbs. She figured her mother may know more and headed inside.

When she couldn't find her mother, she ventured to the ranyi grounds, a massive piece of land filled with ponds and stables behind the large Nuan estate.

Mrs. Nuan was buffing the golden scales of her personal ranyi next to their main pond. The golden ranyi had half its body submerged in the water with the other half standing on land. It stomped one of its six-taloned feet as Halla approached.

"Jin, it's only Halla," Mrs. Nuan assured the large creature, its head the size of a horse's. Jin flicked a forked tongue out to smell the air, relaxing when it seemed to recognize Halla.

Halla had grabbed a microfiber towel and joined her mother in the task of buffing the creature's seven-foot-long body. She thought about Grandma's warning and the fact that it was hidden before deciding to keep that part of the letter to herself. Instead, she was curious about this unknown aunt of hers. "Mom, have you heard of Aunt Sarai?"

Mrs. Nuan's hand paused mid-movement on Jin's body. "Grandma Wen mentioned her?"

Halla nodded before realizing her mother couldn't see her over the ranyi's body between them. "Yes. In the letter."

Mrs. Nuan continued buffing. "I know of Sarai. She's your grandmother's sister's daughter. She's my cousin—your aunt, once removed."

"How come we've never heard of her?"

"Family drama," Mrs. Nuan answered. "Your grandmother's sister, Bing, had a child out of wedlock."

Halla's eyes widened. "Aunt Sarai?"

"Yes. Sarai was the child, and Bing was also already married."

"Grandma's sister had an affair?" Halla was shocked.

"Yes." Mrs. Nuan sighed. "Because Sarai was illegitimate, she took the father's surname instead of the 'Nuan' name. According to Grandma Wen, her sister went to live with her lover and Sarai in Tanheli. Grandma Wen never liked Bing's husband, so she remained close with her sister, but out of respect for the larger Nuan family, she refrained from speaking about Bing and her illegitimate family."

"What about her husband and children?" Halla asked, surprised that the grandmother she knew to be steeped in traditions accepted Grand-Aunt Bing's situation.

"Your Grand-Uncle-in-Law? He maintained their branch of the Nuan business with vertical herb farming. He fulfilled his duties and provided Bing with one child, Tin. I feel sorry for Tin for having grown up without a mother, but he was well-taken care of. We maintain contact with them once a year. As for Bing and her illegitimate family, only your grandmother had contact with them. I don't know much more."

Halla thought about Grandma's words in the letter. "Grandma told me to seek out Sarai if I want to learn more about synthing."

"Synthing?" Mrs. Nuan said. "I thought you didn't want to go down that path."

"I didn't want to take over the family business, Mom." Halla shook her head. "But I've always loved synthing."

Mrs. Nuan frowned. "You haven't synthed in so long!"

"That's because school taught us that we had machines and western medicine for mapping. There was no need to cultivate synthing at school. I never needed it, but... I actually do need it now."

"What do you mean?"

"Rex's ailment," Halla said. "It's... strange. I wish Grandma were here to diagnose her. Everything on the surface seems fine, but Rex clearly is not well. The only way I can see anything is by synthing."

The lack of physical symptoms had pushed Halla to try synthing more extensively again, but now, Halla felt an increased need to boost her knowledge. Since Grandma wasn't around, this could be the next best option. For Rex. For Halla. The sooner Rex was healed, the sooner Halla could put all this behind her.

"Huh. I haven't heard of an illness like that. Even your grandmother did not purely rely on synthing."

"That's true. That's why I thought synthing wasn't necessary. But weren't there stories of our ancestors purely using synthing? Before our family learned traditional medicine?"

"There are stories like that, but I can hardly believe it." Mrs. Nuan moved to rub Jin's head, and Jin ducked into the touch. Halla imagined if the ranyi had eyelids, she probably would have closed her eyes in pleasure.

"I think I need to go find Sarai. To learn more and heal Rex."

There was a long silence between the two women before Mrs. Nuan spoke. "Halla, you can't run from your fears all the time. I let you leave our estate for schooling, but I also know you did it to run from Grandma Wen's expectations. Now, there's trouble in the capital, and you're running again."

Halla frowned and fixated on a spot on Jin's scales, scrubbing fervently. Had she run from family expectations? In a way, she admitted she did. Though at the time, she'd convinced herself she was going purely for school. But this was something different. She wasn't running, she was simply trying to finish the job the Urquarts hired her for.

"I'm not running," she said out loud.

"I think you are," Mrs. Nuan said gently. "Like how Rexford is running."

"You can't compare me to her! She's had her life fed to her with a silver spoon!" Halla retorted, offended.

Her mother waved at their surroundings. "Halla, have you forgotten what family you're from? We may not have the doilies and frills, famous chefs or mansions, but we have our estate, land, beasts, and business. We were never lacking. We live a rich life of open air, fresh food, medicinal knowledge, and being close with nature."

Despite Mrs. Nuan being modern in outward appearance, and having had rejected Grandma's medicinal synthing knowledge in her youth, she still held a reverence for tradition. Halla was surprised to find her mother sounding a bit like Grandma Wen. What her mother said was not untrue, and Halla felt her face flush in embarrassment.

"Besides," Mrs. Nuan continued. "I wasn't talking about upbringing. I was talking about the running."

"I'm not running from this, Mom. Every bone in my body wants to drag Rex and her stubborn head back to the city to explain everything."

"And yet?" her mother inquired.

Halla sighed. "I can't do that to her. Because I know what it's like to finally breathe in some freedom away from home," she admitted. "Because I know if we go back, the Urquarts will likely lock her up in her room and watch her like a hawk. It's exactly what she doesn't want. Additionally," Halla tapped her chin, "even if we do go back and explain Rex put herself in a coma, they may still arrest me for the possession of illegal drugs. Rex's story doesn't explain the drugs and the cash at my place."

Halla's stomach dropped at that realization.

Mrs. Nuan moved to the other side of her ranyi and stood next to Halla. "That's true," she said. After a moment of thought, she followed up with, "I'm afraid this smells like foul play."

Halla nodded and suddenly felt sick. "Going back won't solve anything. I'm sure the inspectors can still run their investigation with me gone. In the meantime, let me try to heal Rex while I consider what to do about the planted drugs and cash."

"While *we* consider what to do about that. We are your family and will fight for you. I'll see if I can go into town and find some clues."

"You'd do that?" Halla asked.

"Of course!" Mrs. Nuan said passionately, her earlier reticence gone. "I was worried you were acting rashly, but I think this is the right move. If someone is framing you, I'm afraid you'll be in more danger if you go back."

Halla felt queasy again, realizing someone was likely actively trying to harm her. But why? Had she now brought danger to her family? Regardless, it would be better if she left soon.

"Thank you, Mom. If you have a map to Tanheli, I think we should head out tomorrow."

"I agree. Time is of the essence. Take Mogi with you."

"You'd have me take a ranyi?" Mogi was the youngest ranyi in the school the Nuans had, and he was the one that had pulled the carriage to The Green Thumb those years back. "Wouldn't that draw attention?"

Mrs. Nuan waved a hand at Halla. "As you get closer to Tanheli, you'll find stranger things. Tanheli's grounds hold more history and magic than this region. Plus, public transit does not reach Tanheli. Fastest way is either a private cab or having a steed, and if we don't want anyone tracing you to Tanheli, then let's exclude any additional third parties. A steed it is."

"I barely know Mogi! And I haven't ridden a ranyi in at least a decade." Halla didn't know if she could stay on a running ranyi, let alone if Rexford could. "How about a carriage?"

Mrs. Nuan shook her head. She'd always been an excellent rider and paid no attention to Halla's concerns. "Mogi's great. A lot of strength. And a carriage is too much maintenance on unpaved roads. On a ranyi, you should reach Sarai in two days. There's a post town on the way that you and Rexford can rest at for the night. I'll prepare a map and ask Ahming to pack food for you two."

"I don't know..." Halla started.

"Are you running away from this now that we've decided?" Mrs. Nuan interrupted.

Halla opened her mouth to retort, snapping her head toward her mother, but then found the older woman smiling with a playful wink.

"Mom, don't tease me like that," Halla breathed, dissipating the anger that had been quick to rise.

Mrs. Nuan laughed. "You take everything so seriously, Halla." She patted Jin's side, and the golden ranyi quickly turned and dove into the massive pond and disappeared. Before Halla registered that the creature had left, Mrs. Nuan had her arms wrapped around Halla. "Please be careful. There is a strange force that's targeting you; tread carefully. Go learn from Sarai and heal Rexford. We'll try to figure things out here, too."

Halla burrowed herself into her mom's scent of sunshine. "I will, Mom."

She had a feeling that instead of running away, she was finally running toward something. Toward what her grandmother had wanted her to learn. Toward traditions. Toward her birthright.

CHAPTER 15

The next morning, Halla rose early at Mrs. Nuan's request to officially meet Mogi and receive his blessing to ride.

"Why do I have to ask permission? I didn't even want to ride a ranyi," Halla grumbled to herself as she dragged her feet to the ranyi grounds. The sun was just peeking over the horizon, casting an orange light into the dawn haze.

Mrs. Nuan, dressed in a beige fit with flowers embroidered along the hems, was already outside with Mogi and Jin. "Finally! The sleepyhead made it!" she announced as she waved at Halla.

"Yeah, I'm here." Halla rubbed her eyes. "Now, how do I receive his blessing?"

Whenever she'd ridden a ranyi as a child, it was usually Jin or another older one that her parents or Grandma instructed to allow Halla to ride. Traveling alone with a ranyi, Halla now needed permission directly from the creature. Otherwise, it wouldn't stay still long enough for even a saddle.

Mrs. Nuan had finished fitting Mogi with a saddle large enough for two. "It's easy. You approach from the side, put a hand out, and ask to be partners."

"That's it?" Halla asked. She had expected something a little more complicated.

Her mother clapped her hands once. "That's it. You know, back in the day of the ancient beasts and when our family first started domesticating them, it was a lot more difficult. You risked getting your hand bitten or getting mauled by their talons." She laughed.

Halla gave her mother a deadpan stare. That didn't seem very funny. She then took a deep breath and called Mogi's name to get his attention. His head swiveled toward her.

"Mogi." She put a hand out. "Will you take me to be your partner in my journey?"

The large creature stood straighter, looking more like a snake than a fish, and focused his rounded pupils on her. *Huh, Jin has slitted pupils. I didn't know they could have different eyes.* The sun was coming up, and the rays bounced off his silver-green scales.

"Well, he hasn't bonded with anyone before, so it should be anytime now," her mother comforted. "Keep your arm steady."

The glittering creature finally took steps toward her, talons scraping over dirt, and pressed his slitted nose against Halla's palm. Halla breathed a sigh of relief.

"Excellent," Mrs. Nuan exclaimed, clasping her hands together. "You can now trust him with your life as long as you don't betray him! And if the heir is with you, he'll allow her to ride, too. Grab some breakfast, and make sure Rexford is packed."

Halla rubbed Mogi's snout in wonder. She'd mounted ranyis for practice, but she'd never looked one in the eyes like this. After a moment, he pulled back his head and then headbutted her lightly, prancing on his six feet.

"Hey!" she said, rubbing her forehead. "You're a prankster, aren't you? I remember you messing with Tomas at my shop!"

Mogi seemed to shake his head in laughter, flicking out a tongue and flapping the pectoral fins on the sides of his head.

Halla knocked on the wood slats lining the door of the guest bedroom.

"I'm here," Rexford said from inside.

Halla slid the door open and entered. She hadn't spoken with Rexford since the girl ran out at breakfast yesterday, but she hoped Ahming spoke some sense into the girl.

"Hey," she greeted.

"Hey," Rexford said sullenly from the bed. "Are we going back?"

Halla shook her head while setting herself on the edge of the mattress. "We're actually heading to Tanheli."

Rexford perked up. "Tanheli? Where is that?"

"A two-day ride away."

Rexford's face fell. "I thought we needed to go back to the capital to explain everything. I don't want to go back, but I know I've caused you a lot of trouble."

Halla softened at that. Rex wasn't a bad kid; she wasn't trying to complicate Halla's life. "We do. Eventually. But going back right now does not solve everything. If you remember, they found some poisonous substances in the herbal parcels I gave you and at my shop. We still don't know where that came from."

Rexford's golden eyes widened. "That's right. But you never gave me any poison!"

Halla sighed. "I know. So, something else is afoot. We'll go to my aunt first, to better diagnose you. If we're on this trip to experience things, we might as well continue treating you, too."

Rexford leaped up in excitement. "I've never traveled! This will be so much fun! Do you have horses or a car for us?"

Halla grinned. "Oh, no. We have ranyi."

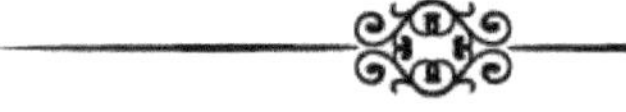

Ahming tied bundles of food to Mogi while Mrs. Nuan handed Halla a jade pendant and a map.

"Stop in Hanashuku for the night. There's one inn there so you can't miss it. Send a bird when you reach Tanheli. The address Grandma had in her note should be accurate, and her jade pendant will prove to Sarai who you are."

"Maybe we should have sent a message ahead so Sarai knows to expect us." Halla just realized how jarring it may be to have a long-lost niece show up at your doorstep.

"Already done," her brother said from behind her. "I found Grandma's *qingniao*. I assume the bird has carried messages to Tanheli for her before, so I sent it with a note." Qingniaos were blue-green crow-like birds that the Nuans used for sending messages. Some within the flock they had were three-legged and some were one-legged. In mythology, it was said that the qingniao were messengers for a major goddess who had an orchard of longevity peaches. These days, numerous peach orchards claimed their peaches tasted like the juicy sweetness of longevity peaches, but no one had been able to cultivate one, much less find this mythical goddess orchard.

"Thank you, Harley," their mother noted. She turned her attention to Rexford. "You take care. Stay out of trouble." She offered her hands, palms up, to Rexford.

"And remember you need to go back eventually to explain everything, for Halla's sake," Harley reminded from behind.

Rexford hung her head respectfully after taking Mrs. Nuan's hands. "I know. Thank you for your hospitality. I'll definitely explain everything to my parents and the authorities once we're back."

Mrs. Nuan nodded approvingly.

With her family's blessing, Halla found herself on the back of a giant, glimmering fish with Rexford strapped securely behind her.

"If Mogi's a fish," Rexford began, "how does he breathe on land? Or is he like the opposite of a whale where he's holding his breath on land and has to stick his head in water? Why does he have talons? Is he part bird, too? What does he eat? Does your family eat them?"

"Woah, Rex. Slow down." Halla shook her head. "Ranyi's have lungs so they can breathe on land and underwater. Mogi needs moisturizing from time to time, so we'll have to make sure to find water for him. I don't know why he has talons—that's just how ranyi are. He can eat small fish or animals. He'll hunt on his own; my family teaches them to do so. The consumption of their meat is known to dispel nightmares, so we sell it. We'll eat them occasionally but not often. We keep the strong ones as steeds or for work, and the weak or older ones are sold when it's time."

"How are you able to eat them when you know them? I would never eat Mogi! He's so pretty. If he's part-snake, does he have venom? Have you ridden one in the water?" Rexford continued.

We have nine hours before we reach the post town. It's going to be a long *ride.*

CHAPTER 16

The last time Herb used a Tracker was at the Academy. He'd never needed one. Today, he carried it with him as he headed to The Green Thumb. With Halla gone, he'd reached out to Cerul, one of her employees, to lock up the shop after Halla ran away and to provide a copy of the keys to him for the investigation.

The small-framed employee met him at the back of the shop. "So, Halla was here?"

"Yes. She and I were speaking."

"Why would she be here if the store was closed?" Cerul asked.

Herb shrugged. "She was probably trying to keep herself busy. Going back to what she knows." *Doa knows I'd be doing the same if I were her.*

The woman seemed lost in thought, and Herb cocked his head. "Have you seen Halla recently?"

"Oh!" She startled and raised her hands. "No, not at all. I was told by the previous inspectors to avoid contact. But if The Green Thumb is closed for long and I stop getting paid, I'll have to start looking for other jobs."

Herb nodded.

"Do you..." Cerul started tentatively, "have any leads on the case with the heir? Did Halla do it?"

Herb looked down at her curiously. "The employees are probably all concerned about your jobs?" She nodded quickly. "I don't know." He sighed. "I'm investigating to get to the bottom of this, but it's probably smart to look around for another job just in case."

Cerul nodded and handed him the keys to The Green Thumb. "Well, Halla isn't here, and I don't want to stand in the way of your investigation. You can hold onto the keys until you close the case."

"I appreciate it," Herb said as he waved her off and turned toward the shop.

It had been a few days since the night he saw Halla run. He'd been so confused and rattled that day that he didn't take the time to investigate. Today, he was going to thoroughly scour the shop.

I was in the kitchen when Halla saw something, or something happened, that resulted in her running. She seemed completely calm before. Which means whatever it was, it was not *in the kitchen. Maybe her office or one of the other rooms? It wouldn't be the storefront either, since she ran out of it.*

He entered through the back again and walked through the kitchen into the hallway with the various examination rooms and the office. Herb decided to start in her office.

Their unfinished tea from that night remained on the table, untouched. Nothing seemed off within her space, so he stepped out, imagining Halla creeping down the hallway after him that evening. Heading toward the kitchen, Herb realized one of the rooms was open: Examination Room 8. *Curious,* he thought as he entered.

This room's aesthetic was different from the rest of The Green Thumb. Light streamed in from latticed windows, and stepping into it felt like stepping into the countryside. He went to check Examination Rooms 9 and 10. Those two rooms were the expected aesthetic with white walls and sterile instruments. Herb wondered why Room 8 was different as he headed back.

There was a chair on its side, as if pushed out of the way. With gloved hands, he rummaged a few drawers before he noticed a folded sheet of paper on the examination bed.

He plucked it from its place and opened it, eyes widening as he read the scrawled message. It was signed 'Rex'.

"'Rex' as in Rexford, the Urquart heir?" he wondered aloud. "And he poisoned himself?"

Could this have been a fake note left by Halla? That would be a strange ruse, though...

He recalled speaking with Halla that evening and her expression when she ran. It felt genuine. A woman who suddenly found herself accused of poisoning a high-profile figure with evidence she'd never seen stacked against her. Herb shook his head. If she truly was innocent, he didn't want to see her convicted. And this note signed by the heir cleared Halla if it was true. First, he'd need the Urquart family to match the heir's handwriting and then a forgery expert to examine it to determine the authenticity. He tucked the note into his pocket and continued his search. For good measure, he checked the other examination rooms before heading back to Halla's office.

He pulled out the Tracker. "Here goes nothing," he said, and he turned it on.

The screen on the handheld device lit up, noting that it was collecting data. He placed the opening of the device on Halla's seat and waved it around her neat workspace. After a few seconds, the screen showed multiple colors in varying band lengths. The lengths of the color bands indicated the strength of the scent the Tracker picked up. Strength of a scent depended on how often someone was there or how recently. Out of the nine bands, two were thickest. Herb clicked on the thickest yellow band and compared it to the saved file on his Tracker that he'd picked up earlier from Halla's apartment. Upon selecting it, the device glowed green, indicating a match.

Herb then selected the 'Follow' button, noting to the Tracker to follow this specific scent, and held the device in front of him. Upon aiming it at the door, the Tracker glowed green again, indicating a path to follow. Herb already knew the general direction Halla went within The Green Thumb but wanted to test the device. As he expected, it took him down the hall to Examination Room 8, and then back down the hallway and into the storefront. He stepped onto the street, aiming the Tracker to his right. No response. He aimed it to his left, and the Tracker glowed in affirmation. He looked down the street.

"I guess it's time to track her down."

The evening in Hanashuku was uneventful. Halla had found the town easily enough, and there were signs for the inn. The hotel staff were a bit surprised to hear they had to stable a ranyi but quickly accommodated.

In the morning, Halla and Rexford gorged themselves on a breakfast of ham, eggs, and rice and headed out. Mogi was waiting for them at the front, pawing his front talons with impatience. A few passersby looked at him appreciatively but left him unbothered.

"How much longer before we make it to your aunt?" Rexford asked, following Halla out.

"Another day's ride," she said tiredly. Halla tied their food stock to Mogi and patted his side. "They take good care of you?"

Mogi turned his head completely around to face her and nudged her body as if to say yes.

"Great," she said, noticing a film of dust on his body. She'd have to buff out his scales when they arrived in Tanheli.

They mounted and proceeded down the road as marked on Mrs. Nuan's map. On their way out of town, Halla observed how quaint Hanashuku was. She hadn't noticed when they arrived in the dark of the night, but there was no time to explore.

After a day of chattering away yesterday, Rexford was uncharacteristically taciturn today. A few hours into their journey, Halla heard the burbling of a stream. She patted Mogi's neck and leaned forward. "Let's head toward the water for a break."

He flicked his forked tongue and changed course. Fifteen minutes later, they were in a meadow with a stream. Halla untied their food bundles but kept Mogi saddled.

"Is it lunch time?" Rexford asked.

"Yes. Giving Mogi a quick water break," Halla said as she unpacked two soy-braised rice balls wrapped in bamboo leaves. "And to check in on you."

Rexford cocked her head in confusion. Halla gave an exasperated sigh.

"Sit with me and hold out your hand." Rexford did as asked, and Halla took her wrist.

"Oh! You're synthing!" Rexford said.

Halla shot her a glance. "Yes, you do remember I'm your doctor, right? I know you're on this journey, but we still need to work on your treatment."

"Right," Rexford said, chastised. "I've just been feeling really good ever since I ran away, so I hadn't thought much of it."

Something about what Rexford said stood out in Halla's mind, but she couldn't pinpoint it. She focused on Rexford's body and instructed the girl to stick out her tongue. As usual, Halla could see nothing wrong with Rexford. Her body looked completely healthy in observation.

"How am I?" Rexford asked.

"Hush," Halla instructed. "I need to focus."

Halla, once again, felt the energy within her core and led it toward where her hand made contact with Rexford's wrist. Halla braced herself for a mosaic of colors to assault her, but to her surprise, the colors within Rexford were calmer today.

That's strange. There are less than twenty shades. There used to be more than fifty. Have my herbs worked that well? The last prescription I gave Rex could treat two symptoms, which may also affect five others, but it wouldn't decrease the ailments so drastically.

There were still too many colors to determine Rexford's base color, but the improved state relaxed Halla. They would be fine, at least until they reached Tanheli.

"How am I?" Rexford asked again, this time in a whisper.

Halla released her hand. "You're looking better. We'll take thirty minutes, have some lunch and some chrysanthemum tea, and pack up for the rest of the trip."

They unwrapped the soy-braised rice balls Ahming had made while Mogi splashed in the stream, switching between throwing pebbles with his talons and submerging himself. As Halla took her first bites of home, Rexford gave a muffled sound of delight.

"There's meat in here!" she said in-between bites.

"Yup. A chunk of fatty pork belly, mushrooms, and a hard-boiled quail's egg," Halla said appreciatively. In all the restaurants she'd tried in the city, she'd yet to find anything that rivaled Ahming's food.

Rexford took more rapid bites while examining her rice ball. "I haven't gotten an egg," she mumbled while chewing.

"Ahming doesn't always put them in. Luck of the draw, I guess." Halla smirked.

"No fair!" Rexford protested. "You knew which one had an egg already!"

"Rex! I would never. You're my patient," Halla said.

However, she indeed already knew which of the two had an egg, but she wasn't going to tell Rexford that. Ahming tied the string that wrapped around the bamboo leaves in a different way than usual to indicate the inclusion of an egg. It was an old code she and Ahming had so Halla would always get one. Her brother had never figured it out over the years, much to his egg-less frustration.

After the meal, Rexford seemed to have returned to her usual chatty self, commenting on everything she observed.

"I didn't know water out here could be so clear. The sky is so gorgeous! I've never met a family like yours. They're so interesting, and your brother is such a straight-edge."

Halla gave a small laugh at the last comment. Harley was indeed a rule follower. She had wondered if it was a result of being a first-born son deemed unworthy of inheriting the business because of his lack of skill. To compensate for that failure, he strictly followed family rules and had stayed home to help however he could. She'd heard stories from Ahming about how carefree and rambunctious her brother was before she was born. However, anytime Halla asked him why he stayed at home, he said it was his duty and wouldn't expand on the topic.

A silence fell over them when Rexford exhausted herself, and Halla got up to pack.

"Do you think my parents are worried?"

Halla turned to see Rexford hugging her knees, as if trying to make herself smaller.

"Yes, they're probably worried," she said.

"I can't help but feel guilty."

Well, you faked your coma and ran away. You kind of are guilty, Halla thought with a flash of annoyance. *You choose to feel guilty while we're halfway to our destination?*

"I'm out here breathing fresh air, experiencing new things, new food," Rexford continued. "And they're home worried that I'm out here dying or kidnapped."

"Yeah, by me supposedly," Halla muttered.

"I've never been away from home for longer than a few hours. What if..." Rexford sniffled. "What if I'm dying soon? What if I never see them again?"

She buried her face in her knees, and her shoulders shook.

"Rex," Halla said as she bent down to pat Rexford's back, shocked at the change from earlier. She had to remember that Rex had been sick for years, never being far from home. Perhaps now that Rex was out and experiencing life's colors, her mortality had finally dawned on her. It was a lot on anyone, much less a ten-year-old. "You made the decision to run from home, and you need to understand the ramifications."

"Thanks for the comforting words," Rexford huffed morosely from between her knees.

"But," Halla said, "you're not dying. At least, you're no longer dying. You've noticed your ailment has been getting better over the last few months, right?" The girl lifted her head slightly to nod. "I just synthed you, and I've never seen your body in such an improved state. You're getting better. I see it."

Rexford lifted her head and met Halla's eyes. "Really?"

"Yes. Once we get to my aunt's, it'll definitely get even better. She's more skilled in Synesthology than I am."

Rexford's countenance brightened. Halla suddenly felt awkward. She gave Rex a small smile and a light pat and got up to finish packing. She'd never been good with kids.

After a few minutes, the three of them resumed the path. Mogi's scales shone again in the sunlight as they rode after his romp in the water. At least that was one less thing for Halla to worry about.

"I hope there's a hot bath and bed waiting for us in Tanheli," Rexford chirped.

"I hope so, too, Rex," Halla agreed, wondering how her long-lost aunt would receive them.

Stars lit the dark purple sky by the time Halla saw the lights of Tanheli. Mogi flapped his pectoral fins as if excited that the destination was near. She patted his neck in response.

When they approached the town, Halla noticed the lights gave off a blue hue and were not fire or electricity.

"They're bugs!" Rexford whispered from behind her.

Halla took a closer look as they passed a lamppost and saw that the container of blue light was filled with movement of small fluttering creatures.

"It's too bright for me to tell," Halla whispered back. "How can you tell?"

"What else would they be? I read about them in a book."

Halla lightly slapped Rexford's thigh. "You and your books. You can't assume everything in a book is true. Like the thorn-apple concoction!"

Halla remembered a time when she had buried herself in books for studies, but those were for a set curriculum, not whatever books Rex seemed to be picking up.

Rexford blew a raspberry at her back.

Since it was night, most shops were closed, and the streets were empty. Halla pulled out Grandma's note with Sarai's address and looked for street signs or a town map.

"How do we know where your aunt is?" Rexford asked.

"Working on it," Halla said between gritted teeth. She was exhausted from their long day of traveling, and Rexford's constant nagging was getting on her nerves.

Halla spotted a light coming from the singular store on the street and nudged Mogi toward it. As they got closer, the sign marked it as a tea shop.

She hopped off Mogi's back and patted his head. "Rex, stay here with Mogi while I ask for directions."

Rexford offered some protest, but Halla ignored her as she entered the shop. The door chime jingled, and the scent of roasted tea and warmth enveloped her. Halla stood for a moment, savoring the smell before searching for the shopowner.

The shop had three occupied tables. One hosted a group of young women murmuring in low tones, another an elderly couple reading, and the last, a boy slumped asleep over his books, glasses askew. Halla made for the register where a tea brewer stood wiping a cup.

The brewer, dressed in a crisp, mandarin-collared shirt and apron, took an appraising look at Halla, the slight smirk revealing he could tell she was not from town. "Good tidings. How may I help you?"

Halla pulled out the address. "I'm looking for this place. Could you point me in the right direction?"

As the man bent toward her to glance at the handwritten address, Halla caught a scent of crushed pine needles with a lingering spice of a warm cup of tea. Her stomach fluttered, but she immediately stomped the feeling as he raised a brow. "That would be near the animated root forest."

"Isn't all of Tanheli next to the animated forest?" Halla said, impatience rising.

"Sure," he shrugged, standing straight again. "But this address is right at the edge. Why are you trying to find it?"

Halla narrowed her eyes at him. "Who said you could ask personal questions?"

The brewer met her gaze with his sharp, brown eyes. Halla thought if he wasn't so nosy, he would have been handsome. "In Tanheli, your business is everyone's business. I'm asking you why you want to go to determine if I should tell you how to get there."

Halla had just about enough. Between being chased for a poisoning she was innocent of, days of traveling by ranyi-back, listening to a sheltered girl prattle endlessly, feeling insufficient with her synthing, and now being accused of something nefarious by this stranger, Halla had been pushed to the edge. She slammed a hand onto the countertop.

"So, you *do* know how to get there? Well, let me tell you that my relative lives there, and I have a sick child who needs her help, and I've been traveling for days, so help me Doa if you don't tell me, I'm going to set my ranyi loose on your shop!" With a straightened arm, she pointed out his front window to where Mogi stood, staring at them head-on through the glass. She was sure Mogi was just watching her out of habit but hoped the stare gave a dangerous look.

The entire shop went quiet as the other patrons, even the previously sleeping boy, stared at her and the brewer. The brewer called over Halla's shoulder. "Don't worry. It's just a lost traveler. Please, continue enjoying your evening."

Out of the corner of her eye, Halla noted the other customers slowly turn their heads back to their activities. She focused on the brewer, unfazed and, once again, cleaning utensils. In fact, no one seemed scared of Mogi. Her mother's words suddenly flowed into her memory. "As you get closer to Tanheli, you'll find stranger things. Tanheli's grounds hold more history and magic than this region."

I guess they've seen ranyi before.

"You say you're a relative?" The frustratingly handsome brewer interrupted Halla's thoughts.

"Yes. My grandmother recently told me about it in a letter," she said tersely.

"And that child," the brewer nodded to Rexford atop Mogi, "is sick?"

"Yes. How many times do I need to say this?"

"She doesn't look very sick to me," he said.

"Well, she is," Halla snapped. "I'm a traditional medicine practitioner and a synther."

His hands stilled, and for the first time, he seemed entirely focused on Halla. "A sensing synther?"

"What about it?" Halla said, slightly retreating from the sudden intensity.

The man slowly nodded to himself. "It's night. It wouldn't do to knock on someone's door at this hour. You'll stay at my shop. Tomorrow morning, I will send a note to the person at your listed address. Once they confirm they know you, I will send you on your way. In fact, I'll personally escort you. If you really are a relative, then this shouldn't be a problem." Halla opened her mouth to protest, but he raised a hand. "No point in arguing. I'm not sending you to a friend's house without confirming who you are. This isn't an inn, but we're open late, and you can sleep on the couch. Bring in the child, and we can stable your ranyi in the town stables."

"No. Mogi stays with us," Halla said. She wanted him nearby in case they had to run. She also didn't know if he'd be safe alone, knowing ranyi meat was a rare commodity.

The brewer shrugged. "Suit yourself. The beast will be more comfortable in the stables, but he can stay outside. I'll bring him a few pails of water and fish and ask my stablehand to buff his scales."

Halla was surprised the man knew general ranyi care but didn't dwell on it. She stomped outside to bring Rexford in and hoped that her brother's qingniao message had successfully reached her aunt.

CHAPTER 17

The tea shop stayed open until 2:00 AM, so Halla and Rexford didn't get much sleep, but Rexford didn't seem to mind.

The girl had shaken Halla awake mid-nap, announcing, "Halla! The lights *are* bugs! Apparently, they have a cave where these light bugs are raised, and when night comes, the bugs are siphoned to light fixtures. During the day, the light containers will be empty because the bugs are sucked back into the cave to be fed."

"Great. Really cool," Halla had mumbled. "How do you know?"

"The old gentleman told me about it!" Rexford had pointed at the elderly couple who waved back, eyes seeming to glitter with the life that Rexford brought.

It wasn't long after that Rexford had found something further to occupy her, and Halla fell asleep once again. Sometime later, Rex had woken Halla to share that the animated forest reportedly boasted *qilin* and *si*, among many other mythical descendents. This piece of information had intrigued Halla because she knew her father was working on their new business branch. Despite being rarely found, qilins were widely written about in mythological literature, so Halla knew that despite their fierce look of a dragon's head with antlers and a deer's body, they were gentle in disposition. Psychics liked to have qilin antlers for their precognitive abilities. Qilin descendents were rare because the ancient creatures themselves were already rare, reportedly only appearing for the birth or death of great rulers or those of great intellect. Halla hadn't heard of a si before, though, but she was too tired to ask what it was at the time.

Eventually, the shop had emptied, and the brewer threw a blanket on the two of them settled on the couch in a restless slumber.

He returned early the next morning, and Halla and Rex woke to the smell of toasted rice.

Halla checked the time before groaning, "7:00 AM? With how late you close, are you not tired?"

The brewer laughed. Today, he was dressed in a light blue shirt, sleeves rolled up to his elbows, and an apron. "I don't need much sleep. That's why I have a tea shop, Miss Grumpy."

Halla knitted her brows. "I have a name, Mr. Nosy Tea Brewer."

They'd already lost a whole night because he wouldn't show them the way. Now, he wanted to joke?

Rexford was already up at the barstools, taking a cup of toasted rice tea from the brewer. "This smells amazing!" She inhaled deeply. "The grumpy one is Halla, and my name is Rexford. It's kind of my fault if she seems grumpy. I dragged her into this."

If Rex felt any guilt about that, she didn't show it, instead opting for a sip.

"It's good to meet you." The man dipped his head at Rexford before glancing Halla's way. "My name's Shylou. I own the town tea shop. I've sent word to the address you had listed."

Halla's stomach flipped. *Please confirm you know us. Please confirm you know us.*

"Sarai confirmed she knows of your coming, so I'll take you there," Shylou said.

Halla breathed a sigh of relief while Rexford whooped.

"But what about breakfast?" Rexford asked.

"Rex!" Halla chided her. *How is she so entitled?* While Rex's outburst had been forward, Halla also didn't want to spend longer than necessary with the annoying tea brewer.

Shylou laughed. "I have to prepare my shop for opening after I send you off. There's no way I'm feeding you. That's your relative's responsibility."

Before setting out, Halla took Rexford's wrist to synth. Once again, Rexford's condition seemed stable. No better and no worse than last time. *How curious. Maybe it's something about the air or magic out here.*

When they stepped out, Mogi swung his head toward them and wiggled his long, green body, tapping his two front talons.

Rexford ran and hugged his lowered head with both arms. "Did you rest well, Mogi?"

He flicked a tongue in response, which Rexford must have taken as positive because she laughed. Halla approached him and patted him fondly, as well, receiving a flicked tongue to her ear.

"Mogi!" She leaped back, swiping at the drool seeping into her ear. The snake-headed land-fish stomped all his legs, seemingly in laughter.

"Whoa," Rexford breathed.

Halla turned to find Shylou on his own steed: a massive horse with a head as white as snow and a body orange with black stripes like a tiger's coat.

"A *lushu*," Halla said. She'd never seen anyone ride one. She made a mental note to tell her father given his interest in other beasts.

"A kind of horse?" Rexford asked.

"In a way." Shylou grinned. "They don't neigh like normal horses, though, and it's said that a lushu's coat can bring luck to one's offspring."

"What do they sound like?" Rexford asked eagerly.

Shylou laughed. *For an annoying guy, he laughs a lot. It's not a bad sound,* Halla thought to herself.

"You'll hear it sometime," Shylou told Rex.

Tanheli was turning out far more interesting than Halla had expected.

The sun rose while they followed Shylou through the town. Halla couldn't help noticing that his dark hair gave a blue sheen in the sun, similarly to how hers had a green sheen.

They exited the main town and walked toward a looming forest. At the edge of it, Halla spotted smoke puffing out of the smokestack of a house. As they approached, Halla saw Grandma's qingniao, that blue-green crow, on the rooftop. They were at the right place.

Shylou bid them farewell as he headed back to open his shop. Halla and Rexford dismounted Mogi and approached the front door. A simple sign hung next to the door read: Apothecary.

I guess it's true we're all in the family business.

She knocked twice, palms sweating, but there was no answer.

"Maybe she's still sleeping?" Rexford suggested.

"Shylou said he sent the message to her this morning, and she confirmed, so I think she'd be awake," Halla said, but she bit her lip in worry.

She tried to peek through a window, but the curtains were drawn. Suddenly, a creak sounded, and Halla snapped her head in its direction. Rexford's hand froze on the slightly open door. The girl shifted her eyes to Halla with a guilty smile.

"What are you doing, Rex?" Halla whispered forcefully.

"I didn't know it was unlocked!" Rex whispered back, throwing her hands up in a shrug. "But maybe we go inside to check it out?"

"No, that's rude," Halla countered, but Rex was nearly inside.

"There's a kitchen in the back with something on the stove." Rexford craned her neck to peer farther inside.

"Let's knock again," Halla said as she approached Rex and caught a glimpse of the kitchen.

It was a traditional apothecary. The interior was furnished in dark woods and filled with tight aisles; shelves held various ingredients in glass jars. The back had a counter with a register and the familiar wall of drawers. It was like Halla had stepped into Grandma's apothecary at the Nuan estate. She spotted a small seating area in the corner like a cafe, very similar to the waiting area she had within The Green Thumb.

Then, the scent hit her. The scent of drying herbs, boiling concoctions, and dried chrysanthemum. Halla closed her eyes and felt a warmth in her heart, thinking of Grandma's kind hands cupping her face.

Without realizing it, she had stepped into the small store, lifted the detachable counter at the back, and headed for the kitchen.

"Halla!" Rex tugged at Halla's sleeve. This time, it was Rexford's turn to chide. "What are you doing? I was peeking inside, but you straight up walk in?"

Halla ignored her and entered the backroom. There were pots on clay stoves, brewing soups, half-opened drawers of various herbs, baskets of mountain vegetables, bundled herbs hanging upside down on racks, and hanging strings of drying persimmons.

"I would hope the Nuans taught you better manners," a voice lilted humorously behind them.

Halla spun, finding a young woman leaning against the door frame.

The woman with the unmistakable green sheen to her clipped-up hair glanced at Grandma's jade pendant hanging around Halla's neck before looking back at her and Rexford. "You must be Halla and Rexford." Her eyes twinkled. "I'm Sarai."

"You're young!" Rexford blurted, voicing Halla's thoughts. Instead of Mrs. Nuan's age, Sarai appeared only about six or seven years older than Halla herself.

Sarai blinked slowly and then broke into laughter. "I can assure you, I'm not *that* young, but I guess you expected someone quite a bit older to be an aunt." Sarai looked to Rex and offered her hands, palms up, in greeting.

Halla glanced away sheepishly, a hand coming up to clasp Grandma's pendant. "Nice to meet you, Aunt Sarai."

"Just call me Sarai," the other woman said, winking before entering the kitchen to tend to some simmering pots. "Go sit in the cafe area at the front. I prepared a light snack for you two."

Halla and Rexford did as they were told, settling themselves into seats at the storefront.

"She's so cool!" Rexford gushed.

As the young girl prattled with Halla giving slight nods and smiles in response, Halla couldn't help thinking the same. A woman living alone on an edge of an animated forest, cooking her own food and herbs—and the way Sarai carried herself! She was so sure, so relaxed. Halla's mother was similar in a way—bold, confident, bright—but Halla had always found it too much, too jovial, too free-flowing. For someone like Halla who liked rules and straight paths, she found it difficult to relate.

Sarai was different. She didn't sport a bold haircut or colors, but her face wore the look of a woman who'd held herself up. She was quietly confident. She wore the traditional clothing and coloring of Grandma's time, yet she had the countenance of Mom and of a modern woman.

After Sarai let Mogi loose, telling him to be back by nightfall, she presented two piping bowls to Halla and Rexford. "Eight treasure congee." She smiled down at them.

Eight treasure congee was made of whole grains, softened nuts, and dried fruit—like an oatmeal. It was nutritious and warming. Halla had loved snacking on the canned versions during her school days. The canned ones were often sold in vending machines throughout campus, some of the machines having heat settings so that they could keep the can warm for a toasty snack, and the lids popped off with a foldable plastic spoon.

Halla had never been happier seeing a bowl of grains. It wasn't until this moment that she realized how much she needed a little touch of comfort. As they sipped on the hot breakfast, Halla let Rex recount their adventure to Sarai. The other woman listened patiently.

When Rexford finished, Sarai put a hand out. "If you don't mind, Rexford, I'd like to synth you."

Rexford glanced at Halla, as if asking permission. Halla sucked in a breath but nodded, and Rex offered her wrist. After all this time trying to make sense of Rexford's body with what little knowledge Halla had, she wondered what Sarai would see.

Sarai furrowed her brows, eyes closed. "This is indeed a rampant illness. But this isn't a body ailment." She opened her eyes. "It's a poisoning."

CHAPTER 18

"How could that be?" Halla exclaimed. "I didn't poison her!"

Rex had made herself a thorn-apple concoction, but that should have been out of her system by now.

"Check again," Halla urged. "You're probably sensing remnants of the thorn-apple."

Sarai gave Halla a steely look while keeping her hand on Rexford's wrist. "Who is the one coming here to seek synthing guidance?"

Halla reeled in her panic and managed to look admonished.

"That's what I thought." Sarai humphed before softening her face. "You didn't let me finish and jumped to a conclusion. You could do to learn more patience."

Halla felt a familiar anger surge within her core but stomached it. She couldn't lose her temper like she did with her employees. She had to stay on good terms with Sarai; it was her only chance to claim any knowledge her grandmother might have left behind. And, as much as she'd like to believe otherwise, what Sarai said about her patience was not untrue.

"I'm sorry," she said between gritted teeth. "Please continue." *Remember your goal. Cool as a cucumber, Halla.*

Sarai turned her attention back to Rexford. "It's a poisoning, yes. But it's not a sudden poisoning like what you're both thinking."

Halla snapped her head back up, and Rexford frowned. "What do you mean?"

Sarai removed her hand from Rexford's with a grave expression. "Your body shows signs of a prolonged, continuous poisoning."

"What!?" Rexford exclaimed, standing. "Wouldn't I be dead if I'd been poisoned for a long time?"

Halla could only sit in shock.

Sarai shook her head. "It's been carefully done in small, calculated doses. Yes, there are poisons meant to kill and some meant to incapacitate. But there are also poisons meant to be slow-acting and to build over time. These are not studied nor considered as often due to the time it takes and the risk. One wrong dosage could result in an immediate death which may not have been the purpose. Not enough, and the victim could clear it out of their digestive system before the next dosage." She met Rexford's gaze. "Has it been about four years of your various illnesses?"

The girl's eyes widened in shock. "How did you know?"

Sarai nodded to herself. "The accumulation of toxins within your body can give me an approximation. I can see some of Halla's work over the last few months," she nodded in appreciation toward Halla, "but some of that had been negated. In these last few days, your body is slowly trying to recover, but it will need some help." She reached for Rexford's hand. "I'm afraid this is no accident, young heir. This is something diligently planned."

Rexford pulled her small hand away. "What does this mean? I don't understand! What does it mean that I've been poisoned over a long time?"

Sarai hesitated, so Halla answered instead, having reached the same conclusion with a cold dread. "It means someone's been intervening in your health. Your illnesses weren't natural, Rex. They were created through poison that you've been ingesting."

As she said it out loud, coldness crept through her body into her fingertips. *Who would do such a thing?*

Rexford choked on her words of denial. "You're saying I've been eating poison everyday? And that's why I've been sick with this strange illness?" She looked at her hands as if betrayed by them. "How would I not know what I'm eating!?"

"Think about it." Halla grabbed Rexford's shoulders. "I told you during our trip that you were getting better. During our travels here, ever since being away from your home, we've been eating different things."

How could I not have seen that Rex's illness was not natural? How could I not sense it was from toxins?

"No." Rexford tried stepping away from Halla, but Halla held firm. "Are you saying the food I had at home was laced? My parents would *never* do that!"

Halla shook her head. "I don't think your parents would either. I can tell your mother loves you very much." Halla thought of Thrum's mechanical smile and his missing pulse, but he seemed very loyal to Mrs. Urquart. It couldn't have been him. *Or was it all an act? Could he be a part of something else?*

"So, you're accusing my kitchen staff?" the young girl said, pulling herself up to her full four-foot-three-inches.

"I don't know." Halla sighed. "I don't want to accuse them of anything, but honestly, any of them could have been easily paid off by some opposing family."

Was the Cru family actually involved? Another family? There was the money they found in her shop. Did they pay off someone, and that person stashed the money at Halla's shop to pick up later?

"The Urquart staff is loyal," Rexford stated. "They've all been vetted. They've been with us for years."

Halla lifted a brow. "Sarai says you've been poisoned for years. Is there anyone who joined around the same time you got sick?"

"They've all been here since before I got sick," Rexford said indignantly. "And excuse me if I don't recall. I've been ill since I was six years old.

"It could be your water supply," Sarai suggested.

"But no one else in her household has been sick like her," Halla said. It had to be something only Rex had exposure to. A personal maid? A tutor? Dr. Kurand?

Halla was scared of the implications. It meant someone inside the Urquart household was responsible for Rexford's shot health. She felt a prickling sensation as the fine hairs on the back of her neck stood. And this person could very well be the same person who was trying to frame Halla.

Sarai hummed in thought, bringing a hand to her chin.

"Stop accusing everyone I grew up with of poisoning me!" Rexford demanded. "I don't believe it. I won't believe it." She stomped her foot, covering her ears with both hands.

"Rexford." Sarai pulled the girl close. "I know it may be hard to believe. I'm not sure what to believe right now. But what I see shows an accumulation of poison over several years. And you need to remember you come from a powerful family: the family that owns and runs our territory. You must know that the Urquart name is not lacking in enemies. You do know that much, don't you? Isn't that one of the reasons your family makes you wear that male disguise?" Sarai patted the pendant lying flat on Rexford's chest.

And she's calm and able to talk a child down from a ledge, Halla considered as she observed Sarai. As much as she had come to care for Rex, Halla had a feeling that her impatience and speed to anger probably weren't good for a child.

The small girl met Sarai's sympathetic look with a momentary hard gaze, and then she broke, her lips quivering as understanding dawned on her.

"Come here, child," Sarai said, and the little girl collapsed into Sarai. Rex wrapped her arms around the apothecary, burying her head into Sarai's shoulder, and cried.

The news exhausted Rexford, so Sarai settled her into a cot, covered with warm blankets, in an empty exam room.

"How did I not sense that she was being poisoned this whole time?" Halla asked as Sarai re-entered the storefront.

"Don't blame yourself," Sarai said. "Prolonged poisoning of small dosages is difficult to sense. It may seem natural to an untrained sensor."

"But I'm a Nuan," Halla said. "I am a trained traditional medicinal practitioner. I've treated hundreds of patients."

That was what was bothering her the most. If Halla had just paid a little more attention, applied herself the way Grandma wanted, she would have been able to catch that detail and avoid this mess altogether. But even so, she was a Nuan. Wasn't synthing in her blood? Shouldn't she have known better?

"I'm well aware of your accomplishments, Halla," Sarai said. "I'm a bit disconnected from Aunt Wen's side of the family, but I looked you up when I received your brother's message."

That caught Halla's attention. "You knew Grandma Wen?"

"She and my mother exchanged many letters, yes. And Aunt Wen visited once every few years, so I would see her then."

Halla remembered when Grandma was more sprightly, she would go on long trips twice a year, saying she was traveling to source rare herbs. She wondered if Grandma had taken those opportunities to actually visit her disowned sister and the fertile soils of Tanheli.

"All that to say," Sarai continued, "I know you're very accomplished, but I heard you weren't properly trained in Synesthology. Do not blame yourself for not sensing the poison."

Halla looked away. "It's my fault I wasn't trained."

Sarai flipped her window sign from 'closed' to 'open' and sat next to Halla. "How do you mean?"

"I refused Grandma Wen's knowledge. Instead, I went away to city school."

Sarai cocked her head. "Didn't you go to Lianou Academy? The top traditional medicine school in the territories? I'm sure you learned a lot."

"I did. But it wasn't synthing. In fact, they told us to not concern ourselves with it. I had a lot of classmates who were sensors who actually found it burdensome. Grandma Wen tried to tell me…"

"Well." Sarai sighed. "With the development of cities and technology, that's where it's going. Us sensors and crafters are increasingly seen as obsolete. The imbuers may still have some use of their skills until technology catches up, and they're the rarest of the Synesthology Triangle. It's a good time to be an imbuer."

Halla hadn't thought of the world and its evolution that way. She wondered if synthers in other territories were seeing the same trend.

"Why did you refuse Aunt Wen's knowledge?" Sarai interrupted Halla's thoughts.

Halla's mind swirled with multiple emotions. Shame, sadness, longing, and even a pinch of anger. "I think," she started slowly, "that I didn't want the family pressures. My mom didn't take the mantle, so the attention was magnified on me, especially when I showed promise. And I think deep down, I felt that if I didn't take the knowledge, then they wouldn't be able to make me stay home and continue Grandma's business because I wouldn't have the skills to. I loved medicine anyway, the thought of a school in the capital excited me. So I moved, and I studied. I've never really needed synthing. Until Rex, that is." When Halla looked up to meet Sarai's eyes, she found Sarai looking at her intently, as if to peer into her soul. She shrunk instinctively. "What're you doing?"

"Halla," Sarai said. "The Nuan family legacy wasn't about keeping your grandmother's business alive. It was about retaining that knowledge for the future. There's a lot the Nuans don't write in books because it's passed orally. You could have accepted her knowledge and continued to city school."

Halla frowned. Of course Sarai wouldn't understand. She lived away from the Nuan pressures and household. She lived here in her cozy house with her mother who chose love over family duties.

"What do you know about the Nuan family legacy?" she spat before she could stop herself.

At Sarai's look of hurt, she immediately regretted her words. "I'm sorry," Halla said quickly. "I shouldn't have said that."

"No." Sarai raised a hand. "It's true that I lived away from the Nuans. I don't even carry the Nuan name. Instead, I carry my father's surname. I wouldn't know what you've been through. But," she eyed Halla, "you *are* here now to learn about the Nuan skills, are you not?"

Halla blinked. "Yes."

"Which means I do know a thing or two about the Nuan legacy." Sarai gave a small, triumphant smile.

The corner of Halla's lips curled upward. "I spoke too soon. If I haven't offended you too much, I really hope you'll still consider teaching me what you know." Halla bowed her head in deference.

"There's no need for such formalities, Halla." Sarai laughed and stood, retreating to the back counter and the shelves of herbs. "We barely know each other, but we're family. And if not for you, I would do this for Aunt Wen. I owe her more than I can repay for continuing correspondences with my mother and for visiting. I think her acceptance of my mother and myself kept my mother sane when she was disowned. Plus, it'll be nice to have more help around the shop."

"Oh," was all Halla could manage.

The front door slid open. "Good tidings," Sarai called out in greeting as a customer entered.

Halla also stood, unsure what to do with herself. She didn't want to take up a seat for a paying customer, and she felt like she should help, but she didn't know where to start.

"Sarai! I found some wood ear mushrooms to harvest. Want to go sometime?" A man with a stocky build and middle-parted wavy, black hair entered with a cheerful expression. If it weren't for his sunny demeanor, Halla would have thought of him as more of a strong ox.

"Attica!" Sarai exclaimed and ran to embrace him.

Halla's brows almost reached her hairline. *That's quite a long embrace,* she thought, bemused before understanding dawned, and she pursed her lips to stifle a smile.

"Halla, this is Attica. He helps out quite often around here." Sarai's smile was practically radiant.

Helps out, huh? "Nice to meet you," Halla said. "I'm Sarai's niece."

"Your niece?" The man looked at Sarai in surprise. "I didn't know you had one. I mean, I know your mother ran away from home and settled here with Mr. Leng. I assume she's from your mother's side?"

Halla frowned. Attica seemed to know a lot about her. But Sarai merely rolled her eyes. "She's a distant niece. My mom lost contact with them. Lots of family drama. I'll catch you up. You'll love this."

And so the three of them sat down at the cafe corner, and Sarai regaled Attica with the story of her family up to receiving the qingniao message and Halla's arrival. The entire time, Attica sat with rapt attention, gasping or widening his eyes or covering his mouth at all the right moments. Halla thought the two must be close if Sarai was telling him everything. *Very* close. But having another person know about her situation made her a bit nervous. She was sure if Sarai trusted him, it was fine. But that was one additional person who could spread the news that Halla and Rex were here.

Halla knew the majority of the story after Sarai had finished the part about her mother moving to Tanheli, so she let her eyes wander around the small shop. She noted the time was 11:00 AM, and there had been no customers yet today. Probably similar to her grandmother's business. It was a stark contrast to the hustle and bustle of The Green Thumb.

For as long as Halla could remember, she tried to maximize her time anywhere, tried to get the most done within the shortest period of time because that created results. But where Halla used to scoff at the sluggish pace of her grandmother's business, she now felt a comfort within Sarai's shop.

CHAPTER 19

When Herb realized the Tracker was taking him out of town, he returned home to pack and gave his captain a call.

"Inspector Mooran," she greeted.

"Captain Asma," he said. "I found a note that I'll need to send in for handwriting analysis for the heir."

"Done. Send me an image, and I'll run it through the Urquart family."

"And I'm packing," he said, holding his breath.

There was a pause on the other end. "You're using the Tracker?"

"Yes. It's taking me outside the capital. I was planning on giving the Nuan household a visit anyway. I can do both."

"Excellent. You have my seal tag for authority wherever the Tracker leads you within the territory. If Halla ran to any of the surrounding territories like Cru or Tripa, then report back. We have no jurisdiction there. She may as well have sealed her fate if she did so."

"Thank you, Captain." Herb didn't think Halla was running to escape, but he hoped she didn't go far.

"And Inspector?" Asma added before hanging up. "Be careful with the Nuans. I'm shielding you from the brunt of it, but there are a lot more politics at play than we may know."

With Captain Asma's blessing and warning, Herb packed his belongings into his two-person car and drove out of the city toward the Nuan estate. To his relief, the Tracker glowed green the entire way. *That means I save time with Halla having gone to the Nuan estate anyway.*

He only hoped the remainder of the tracking was as straightforward as this first leg.

Tires crunched over gravel as Herb pulled up before the largest house he'd ever seen with an imposing gate and walls. There were a few others around, coming and going without visible invitation. So, Herb parked and headed inside.

The hinges creaked heavily as he entered through the massive doors. He had to remind himself not to let his jaw drop open at the sense of stepping back in time. Inside was a gorgeous inner courtyard with a surrounding walkway. It wasn't until he reached the courtyard that a woman in a flowing skirt and long vest greeted him.

"Are you here for an appointment?" she asked.

Herb shook his head, flashing his inspector seal hanging from his belt loops. "I'm Inspector Mooran. I'm here about Halla Nuan. Might I speak with the head of the household?"

The woman's eyes widened before she schooled her expression. "Of course. Please come inside. I'll fetch Mrs. Nuan."

Herb gawked at the numerous florals and the actual river in the courtyard before they entered a massive room. It looked to be some kind of waiting area, with plenty of basic seating and a view back out to the courtyard.

A woman with a short haircut pinned with various jewels floated into the room shortly after Herb seated himself.

"Inspector. We've been expecting you." She smiled. "I'm Gaia Nuan. Halla's mother."

"You've been expecting me?" Herb echoed.

She nodded, causing her dangling earrings to tinkle. "Indeed. I'm sure you're looking for Halla. She was here, but you've missed her."

Herb told himself not to grip the arm rest. "How long ago was she here?"

The woman's expression dropped, a stark contrast to her calm hospitality, and said, "How about you explain what in the spittlebork is going on first?"

"Excuse me?" Herb said sharply. "I'm the authority here."

"And you won't get any cooperation from me until I know more." Mrs. Nuan crossed her arms. "You may have the authority, but let me remind you of my standing. This is the Nuan household. We respect your authority, but we all know the Nuans have always functioned outside of it. Just because my daughter is unaware of that doesn't mean someone can take her case and run with it."

Captain Asma's last warning played in his head. *"Be careful with the Nuans."*

The Nuan family was long-known as a medicinal synther bloodline, but with generations of that reputation came power. In modern times, the Nuans had taken a backseat, opting not to run for any political positions and claiming philanthropic motivations, but there were rumors of a tendril hold the Nuans had somewhere. They'd always publicly denounced any such claims, making Mrs. Nuan's warning the closest confirmation of such Herb had ever heard, which was doubly alarming.

He cleared his throat, trying not to look shaken. *What could this woman do to me anyway?* "Of course. I can explain the situation. That's only natural." He cleared his throat and straightened. "I expect your full cooperation afterward."

Mrs. Nuan sat back in her seat. The woman who had greeted him earlier in the courtyard appeared with two cups of tea and a plate of small mung-bean cakes. "Thank you, Ahming," Mrs. Nuan said before addressing Herb again. "The floor is yours." She waved a hand. "Help yourself to refreshments."

Herb took a breath, thinking this wasn't how it was supposed to go but saw no other way about it. He found himself explaining how the case came to him, the evidence stacking up, what they found at The Green Thumb, finishing with him witnessing Halla run.

"How curious, indeed," Mrs. Nuan mumbled to herself.

Herb nodded. "I think it's why they set me on this case. I'm known to chase down every lead." He gave a small chuckle. "But I need the heir who's with Halla, and I need Halla to come back if I'm to prove her innocence."

Mrs. Nuan's look sharpened. "So, you think she's innocent?"

Herb shrank slightly before straightening his spine. "Well…" He hadn't meant to say that. He actually hadn't realized he thought Halla *was* innocent. The entire case smelled strange, and he had a hunch she wasn't guilty. But innocent?

"What I meant to say is that if you want to help your daughter, help me find her. We can't complete our investigation without her."

"You very well can," Gaia Nuan huffed. "What about the note from the heir that says the heir poisoned himself?"

"I've sent that in for analysis, and it's being considered, of course." He bristled. He had enough of people telling him how to do his job in his own department.

Mrs. Nuan stood. "I'll let you simmer on that. I have a patient appointment at this time. Do you mind waiting or would you like to come back another time?"

"I'll wait," Herb said. He was determined to figure out his next steps, and Halla's mother stepping out was the perfect opportunity for him to look around for clues. "You won't mind if I enjoy your wonderful estate while I wait?"

Mrs. Nuan raised a brow. "I have nothing to hide. Help yourself to the estate. But if you venture outside, be careful with our ranyi school."

She gave a rueful smile, as if she hoped to witness what would happen should he come across a ranyi, and left in a flow of fabric.

"I have no intention of going to your ranyi grounds," Herb muttered to himself. He'd never seen one, but he'd seen their fierce depictions in mythological art. He waited a few minutes out of a semblance of manners, helping himself to a small cake which was quite tasty, then stood. "Time to take a look around."

The corridor he was in was massive. The sign above the entry read: Hall of Central Harmony. The cavernous room with twenty-foot ceilings was broken into smaller sections by furniture, whether it be a rug here or there, or partitions created out of square shelving. He walked through each section, looking through the art and using the Tracker. It confirmed Halla had been there, but it wasn't a strong scent.

The hall was filled with various curios and antique vases. Herb couldn't imagine raising children here as everything seemed fragile or ancient. Among the art pieces were various photos of whom he assumed were members of the Nuan family and their relatives. Several featured two small children, a boy and a girl. Herb assumed the girl was a younger Halla since they looked alike and stood next to a younger Mrs. Gaia Nuan.

There were also multiple photos with an older lady. *Likely the matriarch Wen Nuan.* He had read that she passed a few years ago, which greatly impacted the Nuan income. *Perhaps it would be good for a powerful family to fall.* He shook his head. How could he wish for the downfall of anyone? In fact, their fall would likely create a power vacuum for some other family to seize. The Urquarts kept multiple powerful families in tow, having them struggle with each other to keep the balance. Everything was about balance, just like the tenets of Synesthology.

Synesthology? He suddenly remembered what the Nuans were known for and hugged his arms close to himself, wondering if Mrs. Nuan or the lady she called Ahming had synthed him at any point, like during a handshake or passing off the tea.

He searched the shelves of books, meticulously clear of dust. As an avid bibliophile, Herb had done excellently in school. His attention to detail and the written word was what made him a scrupulous investigator. As such, Herb found himself scouring over the book spines with more curiosity than scruple for his investigation.

"The Neijing Suwen," he read aloud. "Huangdi's Classic of Medicine."

From high school history class, he knew that Huangdi was a legendary emperor in mythology, known to have jumpstarted civilization and many important inventions. Herb shrugged. For a family of traditional medicinal synthers, of course they would have this book, though on second thought, he found it interesting they would study the words of a mythological character.

He continued reading through various traditional medicine titles, all sounding dry and more clinical. He then found a few titles of classic literature such as *Journey to the West* and *Dream of the Red Chamber*. Herb had read the latter in a required school course and found the storyline boring in youth. He wasn't interested in reading about upper-class intrigue, love triangles, and corruption. Although unrelated, that title reminded him of the film *Raise the Red Lantern*; a great film but sad and with a chilling ending. *Journey to the West* was much more exciting: a tale of a monk's dangerous pilgrimage, accompanied by strong disciples, such as the mischievous Monkey King. In fact, this classic tale was so popular there was a video game on the Monkey King that had been recently released.

It was a few titles later when Herb found an unlabeled spine. He hooked his finger over the brown leather and pulled it out. Upon flipping it open, he found that it was an old photo album.

Maybe I'll learn more about the family here. He flipped through pages of aged photos. They didn't show anyone he recognized in the current household, and he found no date listed. However, each image was captioned with cursive handwriting.

'Ranyi Roadshow: 1st Place.' The image showed a massive fish-snake creature standing on a podium with a woman.

'New Home!' The image showed a family of ten standing in front of the Nuan estate front gates that Herb passed through not too long ago.

Herb gave cursory glances over the next several pages, noting multiple photos of people sitting together and shaking hands with important figures such as the Minister of Power, the Minister of Livestock, or the Director of Pharmacology. Near the end of the album, a name stood out. Herb brought the album closer to his face to read the scrawl.

"Tronjone Kurand, Headmaster of The Yan Academy of Medicinal Synesthology," he read. "There was a school for medicinal synthing?" Herb wondered aloud.

For as long as he could remember, the Synesthology schools had long been closed, deemed obsolete multiple decades ago when the technology boom occurred. The man was shaking hands with a woman whom Herb assumed must be a Nuan predecessor.

"Hold on," he paused. "Kurand?"

He ran a finger over the written name. *Was that not the name of the Urquart family doctor?* Herb flipped through the rest of the album, looking for any other photos of the man or any other Kurand labels but found none. This was the only photo.

He took out his work-issued phone and snapped a picture before pulling up his files. From his notes, he confirmed it was the same name as the Urquart family doctor's. Was it a coincidence? Or did the families know each other? Were the Nuans more closely connected to the Urquarts than they all thought?

"Bi fang!" a voice called.

Herb jumped at the sudden sound and whipped around, but no one was there. Instead, there was a white-beaked, blue crane perched on an open windowsill. Herb narrowed his eyes and looked around again for the source of the sound.

"Bi fang!" the crane called again.

Herb raised his brows; he'd never seen nor heard of a bird like this. He took a step closer.

"Bi fang, bi fang!" the crane called loudly.

"Shhh." Herb placed a finger to his lips. "You're going to draw their attention." The crane stared back at him, unblinking, but seemed to decide to stay silent. "Curious," Herb said. "Are you... missing a leg?"

The one-legged, blue crane said nothing. Herb shrugged, knowing his time alone to search was limited. He turned back around and found the crown of a head right in front of him.

"Spittlebork!" He sprang back, reaching for the baton at his belt.

"Sir?" It was the woman, Ahming, looking up at him from an uncomfortably close distance. "Were you looking for something?"

"No," he blurted, realizing belatedly that the photo album was still in his hands. He closed it.

Ahming glanced at the volume and back at him, narrowing her eyes.

"I was just so intrigued by the family, curiosity got the best of me," he stammered. "Very cool history," he added lamely, raising the album in his hand.

"Right," Ahming said slowly. "Mrs. Nuan will be back shortly."

"Thank you!" Herb said a bit too loudly and returned the album to the shelf.

What is the connection between the Nuans, Kurands, and Urquarts? he wondered as he walked back to his seat to wait for Mrs. Nuan, Ahming's eyes boring into his back.

CHAPTER 20

"What do you know about Kurand?" Herb asked Mrs. Nuan when she returned.

She pursed her lips. "I may have heard the name. What about it?"

Interesting reaction. "Are they another important synthing family?"

Mrs. Nuan nodded. "They were. I haven't heard their name in a while, though. Why do you ask?" Mrs. Nuan kept her tone light, but Herb could tell she was curious in the way she was avoiding eye contact, as if feigning disinterest.

"There's a picture of a Kurand in one of your family albums. Excuse my impropriety. It's a part of my job to look around," Herb explained, hoping Mrs. Nuan wouldn't be angry.

"I'm not surprised." She humphed, and Herb wondered if that was her telling him it was truly fine or her being upset at him for assuming. "Show me."

He got up to fetch the album, flipped to the picture, and rotated it around to face her, sitting back down. He waited with hands clasped in his lap. Mrs. Nuan stared at the picture, her expression unreadable.

"I know this must be old, but do you know anything about this relationship?"

Mrs. Nuan sighed and placed the album down. "Tronjone Kurand was the headmaster of a medicinal Synesthology school. With my family's background, of course they'd know the headmaster of a school." Her lips thinned, as if she was hesitating to share more.

"Was there anything else?" Herb asked. "I need to know everything you know to help Halla."

The woman met his gaze before putting out a demanding hand. "Give me your wrist."

"Pardon?" he asked.

"Give me your wrist," she repeated.

She must want to synth me. He tentatively placed his wrist into her open hands, and she closed them. Herb instinctively pulled back, but the woman held on.

"Why did you take this case?" she asked.

"My captain gave it to me, frankly," he said. The woman shot him an exasperated look. "Well, if you're asking why I'm here or taking this seriously," he amended, "it's because I care for the truth. That's why I joined this occupation." *Despite the obsession with case numbers.*

"Are you committed to uncovering the truth behind the heir's coma?"

"Yes," he answered, surprised at finding himself suddenly in an interrogation.

"Are you committed to uncovering the truth behind the illegal drugs and cash at The Green Thumb?"

"Yes," he said.

"Is the inspector department anxious to close this case?"

His head shot toward her. "How did you know? I mean, my captain is supportive of this investigation, so we have her, but that's it."

Did Gaia Nuan have connections back at the department? Just how well connected was the family?

She ignored him, nodding to herself. "Will you fight for this case to be closed fairly?"

"Of course," Herb said. "But there are limits to what I can do. Unfortunately, any higher power could tell me to stop, so I'm hoping to get as much done as soon as possible."

Mrs. Nuan pulled him closer so he had to lean in, and she peered into his eyes. "Do you believe my Halla is innocent?"

Herb had always been taught to go by the books, look at the hard facts, and to not let emotions affect his job. Emotions were misleading and could be manipulated by others. However, one of his mentors at the academy had also said, *"Never disregard your gut. You've got a good head on your shoulders. You don't need to act on it. But don't disregard it either."*

There were facts in this case, yes. But they didn't perfectly line up like they did in textbook cases. It was still too early to jump to any conclusion, but with the Onyx Division eager to close a case of disconnected evidence, Herb's gut was telling him this case seemed very rigged against a certain someone. He met Mrs. Nuan's eyes and answered.

"I do."

The woman stared at him for a few moments longer, as if searching him, and then she let go of his wrist and sat back. "I believe you. You're a good inspector."

"Thank you?" he said, unsure what to make of her as he rubbed his wrist. "Glad you were able to ascertain I was speaking the truth," he said flatly.

Synthers, he thought to himself with mild annoyance.

Mrs. Nuan gave a small smile. "I had to make sure you were telling the truth. Now that I know your motivations, I'll give you unfiltered information. But why do you want to know about some long-gone headmaster?"

"I don't want to worry you unnecessarily," Herb answered, feeling a bit violated for being synthed without his consent. "I'd appreciate it if you could first answer my question. I've answered quite enough of yours."

He was the inspector, and yet Mrs. Nuan felt like the one on a case. Ultimately though, he wanted to confirm his suspicions lest he share prematurely.

Mrs. Nuan raised a brow. "Very well." She grabbed her tea cup and sipped as if settling in for a good story. "I didn't know Tronjone Kurand, of course. He was generations before us. My grandmother knew him."

"The matriarch Grandmother Wen who'd just passed?"

"No, no." She waved a hand. "*My* grandmother. The matriarch's mother. She would be Halla's great-grandmother."

"Oh," Herb said, mentally working through the family tree.

"In addition to being known as great medicinal synthers, the skilled families were also teachers. Many of my predecessors taught at The Yan Academy. The Kurand name was well-known—one of the top families—and Tronjone ran the academy for multiple years. In fact, the Kurands started the academy about one hundred years before him."

Herb almost choked on his tea. "A hundred years? The school was that old?"

"Indeed, it was. It was extremely prestigious and one of a few medicinal synthing academies." Mrs. Nuan set her tea down. "Unfortunately, it closed like many other Synesthology schools because students stopped coming. People were seeing less of a need to cultivate their skills. Instead, technology did what they needed. I sometimes wonder if the school was still open by the time I was born, if perhaps my synthing skills could have been mastered or amplified through education..." she trailed off, then cleared her throat. "I believe my grandmother was the last to lead the school."

"Your grandmother? I thought you said the Kurands ran it."

"That's right. They had been running it for close to the hundred years that the school was operating. But..." She leaned closer to Herb as if sharing a secret. "Something happened to Tronjone Kurand, and he had to leave. So, my grandmother stepped in to run the school."

Herb's eyes widened. What could have happened that forced Tronjone Kurand to leave?

"It's quite a story." Mrs. Nuan settled back into her seat, seemingly delighted she was about to tell Herb something most people didn't know. "My mother told me that Tronjone Kurand made a mistake in a diagnosis. That patient ended up going to my grandmother to be treated correctly. That could have been the end, but I suppose that patient was quite vindictive."

"What do you mean?" Herb asked.

Mrs. Nuan shook her head. "It's really bad luck to get a patient like this. The patient complained, not only to everyone in the village, but also to the academy. He sent letters to the academy and demanded to meet the other board members, calling for Kurand to step down."

Herb raised his brows. "That's a little overboard."

"Quite so," Mrs. Nuan agreed. "But the man was persistent. He claimed that Tronjone Kurand was not qualified to lead the school, and that he'd gotten worse after Kurand's diagnosis until my grandmother healed him."

"And the Board listened to this patient?"

"Not at first," Mrs. Nuan answered. "Kurand had a good reputation. The Board wasn't going to listen to one complaint. But, this man knew a few capital officials."

Herb frowned. "Well, that's unfortunate for Tronjone Kurand." The story was getting increasingly ridiculous.

"It's suspected the patient knew someone high-up because after three months of no movement from the Board, the Assistant Director of Pharmacology and someone from the Secretariat of Medicinal Practices came to the village asking to speak with the academy's Board. It's not often these capital officials take it upon themselves to look into a village matter, much less one of a singular complaint. The academy was also in good standing with the Secretariat of Medicinal Practices."

How would it be possible for a villager to have connections with government officials? Herb's mind briefly flicked to the pages of photos the Nuans had with official figures, but Mrs. Nuan continued. "Once the capital officials opened an investigation, Trojone was forced to step down."

"What happened after that?" Herb asked.

She shrugged. "The Kurands slowly dissolved into nonexistence, and their story became a lesson: Any greatness can fall from the sky at the whims of the smallest bug. Like a parasite incapacitating a bird from the inside."

Herb scrunched his face at the imagery. "Are there any Kurands left here?"

"No." Mrs. Nuan shook her head. "It's quite a pity, really. There was so much knowledge in that family. After Trojone stepped down, no one wanted to go to him for treatment. With no business, he moved himself and his whole family. No one's heard their name in years, so rumors spread that they moved to another territory."

What was the connection between the Kurands and Nuans? Was the Urquarts' doctor related to Tronjone Kurand? Was there even a connection to this case? Herb's mind tried to work through all the possibilities but found no conclusion with his limited information. He would need to give more in order to get more.

Herb pulled out his files and handed them to Mrs. Nuan. "I had a reason for asking about this history, Mrs. Nuan. There may be a connection between that story and Halla's situation. It's still too early to tell, however."

She took the files and her eyes skimmed across, widening. "The Urquart family's doctor's name is Kurand?"

Herb nodded. "It's just a name. Could be a coincidence. Or maybe not."

He was leaning toward it not being a coincidence.

"Why didn't Halla or the heir tell us?" Mrs. Nuan asked.

"They wouldn't have thought to. They didn't know there's a connection. We haven't confirmed if this is indeed a real connection. They probably thought his name wasn't important."

Mrs. Nuan nodded. "That's true. Halla doesn't know this story. There's a lot she doesn't know about our family." She glanced back up at Herb. "Inspector, are you saying this Kurand could be a descendent of Tronjone, and this could be related to the case?"

"I don't know yet," Herb said honestly. "For now, it seemed your grandmother and Tronjone had a civil relationship, right?"

Mrs. Nuan nodded. "They worked together. After he left, she stepped up to be headmaster since she was the next best qualified."

If Douglas Kurand was indeed involved, he could have easily planted the poison into Halla's prescriptions at the Urquart estate. It didn't explain the illegal drugs and cash at The Green Thumb, but with his resources as the Urquart family doctor, he could have easily hired someone to do that. It wouldn't be anyone close because if those items were indeed planted, they were not planted directly in Halla's office.

If this really was a framing, they'd want the evidence to be as indisputable as possible—Halla's office would have been the best place. Instead, it was in easily accessible spaces. Maybe a customer snuck back there. Or maybe it was an employee.

But why would Dr. Kurand do it? To get rid of competition? He was already in the private sector, probably making a ton of money working for the Urquarts.

Mrs. Nuan gasped. "Do you think the Urquart doctor was involved? We don't even know him."

"These are speculations for now, Mrs. Nuan. I'll have to interview Halla's employees again, examine the evidence, and look into Dr. Douglas Kurand. Your family name is famous, so for all we know, any of these people could have merely been paid by someone, especially when the motive isn't clear yet. If there's anything my job has taught me, it's that anyone can be bought for the right price."

Mrs. Nuan narrowed her eyes, as if trying to mentally pinpoint who could have been bought off, when Herb's phone sounded.

"Excuse me," he said as he took it out. It was a message from Captain Asma.

> Mooran, handwriting analysis came back. 92% positive on a match and authenticity of Rexford Urquart's handwriting. Proceed with determining the note you found was indeed written by the heir.

He nodded. A small part of him had wondered if it was a fake note to alleviate suspicions on Halla, but this confirmation set that to rest. Another *ping* sounded, and he looked back down at his screen.

> Hope you're hitting some luck at the Nuans. -A

"What is it?" Mrs. Nuan asked.

Herb paused for a moment, considering if he should share the update, and then sighed. "News. They've confirmed the authenticity of the note the heir left behind saying that he poisoned himself into a coma."

Mrs. Nuan gave him an exasperated look. "That's not news. I knew that already. In fact, I had told you at the beginning of our meeting for you to consider it."

"But at that time, we hadn't confirmed that it was real," Herb retorted. "You know what. I don't know why I'm explaining this to you. Anyway, it's good news for Halla's case. As for this Kurand connection, no one has looked into

Douglas Kurand, so I'll report this back to my captain to run a background check on the Urquart doctor." He checked his wristwatch. "Night will be falling soon. Once I report to my captain, I'm afraid I'll have to head out."

"On Halla's trail?" Mrs. Nuan asked. "Since I trust that you'll chase the truth, I'll save you the trouble and tell you that she should be in Tanheli by now."

"Tanheli? Where's that?"

"The outskirts of Urquart territory, bordering Cru territory..." she trailed off. "That... doesn't look good given the cash from the Cru family found at The Green Thumb, doesn't it?"

Herb pressed his mouth into a thin line. "It can definitely look like she's running to the Cru family after receiving money from them."

"It's just a coincidence," Mrs. Nuan said quickly. "She's not actually leaving the territory. We have a family member in Tanheli. That town is known for its herbs and fertile soils. She went there with the heir for family resources to diagnose him."

Herb ran a hand over his face. "I don't think she ran. Coincidence or not, it doesn't help her case. But thank you for letting me know. I must find her. Rest assured, my captain is running our resources back at headquarters."

As Mrs. Nuan walked Herb out, a framed picture on the wall caught his eye. It was a family photo in the Nuan estate courtyard and consisted of the Nuan matriarch who was Tronjone Kurand's contemporary, a small girl that Herb assumed would be a young Grandma Wen, the lady named Ahming, a few men, and a tall slender man. Herb wanted to inspect it closer, but Mrs. Nuan was on his heels and he didn't want to draw attention.

As Mrs. Nuan walked him out the front gates of the estate, she asked if he needed any refreshments for the trip.

"There's no need. I have a few soybean bars in the car." Herb was eager to get back on the road, but something about that framed photo kept tugging on his mind.

"The path to Tanheli is not paved. Will your vehicle be all right?" She eyed the small, two-door car dubiously.

He patted the roof affectionately. "She's sturdier than she looks. Got me through a lot back in the day, and I've spent many a night in it when I had to."

Mrs. Nuan wrinkled her nose but said no more.

Herb ducked behind the wheel and turned on the Tracker. Mrs. Nuan had pointed him in the direction of Tanheli, but in cases when the road forked, it was best to have a guide keep him on the right trail. He rolled down his passenger window to wave goodbye.

"Inspector!" Mrs. Nuan called from the front gates. "Please help acquit Halla. Please help her so she can come home."

He dipped his head and drove off, leaving the Nuan estate in the dust while he pondered that photo. In his rearview mirror, he spotted Ahming standing at the gates behind Mrs. Nuan. Something was familiar and strange, but he couldn't quite place what.

CHAPTER 21

Halla had thought business was slow at Sarai's shop, but she was quickly proven wrong. Soon after Attica was caught up on the family history, there was a line out the door, and Sarai immediately put Halla and Rexford to work.

"Rexford, bring these drinks out to the customers!"

"Got it!" It was clear the small girl had never worked a day in her life, but she attacked each of her tasks with gumption. Halla noted that Rex seemed to have a great interest in herbs and the like.

"Halla, brew the angelica root with the tea to the left, and take the second batch to simmer with the chicken stock going on the stovetop."

"Yes, ma'am."

Sarai barked orders throughout the afternoon.

"Attica, don't burn yourself."

"Rexford, don't spill on the tray when you're serving the black sesame smoothie."

"Halla, where are the mugwort and lotus seeds I asked for?"

"Bring back the dirty glasses, Rexford, and wash them in the sink there. Yes, wash them. You don't know how to wash dishes? Great Doa, what do they teach you children these days? No, you still need to wash them, and Attica will quality check. Yes, Attica, you will check her work. Show her where the sponge and soap are."

"Halla, do you know how to conduct moxibustion? Yes? Great. I need you for Mr. Huckle in Room 2. Which room is that? There are only two other rooms back here. Go figure it out."

Despite the constant stream of instruction and shuffling around, Halla enjoyed the distraction from the case. She also found that everything flowed smoothly and efficiently, and once she stepped to the storefront, it was as if time slowed. Customers waited patiently at the cafe section or casually perused the shelves. Sarai ran her shop efficiently, and with a metaphorical whip, so that her customers could step into her shop to slow down.

At three o'clock, Sarai ran to the front window to flip her sign to 'closed'.

"Aw, dang it!" came a muffled exclamation from outside. "Please! I just need one thing."

Sarai pushed open the window. "Is this an emergency?"

"Well, no. My wife asked that I grab some more ginger candies and bird's nest soup for our uncle's birthday—"

"Sorry, we're closed. Come back tomorrow!" Sarai shut the window.

"Hey!" the man said, but he hung his head and walked away.

"Is it like this every day?" Rexford asked as she sank to the floor, leaning her back against the wall. "I was on my feet the whole day!"

"Is that a bad thing?" Attica asked her.

Rex looked at the ceiling in thought before breaking into a bright smile. "No! It was fun! I haven't had that much fun in forever!" She waved both arms out in a circle.

Sarai chuckled. "It's good you have energy. It means our treatment is working, and your body is healing from the poison. I'll need your help more as you get better. That'll be payment for your treatment."

Rexford's doe eyes widened. "I can help you more?"

"Of course. I need a smart girl to help me. And you're taking care of your own health by working for treatment."

"Congratulations!" Attica put a hand on the top of Rexford's head as he passed to sit in a chair near the window. "Your first transaction of your own merit. You're getting a taste of the real world!"

Rexford's eyes sparkled. "So, this is what it's like. Making my own life. Experiencing life!"

It was then Halla understood what Sarai and Attica were doing. *Dang, they're good with kids.* They were keeping Rexford's spirits up, especially after learning about being poisoned by someone in her own household, as well as leaning into Rexford wanting to 'live a life' before returning home. *They're* really *good.*

Perhaps Halla could learn a thing or two. She'd never been good with kids, but being good with them probably helped with appointments, as well. She'd usually push younger patients to her employees.

"By the way," Halla started. "Why are you closing so early when you still have customers?"

Halla would never imagine closing The Green Thumb before 8:30 PM.

Sarai smiled with a glint in her eyes. "Didn't you hear what Attica announced this morning? He found a batch of wild wood ear mushrooms."

"You mean?" Attica suddenly sat straighter.

Sarai and Attica looked at each other and said in unison, "It's foraging time!"

Sarai packed them a picnic basket of assorted rice balls, and the four left Sarai's cottage. Halla and Rexford followed Attica and Sarai around the house and toward the forest that sat behind.

Halla stopped in her tracks. "Hold on. Isn't the Cru territory beyond the forest?"

"The Cru territory?" Rexford gulped and clung to the back of Halla's shirt. Growing up as an Urquart, Rexford had likely never heard any good stories about the Crus.

"Their territory is on the other side of the forest. Urquart territory covers two-thirds, which is ginormous. I guarantee you won't get anywhere near the border within this outing," Sarai said dismissively as she kept walking. "They're also not as dangerous as the news makes of them. I've crossed a few times to source ingredients and do trade."

Sarai had been to the Cru territory? Halla shivered and thought of how brave her young aunt was. She and Rexford exchanged a look before running to catch up.

"The wood ear fungus is in the animated forest?" Rexford asked Attica.

He nodded. "It's not far. And they looked plump!"

Rexford seemed to pick up on his excitement, going from looking fearful about the Crus to bouncing in her steps.

They were traveling on a slightly trodden path in the forest of two-hundred-foot tall trees. Halla looked up to the sky and felt small in the massive, silent forest.

"Halla!" Rexford piped from ahead. "Look at how huge these trees are!"

Halla looked toward the girl and found her attempting to hug a tree. Her arms were not close to wrapping around the twenty-two-foot-wide trunk at all. Halla stifled a laugh. Rex had gotten her into this situation, but there was something about the zest for life the little girl had that tugged at her own heart. It was the same wonder she had for synthing and the colors so many years ago, before she started feeling the pressures from her grandmother.

"Isn't this an animated forest?" Halla called to Sarai. "What's 'animated' about it?"

"Yeah!" Rex interjected. "I haven't seen anything move."

Sarai turned her head back toward them as she kept walking. "The roots have been moving."

Halla thought she caught a glimpse of a sly smile before the woman turned back around.

"Where?" Rex asked, searching her surroundings and squinting.

Halla, too, hadn't seen anything move. If something was moving in this silent forest, she was sure she'd see it. Was Sarai messing with them? Halla wouldn't put it past her.

Sarai and Attica walked ahead, engrossed in their own conversation and laughing. Halla trailed a few steps behind them while Rexford varied between running ahead and falling back.

"Halla, Halla, look at this!" Rexford pushed a thick log into Halla's face.

"Whoa, Rex. Watch it." Halla held a hand out to keep it at a distance. "What did you find?"

The girl held the log with both her small hands. "It's a piece of tree bark. Look at how thick it is!"

Halla leaned closer and found it indeed was a piece of bark that was close to five-inches thick. Everything about these trees was huge. She looked back at Rexford's large, expectant eyes, and then cleared her throat.

"That's impressive," she said, and Rexford beamed even brighter.

"Isn't it? I found it on the ground. Can I take it back as a souvenir?"

"If it was on the ground, I don't think the forest would be missing it. But just in case, go check with Sarai."

"Okay!" The girl ran ahead and pushed the bark into Sarai's face to show off her latest find.

After forty minutes of walking, Attica exclaimed, "It's here!"

Halla jogged to meet up and found them standing in front of a massive fallen tree speckled with leafy-looking, brown mushrooms. Joy burst in her chest as she squatted to peer at the gorgeous fungi. Rexford kneeled next to her and yanked one off the trunk, ripping the mushroom cap in the process.

"Rex," Halla chided softly. "You can't force them off like that." She reached into the small pouch she kept habitually on a belt and pulled out a small pocket knife. "Use this to cut them. Like this."

Halla expertly pulled the flexible mushroom tops away to expose the point where it connected with the decaying trunk and cut it off.

"Here." She offered the small knife to Rex and pulled out a larger knife for her own use.

It took Rexford longer to extract a mushroom, Halla having foraged five for every one of Rexford's, but she was fully focused, biting her lower lip in concentration. When Halla's makeshift-shirt-basket couldn't hold anymore, she got up to deposit the foraged mushrooms into the basket Sarai brought and found Sarai looking at her with wonder.

"What?" Halla asked.

Sarai blinked a few times before saying, "Nothing. It's just, I didn't expect a city girl to know how to forage. Much less do it so efficiently."

Halla shrugged but felt pride swelling within her. "Grandma Wen taught me how to forage when I was younger."

"Learning is one thing, Halla. But foraging is an art and skill that requires connection with the earth and patience to listen. You do that."

Halla cocked her head. She'd never thought of it that way. She'd always enjoyed foraging in the estate courtyard and listening to the sounds within it, like the bubbling stream. "What do you mean?"

Sarai held an open palm toward the mushroom patch. "Not all of them are ready for harvest. Some are slightly too young for the most nutritional value. You've been avoiding them naturally, only harvesting the ones at their peak. And your decisive cuts will give them higher chances of spawning another batch."

Halla hadn't realized she was doing that. Like when she was young, she relaxed and had let her body take over as she foraged. As she stood, staring at Sarai, she felt a nudge at her shoulder. She turned around, ready to give Rex additional instruction, when she found herself facing a large, green-silver, spade-shaped head.

"Mogi!" she exclaimed. The creature responded with another headbutt to her chest and then a flick of his tongue.

"Mogi!" Rexford dropped her bundle of mushrooms—to Halla's dismay—and ran to the fish-snake, wrapping her arms around his neck. "What have you been doing, boy?"

Halla rubbed his snout affectionately, and Sarai stepped up.

"He's looking great," Sarai observed.

"I thought you stabled him," Halla said.

"Nah," Sarai said, heaving the basket of mushrooms onto her back like a backpack. "These beasts are best left to nature. Nuans have been domesticating them for centuries, so I knew he'd stick around the house."

"So, he's been wandering in this animated forest?" Halla was shocked.

Attica ran back with his bundle of mushrooms foraged from farther down the trunk and said, "Yup. There are plenty of watering holes and a few small waterfalls around. Given the shine of his scales, I think your ranyi has found them."

"Wow," Halla breathed, looking back into Mogi's unblinking eyes. Although her family had acres of land for their ranyi school, they still had fencing at the edges. She hadn't imagined letting them roam freely.

The wind suddenly picked up, pushing Rexford's small frame as it whipped through everyone's clothing. Mogi stretched his neck and caught Rexford's shirt in his mouth, holding her in place. Within the wind's howling, Halla heard a haunting song clinging to the air. Everyone held their ground while Mogi pawed one of his taloned feet nervously. The wind died after a few moments, and Halla picked some leaves off her shirt.

"Did you hear that?" she asked.

Rexford nodded rapidly. "The weird singing? What was that?"

"Singing?" Attica asked with a confused look. He glanced at Sarai before they both burst out laughing.

"What is it?" Rex asked as they kept guffawing.

"I'm sorry," Sarai said between laughs. "Let me... catch my breath." She clutched her stomach. "It's just that you both look," she laughed some more, "so scared!"

That started a renewed roar of laughter from Attica, which then spurred Sarai into a further laughing fit that she unsuccessfully tried to suppress.

Halla exchanged a look with Rex and rolled her eyes. The girl smiled in response.

When the two finally finished hooting and wiping tears away, Sarai explained, "It sounded like people singing folk songs, right? That wasn't singing. It was a lushu. Maybe two of them actually."

"A lushu?" Rex echoed.

Halla recalled Shylou, the rude tea brewer's mount. "The horse with the tiger's pelt pattern."

"They don't neigh?" Rex blurted what was on Halla's mind.

"They don't. They howl, and their howls sound like humans singing folk songs."

"I didn't know that," Halla said.

"A lot of people don't. Even if they did, people seldom believe it until they hear it themselves. Anyway, it's nothing to be concerned about, though the sun will set soon, so we should head back before any wild creatures come out." With that, Sarai motioned for them to follow her back onto the trail toward her house.

Halla looked back at her ranyi. "Why were *you* acting so skittish about the lushu? You've seen it. It's a beast like you."

Mogi gave her a flat, unmoving look, as if telling her he didn't know lushus sounded like that either, before using a talon to grab the bottom of her top, pinching a one-inch thick hole into it.

"Hey!" Halla exclaimed angrily.

She looked back at the towering fish-snake, flapping his pectoral fins, and thought better than to pick a fight. Instead, she opted for a silent glare, pointing with her index and middle finger from her eyes to him.

"You watch yourself," she said under her breath before following Sarai, Attica, and Rex.

For a large animal with six legs, Mogi moved quietly through the forest behind them, occasionally tossing a stick at Halla's hair, making their trek back quite eventful as she defended herself from Mogi's antics while Rex giggled.

The sun had just set by the time they broke clear of the forest. Attica wished them a farewell and gave everyone a bear hug before heading for town. Mogi refused to leave, so Sarai allowed him to stay in the back, screened porch. He made a few circles, deftly avoiding any shed tools or hanging cooking utensils, before lying down, snaking his head through the doorway so he could watch them in the kitchen.

"Rexford, go wash up for dinner," Sarai dismissed the girl.

Halla found herself quietly soaking and washing the dirt off the foraged mushrooms in the kitchen while Sarai threw a few mountain vegetables into the wok to stir-fry.

"Sarai?"

"Hmm?"

"Why haven't you taught me any synthing? You know that's why I'm here."

Sarai smiled. "You don't think I've been teaching you?"

Halla looked up from the mushrooms. "No, you haven't been teaching me."

Sarai *tsk*ed. "You formally educated people. Always looking for direct instruction. You're right. I haven't sat down with you and held your hand. But before teaching you, I need to know what you know."

"Can't you ask me what I know?"

"The best way to determine your true knowledge is through observation, Halla. Over this last day, as you've been helping me around the shop, I've watched how you interact with customers, how you take and interpret my instructions."

"You were telling me what to do," Halla said, still confused, focusing on the mushrooms.

"Sure, I was telling you what to do, but some details aren't given, yet you knew how to do it. For example, I asked you to go help a customer. I didn't tell you how, and I observed that you provided the correct herbal recommendation for his issues. I asked you to brew the angelica root into the tea, but I didn't say at what temperature or for how long. You already knew how. These tell me the level of your medicinal education, so I know where to start. Then I asked you to come foraging with us to see your skills. You displayed excellent skills. In fact, you used synthing while foraging."

Halla paused. "I did?"

"You sense the mushrooms to know which ones are at the best balance."

Halla knit her brows. "That doesn't sound right. I don't see colors when I touch the mushrooms, like how I can see colors when I touch someone."

"That's because you haven't honed the skill, or 'art' as Aunt Wen liked to call it. But clearly, you're a natural." Sarai finished preparing the dishes for dinner and sat on a stool, motioning for Halla to join her.

Halla set the mushrooms to one side, dried her hands, and joined Sarai.

"When it comes to sensing, it's most natural to sense through humans. It's the easiest because you yourself are human, so it's the most recognizable."

"Are you saying," Halla started slowly, processing as she spoke, "sensors can also synth on non-humans?"

"That's right. We can synth anything organic." Halla's jaw dropped as Sarai continued. "A fully realized sensor can synth anything they touch. Those that have trained are able to control the focus of their sensing. That means that we learn how to block out some of the items we touch and focus on others. You've clearly learned this much control from Aunt Wen, hence you don't wear gloves. But this control is even more necessary when one is able to synth on anything organic. Those who are untrained get blinded or distracted by colors. Hence, these days, the untrained wear gloves to minimize direct contact."

"And you can teach me that control?" Halla asked.

Sarai smiled. "I can teach you about it and tell you what's possible, yes."

Halla's stomach did a jubilant flip. She had basic control of her sensing, but the more her abilities grew, she knew the more she'd need to control it. "And you're saying I synthed the wood ear mushrooms?"

"You did. The way you're doing it is very natural. So natural that you didn't realize it. You let your hands reach for what was balanced at the peak of its growth. As you know, Synesthology is the ability to pinpoint balance via colors, whether it's touching, smelling, or hearing. You weren't fully synthing the mushrooms, which is why you didn't see the colors, but your body knew already. If you fully synth the mushrooms, then you could see the color of it, and any discolorations would indicate incomplete growth or even illness, just like within a human body."

Halla couldn't believe it. "How can I expand my skills?"

"We start small. I see the extent of your medicinal knowledge, which is good. And I see now that you have an innate talent for synthing. We just have to tap into it and embrace it. I will warn you; once we start expanding the breadth of your sensing, it may get disorienting touching anything. I advise against using gloves to stave off the effects. It creates a crutch and makes you dependent on it. The disorientation will drive your motivation to control your sensing, so that you can dull whatever you don't want to focus on."

Halla nodded gravely as she realized that her grandmother was right; there was *so* much she hadn't been able to teach her.

"Expansion isn't the only thing we'll work on, though. Your sensing of humans needs some work as well."

"How long will this take?" Halla asked.

"It depends." Sarai shrugged. "Depends on how much you practice, your motivations and persistence. Most sensors take many years to hone their skills."

"Years?" Halla repeated, crestfallen.

She didn't have years to stay in Tanheli. She had to go back to the capital. She had to clear her name, heal Rexford (though she was sure Sarai would help with that), and she had The Green Thumb to run.

"Some," Sarai continued, "with a good teacher, will pick it up more quickly. Luckily for you, I had an excellent teacher, and I am a decent one myself." She winked and the dread in Halla's racing mind eased. She had come to the right place.

For dinner, Sarai pulled out a foldable table in the middle of the stone-and-wood kitchen, placing stools around the table. After dinner of seaweed soup, various side-dishes, and rice, Rexford cleared the dishes while Halla brought Mogi three fish and a pail of water. When Halla turned away from the screened porch back toward the kitchen, she found three lidded porcelain bowls on the table.

"I prepared some dessert as a reward for a good half-day of foraging," Sarai said with a hint of a smile.

"I love dessert! I barely ever got them at home," Rexford exclaimed, plopping herself onto a stool after tossing a dish rag into the sink. "What is it? A souffle? Small cake? Oh, I know!" She put up an index finger. "It's crème brûlée, isn't it?"

She squealed in delight. She lifted the lid but immediately dropped it back onto the bowl, placing her index finger and thumb into her mouth to nurse them. "It's hot!" she said with a mouthful of fingers.

"Of course it is," Sarai laughed. "Let me see your hands." She snatched Rexford's wrist and pulled the girl's hand to her face. "Your fingers will be fine. We won't have to amputate them."

Rexford's eyes widened as the color drained from her face.

"I said, you're fine." Sarai chuckled. "I was joking. Your fingers are totally fine. I'd just taken these bowls out of the steamer, but it wasn't scalding."

As Halla approached the table, Sarai lifted the lids of hers and Rexford's bowls. Halla's breath hitched as she caught a glimpse of the contents.

"Is that... poached pear?" Grandma Wen used to make it for Halla as a treat.

Sarai smiled. "Come have some." She turned to Rexford. "And you be careful. It could scald your tongue." Rex's spoon hovered in midair, ready to dig in.

As Halla seated herself, she lifted the lid of her bowl and observed an immediate difference between Sarai's poached pear and Grandma Wen's. Grandma had always peeled the pear and cubed it. Sarai's looked fully intact, sitting in its own poaching liquid. She noticed the top of the pear had a cut around it. Curious, she grabbed the pear stem and lifted the top to reveal a hollowed inside filled with liquid, dates, and goji berries. Instead of cubing, Sarai had cored the pear and placed the other ingredients inside. It made for quite an aesthetically pleasing dish. Halla used her spoon to cut into the softened pear flesh and took a bite.

A warmth and giddiness danced over her tongue. It tasted just like Grandma's. She felt the prickling at the backs of her eyes as she ate. *It's been a while, Grandma,* she thought as she sipped the warm liquid.

CHAPTER 22

Herb sent Captain Asma a message that he was headed to Tanheli when he left the Nuan estate. Fifteen minutes into his journey, his phone rang. He picked up the call with the click of a button on his car to take it hands-free.

"Herb Mooran speaking."

"Inspector, isn't Tanheli on the border between the Urquart and Cru territory?" It was Captain Asma.

"Yes, separated by the forest," he confirmed.

"And Halla is there?"

"Yes."

There was a pause on the other end before Captain Asma spoke again. "This doesn't look good for her."

"I know." Herb sighed, running one hand over his face. "I don't think she's running, though. She has a relative there. They claim she went to better diagnose the heir. Apparently, that relative has some of the Nuan synthing skills, but I won't know for sure until I get there."

"Have you checked the Tracker?"

"Yes. The Tracker confirms Halla is in this direction, so it checks out so far. I should arrive at the post town, Hanashuku, in a few hours. I'll call you then with any other updates."

"Ah, Hanashuku," Asma said fondly.

"You've been?" Herb asked.

"About twenty years ago. I was posted there for the Martial Corps."

"You were in the Martial Corps?" Herb said incredulously.

The Martial Corps was a program spanning the five territories of their land-mass and was a collaboration between the numerous Doa temples. Other than practicing the Doa religion at such temples, the monks and nuns also practiced their form of martial arts as a kind of physical training that supplemented their spiritual growth. If they weren't dedicated to peace and balance, this network of temples could have made a formidable army. The Cru territory had been trying for decades to convince the temples within their territory to join their army but were unsuccessful. Herb knew the admittance rate was famously low and was surprised Captain Asma had been in it. *She might be quite deadly in hand-to-hand combat.*

"I was," Asma said. "I joined a temple after high school for personal reasons.

Herb was curious about her reasons but didn't pry when she didn't expound on it. Instead, she changed the topic.

"It's a lovely town. Small streets full of local mom-and-pop shops. The architecture is quite charming as well. If you see a shop called Kihachiro, definitely check it out. Their meat buns are the best you'll have."

"That's quite a statement," Herb said, but his mouth was already watering thinking about it.

All he'd had today were copious cups of tea and some small cakes. They were delicious but didn't quite have the same satisfying hit as biting into a juicy meat bun.

"You'll know when you try it," Asma said.

"By the way," Herb said, remembering what he'd learned from the Nuan estate. "I found what may be an interesting connection."

He updated Captain Asma on Tronjone Kurand and the story he heard.

"You think he could be connected with Douglas Kurand who's employed by the Urquarts?" Asma asked.

"He could be. The relationship between Tronjone Kurand and the Nuan doctor at the time seemed civil, but she did take over being headmaster after he left, so it could be motive. It's tenuous, though. Do we know anything about Douglas Kurand?"

Papers shuffled on the other end. "It seems the Onyx Division didn't run a file on him other than the fact he's employed at the Urquart residence. I'll run a background check and see if we have anything on these two Kurands. If capital officials were involved in that incident, there should be some old records."

"Thank you, Captain Asma. Anything else new over there?"

"Other than managing the Green and making sure the Onyx's investigation of Rexford Urquart's disappearance doesn't interfere with ours? It's stellar." Her sarcasm oozed through the line with a hint of a smile.

Herb laughed. "Do we know how the Onyx Division's investigation is going?"

"They've taken out two Trackers. It took them to Halla's shop, so they searched it. Of course, they didn't find the note left behind, so I gave them a copy of it."

"You told them about the heir's note?" Herb wasn't upset, just surprised.

"Of course. I will not outwardly impede on their investigation. I'm concerned with making sure they don't impede on ours."

"How did they take that?"

"They were not happy that we had a piece of evidence and didn't tell them. They're running their own handwriting analysis. Their result will be the same, and they'll have to think about what that means for their investigation if Rexford Urquart wrote that note. They may pivot and ask the family if the heir had any connections anywhere or spoken of places he wanted to visit."

"The Nuans confirmed the heir was with Halla," Herb said.

"Indeed. And I have no reason to doubt it. But best not to tell the Onyx for now. They may step into our investigation if that's the case, and I want them focused more on the heir than on Halla. I did tell them that the note implies the two may be together, of course. Especially after you heard Halla say she was going after the heir. But because you didn't actually see the heir, it's not confirmed. What they do with that information is their problem."

"Where are they now?" Herb asked.

"Probably on your trail," Captain Asma said lightly.

"What! You could have started this whole discussion with that!" Herb exclaimed as he accelerated as much as his car would allow.

"It wouldn't have made a difference," Asma responded.

"I would have been driving faster," Herb retorted. His car gave a whine at the sudden increase in speed, so he let his foot off the pedal reluctantly.

Captain Asma gave a hearty laugh. "Don't worry, Herbert."

"Don't worry?" Herb spluttered. "I have to find Halla before they do!"

"Yes, that's true. But you have a head start. I've also sent a missive to the Nuan household about Onyx Division inspectors heading their way. If Gaia Nuan is as smart a woman as the Nuans are known to be, then she'll try to hold them up for as long as she can."

Herb thought about the well-dressed, stylish woman with a smart mouth and keen senses, turning his interrogation on himself not so long ago. *She'll do a great job keeping them occupied,* he thought with a tinge of annoyance.

"I'll keep you posted on what I hear, but you focus on tracking down Halla." Asma hung up.

Herb grabbed a protein bar, ripped the packaging open with his mouth, and continued toward Hanashuku and Tanheli.

The second day in Tanheli was just as busy as the first. Sarai woke Halla before the sun rose and had her brew and prep various ingredients. The Green Thumb had machines to freeze dry or flash dry ingredients and package many concoctions for people to take home or for longer shelf life. Sarai's unnamed apothecary didn't have the fancy machines Halla's did, but it did prepare dishes or concoctions for people to consume in the store. Halla had never considered something like that because it took too long to cook everything. On top of running a clinic, it would be like running a cafe. But Sarai somehow made it work. Sarai's shop served ready-made prescriptions three out of the six days per week her shop was open.

They kept Sarai's best-sellers brewing on low heat after an initial boil in large vats. Other ingredients had been pre-soaked for quick preparation when an order came in. Sarai had several traditional mortars scattered throughout the kitchen, having been used for various herb grinding. These weren't the usual mortar and pestle setup with stone bowls and a grinding stick, but a U-shaped, elongated bowl. It had a stone wheel set within, held by a stick through a hole in the middle. Sarai also had electric blenders in the corner for quicker preparation. Halla took various mental notes for The Green Thumb, already brainstorming how Sarai's process could be scaled.

After she helped Sarai get everything going, she sank into a low stool in the kitchen, wiping the sweat that had beaded on her forehead.

"Don't sit down just yet," Sarai said as she rushed through the kitchen. "Time for us to check on Rex."

Halla groaned but got up and followed the other woman into the bedroom. This was Sarai's bedroom, and she'd set up some floor futons for Halla and Rex to share. Sarai had another room with some cots, but she said that as family, Halla shouldn't be staying in there.

Sarai's room was cozy. It had a window with open slats into the kitchen so that she could monitor cooking ingredients. She had a small desk in the far right corner with leather-bound books and scattered papers. There was an unused electric heater in the opposite corner with two chairs and a small, round table. Sarai's bed was in the last corner, flanked by a nightstand, and surrounded by shelving filled with tchotchkes and books. Rex was still bundled within thick blankets on the futon on the floor next to Sarai's bed.

Sarai flipped the bedding in one movement. "Rise and shine, child!"

Rexford rubbed her eyes as she squinted up at them. "It's morning, already?"

"Yup, and time for your appointment. Sit up."

Rexford did as she was told, hair tangled like a bird's nest. Sarai motioned for Halla to join her kneeling next to Rexford.

"You first," Sarai said. "Tell me what you see."

Nervously, Halla took Rex's wrist to synth. The only person she'd ever synthed in front of was Grandma Wen. She closed her eyes and focused her energy, seeing the colors within Rex as it mapped out her small body in Halla's mental image.

"There are less colors than before," she said while focusing.

"Right. That's good news. Can you determine what Rexford's base color is?"

Halla tried to find it, but it was still too difficult. "I can't."

"That's fine," Sarai assured her. "You'll be able to soon enough. For now, are the colors analogous or contrasting?"

Halla recalled the color wheel Grandma Wen showed her years ago, telling her this was the basis of analyzing the colors they synthed. "A bit of everything," she said, wrinkling her nose. "There are analogous colors around, and then there are some pairs of contrasting ones near each other."

"The reason you see them all over is because the toxin ailing Rexford for years is still running through various parts of her body. In addition to separating her from that toxin source, we now need to help her dispel the toxins."

"In traditional medicine, detoxing is usually done through sweating or vomiting while nourishing the body," Halla recited.

"Exactly." Sarai nodded.

Rexford was fully awake now, looking between them. "What does that mean? I need to make myself vomit?"

Sarai laughed. "Usually, the vomiting is induced by the body if it needs to. Don't make yourself vomit, please. We will focus on sweating and nourishing your body." She looked at Halla. "Can you cook?"

Halla looked away in embarrassment. Many thought cooking and medicine went hand-in-hand, but to her, brewing her prescriptions was drastically different from cooking. "No. Ahming cooked when I was at the estate, and I cook very simply when I'm in the capital by myself."

"I've heard great things about Ahming's cooking from Aunt Wen. I believe that's why they brought Ahming into the family long ago; she had a talent with cooking and incorporating Nuan medicine."

"I didn't know that," Halla admitted.

Ahming had been around ever since Halla was born, and she never questioned why or how Ahming came to be at the Nuan household. *There's probably a lot I don't know about my own family.*

"Would you know what to do if I handed you some broccoli, bamboo, garlic, eggplant, and ginger with some angelica root and astranagus?"

Halla shook her head.

"That's fine," Sarai said, undeterred. "I'll prepare some dishes to help Rex with detoxing, though you should learn some cooking. That's a problem for another day. I have a different task for you."

"What is it?" Rexford asked in Halla's stead. Halla shot her a glare but let it go.

"You two will be going to the thermal caves," Sarai said.

Rexford jumped to her feet. "That sounds awesome! What is it exactly?"

"It's a network of underground caves a bit to the east of here. There are geothermal waters there that people like to soak in, but those waters also run through the walls of these caves, making them warm, like a sauna. I'd like you to sweat some toxins out," Sarai said. "As for Halla, she will accompany you, of course, but also work on synthing other organic beings on the way."

Twenty minutes later, Rexford was riding Mogi with a large jug of water, heading toward the caves while Halla walked beside them. Sarai instructed them to follow the carved signs of a black tortoise, and sure enough, they found one with an arrow pointing ahead as they walked the edge of the animated forest.

Sarai told them of some herb patches on the path and requested Halla harvest some while practicing synthing, which was why Halla opted to walk. The first patch Halla noticed was a group of aromatic mugwort.

"Hold on," she said to Mogi as she walked to the edge of the path and stooped.

Her hand hovered over the mugwort as she practiced synthing. From visual observation, she could see which leaves were ready for harvesting, but she wondered if she'd see more by touching, like what Sarai said she did to the wood ear mushrooms.

Halla slowly extended her fingers toward the leaves and closed her eyes, focusing on the energy in her core and extending it. At first, she saw her own base color of orange and felt it at her fingertips. There was nothing to push it into like she could for a human body.

She recalled Sarai's words that they could synth the balance in anything organic. Halla relaxed her previously knit brows as she listened to the forest and the plants and, finally, the mugwort right in front of her. A pulse of energy within the patch shot through her, and she held onto the feeling, pushing her own energy into it. There was a pop as she fully grasped the mugwort, and her energy spilled into the plant, her orange turning into the plant's green energy and mapping into the form of the mugwort's stem and leaves within her mind.

"Whoa," she breathed with a sense of pride and wonder, viewing the patch behind her closed lids.

Through synthing, she could see which ones had slightly burnt leaves, which ones needed a little longer, and which ones were ready for picking. With a fat bundle of mugwort a few moments later, Halla continued with Rex and Mogi.

The next time they stopped was for mountain yam. Halla noted the conditions were ideal, walking off the path with a discerning eye before squatting to place her hand flat on the ground. She closed her eyes and pushed her energy into the earth. *Worth a shot.*

At first, she saw nothing. After a few moments of concentrating, her fingers tingled. She scrunched her face as she focused, a sudden disorientation hitting her mind as she sensed multiple inputs before the crawling of thousands of small legs impressed on her mind. She shrieked and fell backward.

"What is it!" Rex slipped off Mogi and ran for Halla. Mogi shook his head side to side but stayed put on the path.

Halla got up, brushing dirt and leaves off her bottom. She shuddered. "Bugs," she said. "Or organisms. Whatever it is in the dirt, I sensed them."

Halla felt as if those creepy crawlies were still scuttling up and down her skin and shook out her arms.

Rex's eyes widened. "You can synth bugs? They're so tiny! I've never heard of anyone doing that."

"Probably because no one *wants* to synth bugs," Halla said. "It was an accident. I was trying to find some mountain yam. It's a root so you have to dig it up without harming the rest of the plant. I thought it may be easier to synth for it, so I don't have to dig up everything. I didn't realize there were so many other organisms in the dirt."

"That's so cool!" Rex exclaimed, throwing both her arms up.

Halla blinked and then broke into a smile. "I suppose it kind of is. But I bet if you synthed some bugs, you'd be grossed out, too!"

She jumped forward, pulling the smaller girl into a hug and ran her fingers along Rex's stomach, imitating crawling bug legs.

"Ew!" Rex shrieked with laughter and tried to protect herself from the tickling onslaught. "I'm being eaten!"

At that, Mogi bounded toward them, fallen leaves flying as he circled the two, occasionally flicking his tongue into Halla's ears.

"Mogi!" Halla exclaimed. "You're taking Rex's side? It's two against one now?"

She laughed and released Rex, feeling so light for the first time in years. This joy reminded her of the days in the garden with Grandma before lessons began. Halla paused at the thought. Mogi pushed Halla firmly but gently with his tail and rested his large head on hers. She stroked his neck contentedly in a truce.

"How did you synth the bugs anyway? I thought you needed direct contact to synth," Rex asked after putting some distance between herself and Halla.

Halla tapped a finger on her chin. "Sarai told me that the earth is like a giant organism that can conduct energy. If you know what you're looking for, you could use the earth like a conduit. So, I tried doing that to sense for the yams I knew should be there. Instead, I found bugs."

Rex laughed. "Can you try again? Synthing the bugs?"

Halla shook her head. "No way. I'll try again for the yams."

She had a feeling she would have to steel herself against the bugs during her search. She approached the patch again and placed her hand there.

Because she had done it once, feeling for the other organisms came much faster. Once again, with the multiple inputs of energy, her legs felt unsteady. She tried to shut them out while searching, and she felt a slight tug to the left. She shifted her attention and found something larger to latch onto. Halla pushed her energy into it, and before her closed eyes, she saw the colors forming into the shape of roots. *Mountain yams!* With the mental image, Halla pinpointed where to dig and harvested three fat tubers. With synthing, the ordeal of finding these yams was a lot more efficient than usual—if she could get over the initial nausea.

With the roots proudly tucked into a large pouch, the three of them continued toward the caves.

"Since the caves are heated with water, do you think Mogi would be able to find some water to relax in, too?" Rexford asked.

"Probably," Halla responded, looking up at Rexford now mounted on Mogi again, thinking about how far the girl had come since the first time they'd met months ago.

Halla had noticed this morning that Rex had a slight pink flush to her cheeks, and her personality was brighter, not like the austere, understanding child she was during their appointments or when Mrs. Urquart was present. *She must have a lot of family pressure, too.*

Here, Rex was more herself. It had started with her shedding that male disguise in the noodle shop. Then, Halla wondered if she, herself, had changed during this time.

"I wonder if he'll like hot water," Rex pondered aloud, interrupting Halla's reflections.

"Well, most fish and reptiles are cold-blooded, but I think ranyi are partially endothermic." Halla paused to see Rex cock her head, eyebrows furrowed. "Meaning," Halla continued, "I think as long as the water isn't boiling, Mogi will enjoy it."

Rex broke into a bright smile. "You hear that, boy?" She rubbed Mogi's neck.

The ranyi seemed to sense the waters the closer they got as his pace quickened. The air around them warmed.

"Is it getting... hazier?" Rex asked.

"It's the steam from the geothermal waters," Halla said, quite impressed.

Tanheli held more gems than she'd imagined. She'd only known of it for the high quality of its herbs and vegetables, but she hadn't known it also had geothermal waters and caves.

They eventually made the outline of cavern openings and the sound of water flowed from somewhere unseen. Mogi stopped at the closest opening and flicked his tongue. Halla helped Rex down and untied the jug of water from Mogi's back. When soaking in hot baths or sitting in saunas, it was important to stay hydrated lest one faint.

Mogi snapped his long, finned tail, tongue darting in and out.

"All right," Halla said. "Go have your soak while we sweat in a cave. Come back to get us once the sun is just above the horizon."

She patted his side as he pushed her with his head and ran off. She didn't know if he understood time, but he was already gone. Per usual practices, Halla would time how long they were in the caves in twenty minute intervals, taking breaks outside before entering again to ensure they didn't cook themselves.

The cavern they stood in front of had the same black tortoise carved into the stone.

"I don't know if I want to do this," Rex said from beside Halla. "It's kind of stuffy."

"It'll feel harder to breathe when it's warm like this," Halla said. "But we'll do it in short stints. We want to make sure you're sweating. If you start feeling lightheaded or anything, let me know, and we'll step out to take a break."

They entered the steaming cave, and immediately, the damp, heated air closed in around Halla. Rex coughed.

"It's hard to see so use the walls to guide you," Halla instructed while reaching for the wall to her left and Rex's hand on her right. The stone was slick with water but warm to the touch.

After a few seconds of walking, they entered a larger room and were hit with the scent of sandalwood and patchouli that had Halla feeling like she'd entered a spa. Light spilled from a hole above them, allowing some steam to escape and increasing visibility. A stone bench was carved around the perimeter, accented by symmetrical ridges along the top of the walls.

"This is nice," Rex said, surprise marking her tone. "It's much easier to breathe in here than it was earlier."

Halla nodded her agreement. "Time to get sweating."

The two drifted into a comfortable silence, and Halla's mind wandered back to the yams. She couldn't believe she had started to synth other organic matter in such a short period of time. Although they'd originally come to Tanheli to better diagnose Rex, Halla had gotten so much from this town. It felt like coming home to be learning what Grandma had wanted her to learn.

CHAPTER 23

A few days had passed since Halla and Rexford visited the caves, and they'd settled into a rhythm at Sarai's shop. Each morning, Halla helped Sarai prepare ingredients for the apothecary, starting the fires and brewing, surrounded by earthen scents. Sarai prepared a simple breakfast in the morning while Halla brewed concoctions. Then the two women woke Rexford to synth her and determine her condition, which was improving each day. By now, Halla could see that Rexford's base color was a blueberry purple.

The days always started slow in terms of business but picked up by noon. Their afternoons and evenings consisted of lessons from Sarai. Rexford sat in on the lessons and learned the usages of herbs eagerly. Seeing as Rex somehow successfully created the thorn-apple draught and antidote, Halla wasn't surprised to see the girl learn quickly. It reminded her of herself when she was younger.

On the days of Synesthology lessons, Sarai sent Rexford out to play with Mogi or Grandma Wen's qingniao if he were present. Otherwise, Sarai sent Rexford to town to gather supplies or deliver medicine packets. The synthing lessons were a combination of direct instruction and hands-on training, including synthing plants, trees, the chickens Sarai had wandering around, or even the chicken eggs to see which ones were fertilized and which ones were safe to consume.

Attica stopped by each day, sometimes to drop off some food from town, sometimes to help out for a few hours. Today, he came by earlier than usual, saying he had some free time and that he could help with the shop.

Attica walked through the shelves with a clipboard and pen, checking inventory. Sarai moved among the small drawers on the back wall, weighing ingredients to pack into paper parcels. Rexford and Halla wiped down the tables and windows in the cafe area.

Rex glanced between the Sarai and Attica while wiping a table. "So," she started with an impish grin. "Are you two a thing?"

"What?" the two said simultaneously.

Attica dropped his pen and bumped into a shelf, causing some of the items to rattle. Sarai ran into an open drawer, sundries spilling out. Halla snorted.

Attica and Sarai glanced at each other before quickly looking away.

"So, are you?" Rex asked again.

"Go wash the dishes in the kitchen," Sarai demanded, avoiding the question. As Rex retreated to the kitchen with a smirk, Sarai said, "You can't just ask that question out of the blue! What if you make Attica uncomfortable?"

"Oh, I... uh... I'm not uncomfortable with that question..." Attica started, but Sarai continued without hearing him.

"Where did that question even come from anyway? You haven't been here that long."

"You don't need to look very hard to see how you two look at each other," Halla added.

Sarai shot her a glare, and Halla shifted her focus back to wiping the windows, but she could hear Rex giggling in the back. She suppressed her own smile.

"We've been friends for years," Sarai said. "And Attica knows herbs and this shop like the back of his hand."

Attica nodded. "Yeah, I love her."

Everyone's eyes shot to Attica in shock. Even Rex peeped one eye from the doorway.

"I... mean... you, know. As a friend, of course. We've been through a lot together," Attica stuttered. He met Sarai's gaze with a soft smile.

"Aha!" Rex popped out of the doorway. "I saw that look!"

Attica looked like he wanted to melt into the floors and through the seams. Sarai on the other hand, flushed red in her cheeks.

Halla laughed. "Give them a break, Rex."

"You see it, too!" Rex said.

"Shhh!" Halla put an index finger to her mouth, and the little girl ran back into the kitchen.

Sarai opened her mouth to say more, but she was interrupted by the sliding of the front doors.

A man uniformed in an emerald fit entered. Halla's stomach dropped. It was Inspector Mooran, the same inspector who'd visited The Green Thumb the night she ran from the capital.

CHAPTER 24

"Good tidings. How may I help you today?" a woman with her hair tied in a loose bun called from the back wall. She had the unmistakable green sheen to her hair that identified her bloodline.

"Good tidings," he responded. "I'm Inspector Mooran, here on official capital business." He presented his seal tag.

Another man within the shop placed the pen he was holding behind his ear and stepped forward, almost protectively, examining the seal tag. The loud scraping of a chair along hard floors sounded. Herb glanced over to find Halla in the corner of the shop, rag in hand trying to cover her face.

"Halla!" He took a step toward her, but the other man side-stepped into his path.

This man was not as tall as Herb, but he was built with a large chest and wide back. Herb decided not to test the man, even though his own fingers flinched for his black baton.

"What's your business here, Inspector?" The other woman left the register and approached him.

The tension in the air was palpable. Herb held up both his hands. "I'm here to help. I'm the inspector tasked with Halla's case, and I came looking for her. Albeit, I got a little lost along the way."

"So, you're going to take her back?" The woman narrowed her eyes.

"No! You can't take her back. You can't take me back!" a child's voice rang out.

Herb turned to find a small girl standing at the doorway to the back, clutching a soapy sponge.

"Who—?" Herb started, but Halla interrupted him.

"Rex, stay back! Find Mogi."

"No! I won't leave you," the girl said petulantly, lower lip quivering.

Rex? As in 'Rexford'? Rexford Urquart? Herb's attention swung between the girl, Halla's hand flying to her mouth, and the eye rolls from the others in the room. He furrowed his brows as his mind processed.

The Urquart heir was a son, not a daughter. Or perhaps the son looked particularly feminine? It wouldn't be abnormal for a young boy. But then again, Herb had seen images of the Urquart heir in public settings, and this child was not him.

A silence fell over the shop, occasionally broken by the girl's sniffles.

"Let me start over," Herb said. "I'm Inspector Mooran, and I'm here to help Halla. I've spoken with her mother at the Nuan estate, I've seen the note left by the heir, and I think something else is afoot. I've been tracking Halla so that I can get to her before my counterparts find her and the heir."

The woman cocked a brow. "If we're going this route, then sure. I'm Sarai Leng, Halla's aunt. And I don't believe you. I know capital inspectors are on their trail. In fact, you got here sooner than I expected."

"Sooner than you expected?" Herb echoed.

He recalled some of the dirty looks he received in Hanashuku when he asked how to get to Tanheli, and how the locals' instructions had led him to another post town to the west before he realized he was in the wrong place. His Tracker had mysteriously disappeared in Hanashuku after he stepped out of his car to order some of those famous meat buns Captain Asma had mentioned, so he couldn't even use it to check his path. Only after he'd made it to the other town was he made aware that it was called Chuli, and a nice passerby pointed him in the direction of Tanheli.

Herb narrowed his eyes as realization dawned. "You! You somehow had people point me in the wrong direction. And steal my Tracker!"

A smug smile emerged on Sarai's face. "I sent a note to some of my contacts in Hanashuku to let them know that my niece was being wrongly accused of a crime. Whatever they did with that information was on them."

Herb groaned. "You wasted precious time! There are others on my trail for Halla. I could have gotten here earlier to help."

Sarai opened her mouth to retort, but Halla finally entered the conversation.

"Wait." She stepped forward and looked at Sarai. "I believe him. I met him at my store right before we left. I sensed his sincerity."

Sarai regarded Halla closely before sharing a glance with the man who was still standing quite close to Herb, as if ready to tackle the inspector whenever given the order.

"Fine," Sarai said when the other man nodded. "One way to settle this is to let me synth him."

"Excuse me?" Herb said.

Sarai gestured to the table Halla had been wiping down. "Take a seat, and hand me your wrist."

What was up with this family and the need to synth everyone? Couldn't they just believe him? "You're going to synth me?"

"I can see if you're telling the truth and whether to trust you," Sarai said.

Herb threw up his hands. He had been synthed more in a few days than he'd ever been in his entire thirty-one years of life. "Gaia Nuan already synthed me for the same reason but fine."

He sat, accepting his fate. It seemed faster to convince them this way than it was to talk through his logic.

Sarai took the hand he offered and stilled. Similarly to his experience with Gaia Nuan, Herb felt nothing out of the ordinary as he answered a slew of questions regarding his purpose. When he answered Sarai's questions to her satisfaction, she leaned back, hand still on his wrist.

"What do you intend to do now that you've found Halla?"

Herb took a breath. "I want to question her. Get her side of the story. And," he looked at the small girl again, "if the heir is here with Halla, I'd like to get his side of the story, too. Then I'll collate the facts as I continue my investigation

and my captain digs up some background. I—" he paused and took a breath—
"I want to prove her innocence."

Sarai met Herb's eyes and said, "He's telling the truth."

The tension in the shop dissipated almost immediately as everyone collectively heaved a sigh.

"Thank you," Herb said, taking his arm back from Sarai's hold. "And it's also true that there are other inspectors on the heir's trail. If the heir is here, then they'll find Halla, too, and they are of the mind that Halla is guilty. They won't be as kind as me. We need to work efficiently."

Sarai waved a hand dismissively. "The people in Hanashuku will hold them up somehow. The same they did with you. I'll send a qingniao message to Chuli as well so that they're aware. We may be short on time, but we have more than you may think."

"That doesn't mean we don't need to work quickly," Herb said.

Sarai nodded as Attica introduced himself to Herb, jovial and cheery now that it had been confirmed Herb was here to help. Herb found himself quite liking the man. Then all attention was on the little girl.

After a moment of thought, she stepped forward. "I'm Rexford Urquart."

Herb stared at her, already suspecting she was the heir but still uncomprehending. All he could manage out of his mouth was "How?"

Halla was relieved to hear that Inspector Mooran believed in her innocence. She and the others sat down with the inspector to run him through any case updates, including Rex demonstrating the abilities of her Synesthology pendant, to which the inspector stared slack-jawed as if questioning everything he knew. Sarai finished the debrief by detailing how Rex had been slowly poisoned over time.

"It's alarming to hear of your diagnosis, Sarai," Mooran said. "I must admit, this case is getting increasingly nefarious."

"It has to be someone near Rexford," Halla pressed. She still didn't know if it was a random staff or housecleaning or Thrum or Dr. Kurand.

"Right," Sarai added. "Someone who's had access to her for years. And someone meticulous and careful."

Halla noticed Rex clenching her small fists and reached out to touch her leg momentarily. The girl didn't meet her gaze, but her hands relaxed.

When the inspector didn't respond, Halla thought of the strange, slender man who shadowed Mrs. Urquart. "What about Mr. Thrum?"

This elicited a reaction from the inspector. "Thrum?"

"Yeah. He's like the butler to their family."

"He's their Chief of Staff, Halla," the inspector said. "Why do you suspect Thrum?"

Chief of Staff? Halla thought. *No wonder he's so chummy with everyone, including Mrs. Urquart.*

"Well," Halla hesitated. "I haven't told anyone, but when I synthed him, I saw no colors."

Sarai stiffened across from her.

Attica scrunched his brows together. "Are you sure?" He turned to Sarai. "Is that possible? For a living being to not have colors within their energy?"

"Some people may have near-clear or translucent coloring, which a sensor could mistake as having no color." She looked at Halla almost hopefully.

Halla shook her head. "No. I'm quite sure. Plus, his pulse was mechanical. It was strange. I'd never felt one like it."

She shuddered involuntarily as she recalled the cold feeling.

"But Mr. Thrum is alive," Rex said. "Shouldn't he have a base color like you say in Halla's lessons?"

Halla looked at the girl, impressed. First, Rex was able to concoct draughts and antidotes, as well as learn quickly within Sarai's shop, and now she was absorbing Halla's Synesthology lessons?

"He should," Sarai said slowly. "If he truly has no color and has a mechanical pulse, then there's only one thing I can think of him being."

"What is it?" Halla asked as both she and Rex leaned forward.

"A morph."

"A what?" Rex said.

"Morphs don't exist," Mooran interjected and then looked at Rex. "My apologies for the interruption, heir. Sarai said Mr. Thrum is a morph. Morphs are of myth," he said, directing the last sentence at Sarai.

"What's a morph?" Halla asked.

Sarai sighed. "There haven't been records of one in centuries. They were first created to deter the abilities of synthers, particularly of sensors. Though, morphs are also immune to the effects of imbuers. This was particularly effective during the time of the Warring Territories. When synthers could be used to spy or create weapons, the creation of morphs completely turned the tide. This was a being that was the perfect soldier. One that was immune from all the magic of Synesthology. You couldn't sense their emotions, and weapons made purely by Synesthology were ineffective on them."

Halla's eyes widened. They'd learned of the Warring Territories period in school, but it took place centuries ago. Synesthology had been weaponized during that time, but the curriculum seemed to have missed mentioning morphs.

"How come we were never told of morphs in history classes?"

"They're illegal," Sarai whispered. "There was an effort to ensure morphs weren't ever mentioned to ensure they couldn't be recreated. And with Synesthology dying out, the knowledge of morphs naturally dissipated. I only learned about this from my mother."

"Tall tales," Mooran said. "The reason you don't hear about morphs is because they're nonexistent. Stories were crafted to scare enemies centuries ago."

"There's a lot in our world that comes from tall tales, Inspector," Sarai said coolly. As if on cue, Mogi's large, green head appeared at the front window next to them.

"Great Doa!" The inspector jumped in his seat.

"Ranyi and many other beasts were said to be from legends before the Nuans started domesticating them," Sarai continued while signaling to Mogi to come by another time.

The creature drooped his head and disappeared from the window. Halla mentally noted to bring him a snack later for the dismissive treatment.

"Fine," Mooran acquiesced. "But a morph? A living being created through banished Synesthology arts who's immune to its effects? Even if they did still exist, there's no reason to go through the trouble of making a morph when synthers no longer dominate society. No one really uses their synthing skills anymore. Why would someone create a morph whose purpose was their immunity to synthing?"

Sarai shrugged. "Beats me. But it sounds like they could make great Chiefs of Staff."

Inspector Mooran ran a hand down his face. "We have no evidence that Mr. Thrum is one other than Halla's observations. And we have no evidence morphs even exist, so let's table that. I need to ask you all about another matter."

"What could be more important than investigating every suspicious person in the Urquart household?" Halla countered, annoyed that the inspector didn't believe her.

Thrum was the perfect suspect. He not only had a strange pulse, but he was also in a high position, close to Mrs. Urquart and Rex. It was probably easy for him to move about and make nefarious deals.

"Another connection which makes another potential suspect," the inspector responded.

Halla's eyes widened. "Who?"

Inspector Mooran inhaled deeply before speaking. "Dr. Kurand."

Halla inhaled sharply. She'd considered Dr. Kurand as a suspect but didn't think it was as strong a possibility as Thrum.

"What?" Rex popped out of her seat.

Inspector Mooran explained to Sarai and Attica that Kurand was the family doctor and recounted what he found at the Nuan estate: the Kurand-Nuan history he learned from Halla's mother.

"I didn't know about this," Halla said after Mooran finished. "If I knew, I could have put the puzzle pieces together sooner."

"I think there's a lot we don't know about your family, Halla. What you don't know is not your fault," the inspector said, not unsympathetically. "Even then, this may not be connected. My captain is running a background check."

"So, you're saying that Dr. Kurand could be a suspect?" Sarai said slowly.

"It's possible," Mooran said. "What we know right now is that there's no motive for Halla to commit this crime. Other than the bribe money from the Cru family, which we are saying she has no connection to. Usually when you find the motive, you get close to the true culprit."

"You know," Attica spoke up. "The name 'Kurand' sounds somewhat familiar." His gaze grew glassy. "I think Shylou may have a distant relation with them."

"Oh!" Rex said. "He has the cool horse!"

The annoying tea brewer? Halla rolled her eyes.

"I wouldn't be surprised," Sarai said. "Shylou comes from a line of known crafters."

Halla looked up in surprise. That man was a synther? And he worked in a tea shop filled with sounds, whether it be clinking mugs, tea kettles whistling, or customer conversations. As a crafter who synthed colors via sound, how did he do that in an aurally busy space? *He must be incredibly skilled.*

"Then that's the next place to go." The inspector stood.

"Let me accompany you, Inspector Mooran," Halla said, also standing.

"Me, too!" Rexford piped.

The uniformed man gave them a look that clearly said 'no', but Sarai intercepted before he could verbalize it.

"It'll be nice for them to go to the main town. Attica can take you to the tea shop. Though, I think Rex is quite familiar with the way now, too, right?"

"I am!" The little girl puffed her chest proudly.

"Then, it's settled. I have to stay here to watch my shop, but you all go ahead. Give Shylou my regards."

The inspector stared at Halla's young aunt with a flat look before throwing up his hands. "Fine. Come along. Let's go to the tea brewer's. But I'm asking the questions."

CHAPTER 25

Attica talked nonstop about Tanheli and its community, so much so Halla almost thought he was a real estate agent trying to sell them property. To her surprise, Inspector Mooran seemed genuinely interested in the small town.

"Not only the tea shop, but we also have an incredible coffee shop bookstore," Attica gushed.

"Do you, now?" the inspector said. "I'll have to check it out while I'm here."

"There's also a lot of local artisans here. Some are crafting synthers, and some are simply skilled artisans with generational knowledge. If you like leather, there's Trina's leather shop. She actually provides the sheepskin leather that Sarai uses for medicated plasters. But they also have wallets and belts and such. Then we have Sammo who does gorgeous lacquerware. Great as gifts."

There's much to Tanheli, Halla thought with a warmth but then shook her head. Was Attica trying to convince the inspector to move here, or was he taking them to a potential lead? How could he just chat about the charms of the place when a very important issue hung above their heads? She looked around at the various shops and supposed it was easy to love a place that was so quaint.

"Really? I'd love to take a look at their wares." The inspector seemed to remember himself and cleared his throat. "After our investigation, of course."

"You didn't strike me as a small-town person, Inspector," Halla finally said.

He turned to her as they continued walking. "I'm not, usually. But I love a good bookstore, and I enjoy handmade goods. Many of the goods we have in the capital are mass-produced. It's convenient but not as pretty, in my opinion."

Halla hadn't compared town to city life in that way. Having grown up on the edge of the capital in a family entrenched in traditions, she'd always found town life dusty and inconvenient. The city was sparkling with life and consumer items anywhere at any time of the day.

"There's a really delicious sweets shop, too!" Rex chimed in.

"Shhh." Attica put a forefinger to his lips. "You weren't supposed to let anyone know I take you there sometimes during our errands for Sarai!"

Rex giggled and put a finger to her mouth, too. "It's really good, though," she whispered.

Halla found herself smiling and cupped her mouth, whispering, "I'd like to try it sometime."

Rex's returning smile was radiant.

"This town really has everything, huh?" the inspector said in wonder. "I'd stopped by Hanashuku on the way, and it was quite charming other than the dirty looks Sarai's friends gave me. I can see the appeal."

Attica nodded enthusiastically. They'd entered the main street, people coming and going. A few shot looks at Inspector Mooran's uniform but didn't linger.

The four stopped in front of a shop with what seemed to be a constantly revolving door. Mounted above the entry was a wooden sign carved in the shape of a teapot—a detail Halla hadn't noticed the first time through.

Attica entered, and the party followed suit.

Shylou looked up from behind his counter and raised a free hand in greeting. "Hey, Attica! You're early for tea leaf pick up."

The man was dressed in his usual mandarin-collared shirt and apron. This time, the shirt was white with orange threaded frog buttons, paired with a pastel mint green apron.

Attica shook his head. "I'm not here for that. You know Rexford and Halla, right?"

Shylou shot Rexford a grin before his gaze lingered on Halla. Her stomach fluttered, but then he gave a curt nod. Annoyance flared in Halla.

"Well, let me introduce you to Inspector Mooran," Attica continued.

Shylou glanced at Halla before holding out a hand to shake the inspector's. Mooran reached out instinctively but hesitated. Shylou laughed as he firmly shook the man's hand.

"Inspector, I'm a synther, yes, but I'm not a sensor. I know with the two words, it can get confusing with how similar they sound."

Inspector Mooran frowned. "I wasn't confused about that," he said. "I'm—" he paused. "I've been synthed by sensors throughout this entire case, so I guess I overreacted. Sensors *are* the predominant synthers out of the Synesthology Triangle, though."

"Fair enough," Shylou said. "You can be at ease, though. I'm a crafter. I don't synth through touch."

"How does synthing through sound work for you to make stuff?" Rex asked, seating herself on a bar stool.

Halla had met a few crafters at the Academy, but they either didn't use their innate skills or she didn't befriend any close enough to ask questions. As much as Halla was curious about crafting synthing, she didn't want them getting off topic.

"Actually, Shylou," she interrupted. "Inspector Mooran wanted to speak with you about a case."

Inspector Mooran gave her a flat look. "I did. Could we speak somewhere more private?"

Shylou maintained eye contact with the inspector as he considered the request. Then he called back over his shoulder. "Katia, can you watch the shop for a bit?"

A woman with one long braid emerged from the curtains leading to the back. She was tall with high cheekbones, a proud countenance, and leaves woven into her hair. If it weren't for the bored look in the woman's eyes and lethargy in her limbs, Halla thought she would have been gorgeous enough for nations to fight over.

Great Doa. Is everyone who works at this tea shop incredibly good-looking with fatal flaws?

"Do I have to?" the woman, Katia, groaned. "I like it in the back; I don't have to interact with people."

"Then don't work in customer service," Shylou said simply, washing his hands. "I won't be long. And I'll give you first dibs on the new tea shipment I have coming in."

At that, Katia brightened. "Aye, aye, Captain."

She stepped out from behind the curtains with a spring to her step.

Shylou motioned for the party to follow him to a side door leading to a private patio. When they exited and the sun's rays hit Shylou, that blue sheen shimmered across his hair again, and Halla thought about the green of her own. It was said the Nuan family developed that sheen from prolonged exposure with the ranyi over generations. Did Shylou's family have something similar with lushu?

The scent of pine needles and spice washed over Halla like a gentle wave when Shylou passed to sit at the table, and she found herself turning slightly toward him before she caught herself.

"What can I help you with, Inspector?" Shylou asked once everyone had settled.

"I have questions about the Kurand family. They may be linked to a case I'm investigating, and I'm told that you may be distantly related."

The inspector flashed his official seal. Halla internally rolled her eyes. Frankly, she thought Thrum was a better lead. There was something weird about his pulse, and if what Sarai said about morphs was true...

Shylou shot a glance at the rest of the party. "And I assume your case involves the Nuan family member here?"

The inspector shared a look with Halla as if wondering if he should tell Shylou that Halla was basically a fugitive.

"Look," Halla suddenly slammed her palms onto the table a little too loudly. "Yes, Inspector Mooran is here for me, but," she put up an index finger, "something is very strange with this case and all the circumstances surrounding it, so we're investigating *together*."

Shylou cocked a brow with a slight smile, and Halla narrowed her eyes in response. Since day one, he hadn't failed to annoy her.

"A little help here?" Halla looked to Rex.

The usually chatty girl put up her hands. "I think you covered it."

"It's true," Attica added, looking at Shylou. "Halla is innocent of what she's being accused of. Fortunately, Inspector Mooran believes her. Some of the facts he presented don't make sense, so we're trying to figure it out."

Shylou's gaze softened at Attica's earnestness. "In Tanheli, we're a community." He addressed Mooran next. "What do you want to know about the Kurands?"

He crossed his arms.

"Have you heard of Douglas Kurand?"

Shylou shook his head.

"What about Tronjone Kurand?" Mooran pressed.

Shylou's expression turned grim. "Yes. He was disgraced, and as a result, he left Urquart territory."

Everyone nodded, and Rex piped up. "Do you know where he went?"

Shylou gave her a long look before exhaling. "No one knows."

Halla's expression fell, but Inspector Mooran managed to mask his disappointment.

"How are you connected to the Kurands?" Mooran asked Shylou.

"My family is a branch family of Kurand."

Halla managed to suppress her gasp, but Rex next to her inhaled sharply.

"But Kurands are sensors. You're a crafter. Is it possible for families to have different kinds of synthers?" Halla asked, thinking of her own family lineage of powerful sensors.

Shylou gave her an exasperated look. "I'm not a direct descendant of the Kurands. Like I said, I'm from a *branch* family. Someone within Kurand married out and created a family of skilled crafters. This started the Pexia line, which is my family. But my family denounced the Kurand connection after Tronjone's mistake. Kurand lost their right to be the lead family. That's probably why I didn't know that other name you gave me. I assume this Douglas may be a descendent of Tronjone after our families split."

"Yeah, Douglas Kurand is Rex's family doctor," Attica said. Mooran shot Attica a dirty look.

"Oh," Shylou said nonchalantly. "That's an interesting fact, I suppose. He'd probably be an uncle or cousin of mine many times removed."

"And—" Attica's eyes grew shifty— "Sarai says Rex was being poisoned at home for years."

"Ohhhh," Shylou said, fully focused. "Now, *that's* interesting."

"We can't be making assumptions." Mooran frowned at Attica who paid him no heed, seemingly satisfied he'd let Shylou in on the drama.

"But Dr. Kurand isn't a synther!" Rex chimed in. "Maybe he's not related to this big Kurand family."

"Just because he doesn't display synthing skills doesn't mean he's not part of the family. There will be nonskilled family members, or maybe he's not trained in it," Attica said.

"We're not saying it's Dr. Kurand who poisoned her," Mooran continued a bit louder to drown out the interjections. "But the Kurand history with the Nuans and some of the case details do make this connection seem more significant."

Halla rolled her eyes. With Inspector Mooran saying he believed she was innocent, she didn't know why he still had to state things so ambiguously or try to seem neutral. "There's another potential suspect," she interjected. "I personally think this one is more likely, and it brings up the question of if morphs exist. There may be one in Rex's house." She wanted to make sure Inspector Mooran didn't forget about the other suspect.

At that, Shylou's expression sharpened. "A morph? Do you have proof?"

"No." Inspector Mooran gave Halla a disapproving look. "I'm here to ask about Kurand, not fake synthing creations."

"Halla sensed him! She says he has no color and a weird pulse," Rex piped up defensively.

Halla thanked the girl internally.

"A weird pulse?" Shylou turned to Halla. "How so?"

Halla found herself suddenly shy with the intensity of Shylou's attention on her. "It was mechanical. Like the dolls we use at medical school."

Shylou put a hand up to his chin in thought, and Halla couldn't help but notice his exposed, muscled forearm. She chided herself quickly. *He's annoying, remember?*

"It's possible," he said.

Halla looked up in surprise. "You believe me?"

He met her gaze. "I don't think you'd lie."

Halla's stomach fluttered at that, but she squashed it down. Now was *not* the time.

Inspector Mooran frowned. "But there are no reports of any. All must be registered. Any old ones from centuries ago are gone."

Shylou shook his head. "Just because none are reported doesn't mean none are being created illegally. In fact, crafters are critical for the creation of morphs. I can tell you from family manuals I've read that morph lifespans are unknown. They could live for centuries, for all we know."

Inspector Mooran dropped his pen, color draining from his face.

"What is it?" Halla asked.

The inspector slowly turned to Halla. "How long has the lady named Ahming worked with your family?"

Ahming? Why's he asking about her? "I don't know. As long as I can remember," Halla responded.

"Who's Ahming?" Shylou asked.

"She's the Nuan family cook," Halla said. "Though, she's more than that. She took care of me and my brother when my parents or grandparents were too busy. She's more like an aunt." Halla thought fondly of the matronly woman who cooked delicious meals.

The inspector shook his head. "I don't know. It seems impossible, but if what Shylou said is true..."

"What is it? What I said about what?" Shylou asked.

"If it's true that morphs could live for centuries, is it possible Ahming is one?"

"What!?" Halla exclaimed.

Caring, loving Ahming being a synthing creation? Halla was so convinced that Thrum was a morph that imagining Ahming being the same thing made her balk. They couldn't possibly be the same. Halla was sure she'd felt Ahming's pulse at some point while growing up, right?

Though, as she thought about it, she realized the woman always wore gloves and high-necked clothing. Halla had thought Ahming couldn't control synthing, so she covered herself up, but that wouldn't make sense. Ahming never said she was a sensor, and if she was, she could have easily learned more from Grandma Wen when she was still alive. Had Halla ever sensed Ahming in passing?

"I saw a picture as I was leaving your family estate, Halla," Mooran said to her. "I saw an image of your great-grandmother and other older members of your family but with Ahming looking almost the same. Do you know how long she's been with your family?"

Halla's tension released as she realized which photo the inspector was talking about. Shaking her head, she said, "You're mistaken, Inspector. I've seen the photo you're talking about multiple times. That's not Ahming in the photo. It's another person they hired back then."

Inspector Mooran cocked his head. "Are you sure? It looked exactly like the Ahming I saw around your house."

"Quite positive. I grew up with that picture hung there. Plus, I know Ahming. She's most definitely not the same as Thrum."

The inspector pursed his lips. "I suppose I could be mistaken. I saw the photo in passing as your mother was walking me out."

"I think it's highly likely," Halla said while nodding. "But speaking of morphs," she turned to Shylou, "you're saying it's possible Thrum could have been living for centuries?"

Shylou's gaze shifted between Halla and the inspector, who seemed deep in thought, before answering. "It's possible. Or he could have been made in the last decade right before the heir was born."

"Do you know of any illegal morphs, Shylou?" Attica asked.

Halla didn't miss how the inspector snapped his focus back to Shylou at that question.

Shylou glanced at the inspector. "I personally don't know of any. But my great-grandfather spoke of a morph. We all thought he was delirious on his deathbed. That's the last I heard of them other than from some family books about the concept."

They continued to discuss, with Shylou telling them everything he knew about morphs (which wasn't much). Rex chimed in here and there with questions, and Inspector Mooran took notes.

While Inspector Mooran wavered between different conclusions depending on his clues, and the men disagreed about who was the most-likely culprit or if a morph could exist, Rex had gotten up to stare at a trail of ants. Halla checked her phone to find three messages. The first was from Cerul earlier this morning:

> Hi Halla, we heard you disappeared? Where are you? Do you need help?

There was another message from Cerul only a few minutes ago.

> I can send for a car if you need? You're my boss after all. I'm sure if you explained everything to the inspectors, it would all work out.

The third message was from Brandus.

> Boss, it's insane. People line up outside The Green Thumb wondering when you'll be back. The inspectors aren't telling the employees much other than you're on the run!? I don't believe it. I've never liked the inspectors. Anyway, stay safe wherever you are.

Halla smiled. She hadn't expected her two long-time employees to reach out, especially when they'd been advised to minimize contact with her, so it was nice to receive messages from familiar people.

There were also twelve missed calls from Justine. Halla groaned internally. She hadn't realized the signal would be so bad at Sarai's apothecary, only receiving these messages once she was in the main town. She crafted a response to Justine, saying she was well and out of town and not to worry. Halla was handling it.

At least, she hoped she was.

CHAPTER 26

Herb was back in his room at the Tanheli Inn, poring over his notes. After thanking Shylou for his information and bidding the others goodnight as they headed back to Sarai's place, Herb had retired to the inn for a bite to eat and to contact Captain Asma.

"Captain," he said to his mouthpiece. "I found them."

"Good. And?"

"I don't think it's her. Plus the heir," Herb paused, wondering if he should tell his captain that the heir was actually a daughter. "The heir is here."

"Good work. You have some time before the Onyx are in Tanheli. Did you learn anything new?"

"Well, some bad news and good news," Herb hedged, thinking about the Tracker he lost.

"Out with it then," Asma demanded.

"Good news is that I do believe Halla is innocent. Bad news is I lost the Tracker. I also found a link with the Kurands." Herb decided sandwiching the bad news between two pieces of good news would lessen the blow.

There was a deep breath on the other end of the line. "You lost the Tracker? You do know how much those cost to make, right?"

Herb nodded gravely before realizing that Asma couldn't see him and said, "Yes."

He wasn't about to tell her that Sarai had her friends steal it because ultimately, it was his own fault for not watching it closely enough.

"We'll discuss when you get back. What's the Kurand link?"

Herb gave her details on what he'd learned about the Kurand history via Shylou.

"Interesting, but it doesn't tell us much," Captain Asma said after Herb finished. "I also completed running a background check. I found two very old documents about Tronjone Kurand's case. One's a case file that, frankly, lacks a lot of information. It only notes that he was found guilty of malpractice. The other document is a warrant for his arrest, but some information is redacted.

"As for our Dr. Kurand, there are no documents on Douglas Kurand before he entered the Urquart estate, so I'll try to liaise with Urquart press management to ask them about that. When there are no documents, it either means they immigrated or someone had a trail deleted. Either way, I'd like to know. I'd also like to collect a DNA sample to genetically test if they're related, which I'll only procure on their estate."

"Is that allowed? Taking a sample?"

"I'll ask, of course. But I won't mention Tronjone. I'll be asking all the staff for DNA."

Herb nodded to himself. He didn't want anyone getting overly suspicious of his and Captain Asma's moves. "Also," he said after a moment. "Do you know anything about morphs?"

"A morph? I haven't heard that term in a while," Asma said.

"Well, according to Halla's observations and some local information, they may still exist. I find it hard to believe, of course." *But I think it's worth an ask.* "Do we have any background on the Urquart Chief of Staff?"

"Mr. Thrum? We haven't looked into him because there's been no reason to. But I was going to ask for a DNA sample anyway, since he's part of the staff."

Herb wondered what a DNA sample of a morph would show. Would it be indiscernible from a living person's DNA?

"So, you're saying," Asma started slowly, "that Halla and some locals think Mr. Thrum is a morph? Something we haven't seen in centuries? Something that has no reason for existing in our world? And he is somehow involved in this whole affair?"

"Well," Herb said. "When you say it like that, it seems extremely unlikely. But I think it's something not to dismiss until we can say for sure that it's not true."

There was a pause as the captain pondered. "I'll run a background check on Mr. Thrum, as well, to see if there's any connection to the Cru family, too."

"That bribe money could be a red herring," Herb said.

"That's also true," the captain responded, and they both fell silent.

Herb was frustrated that it felt that they were making snail-paced movement on the case and they were no closer to the suspect framing Halla. He was sure Captain Asma was feeling the same, given her silence.

"Get some rest," the captain finally said. "I'll do what I can here. Tomorrow, you may need to close some Green Division cases remotely. Your numbers are starting to be impacted by this case."

Herb groaned. *Not this again.*

Captain Asma laughed. "Unfortunately, we have numbers to meet to keep our funding. As much as I appreciate your investigative skills, Mooran, I also want to make sure you're not getting attention from my leadership. In the bad way. It's been a few days of no cases from you while you've been on Halla's trail, the numbers are stacking. Best to close a few."

Herb wanted to focus solely on this case, but he understood Captain Asma was already being quite flexible. "Yes, Captain," he said sullenly and hung up.

Before tomorrow's uninspiring task of closing cases, he planned to continue looking through his notes on Halla's case over a bowl of hot oxtail stew from the inn. After days of soybean bars and one meatbun, Herb was ready for a proper meal.

CHAPTER 27

Halla took Rex's hand, and without thinking, immediately synthed Rex's blueberry purple hue. Just a week ago, Halla would never have believed that synthing could come so naturally. *Sarai really is a good teacher.*

She immediately pinpointed some orange splotches in Rex's lung area, which she knew to be some dampness. There were some in her liver and kidneys as well, which was to be expected as the girl's body expelled accumulated toxins. Overall, this was a drastic difference from Rex months ago when her body was a pulsating tangle of colors. Rex was healthy overall. Halla reported as much while Sarai took Rex's hand to check. After a few moments, the other woman nodded her approval.

"You learned fast," Sarai said to Halla while Rex jumped with glee at the proclamation.

"I had a good foundation," Halla said, thinking of Grandma Wen. "And a patient teacher," she said to Sarai.

The woman with the low bun smiled back. "Aunt Wen would be proud of you. There's still a lot to learn, but your mastery of control has been honed, and you're improving on synthing other organic items."

Before Halla could respond, Rex stood with both arms thrown wide and announced, "I have the best doctors in the world!" before she cackled and ran out the room, presumably to find Mogi to play.

"You still need to be careful!" Sarai called after the girl.

"It's really amazing how much she's opened up," Halla said, more to herself than to Sarai.

"What do you mean?" Sarai got up to fold the blankets.

"When I first started treating Rex, she was like a small adult. She gave a few remarks here and there, but she never emoted like this."

Sarai hummed in thought. "I would think growing up sheltered in the Urquart house may have something to do with that. With how she presents herself to the public. I'm sure they all go through public affairs training. Perhaps that, with the knowledge she was dying, were a part of her more reserved nature."

Halla nodded. "I think she was also keeping it together for her mom, Mrs. Urquart. Maybe to not worry her as much."

"She's a good daughter," Sarai said.

An old but familiar dull pang hit Halla's chest at that statement. "But being a good daughter shouldn't be the only thing she tries to be. She should be herself. She should live her childhood," she said quietly without realizing Sarai had approached her. She started but relaxed when Sarai touched her arm.

"I think she's found a bit of her childhood back. Thanks to you for taking her out of the capital."

Halla felt a warmth in her stomach before she frowned. "Yes, which resulted in me being a fugitive. I'm sure there may have been a better way."

Sarai laughed. "We have a few more leads now, and Inspector Mooran seems to believe you. I think it's not looking so bad. Now, let's make some breakfast. Speaking of the inspector, I invited him over."

The two women and Rex were setting the table with a large pot of duck soup, fermented tofu, pickled cucumbers, warm soy milk, and meat sandwiches when there was a frantic pounding at the front door. The three exchanged looks before hurrying out the back to the storefront.

Inspector Mooran waved from the front window with muffled shouts. As they shuffled to open the door, there was a flash of pale green scales and a yelp.

Halla yanked open the door to find Mogi pinning Inspector Mooran to the floor, one of his massive claws on the man's chest and one talon dangerously hovering above his throat.

"Hey! Get your beast off of me!" Mooran exclaimed.

As his right hand neared a baton at his waist, Mogi caught the movement and lowered his head, baring his five-inch fangs a breath away from Mooran's face, hissing. The inspector slowly withdrew his hand.

"Easy, boy," he tried appeasingly.

"Mogi, it's okay!" Halla said quickly. "He's a friend."

His snake head cocked slightly, and he flicked his tongue before stepping off of Mooran.

Rex rushed forward to hug Mogi's neck. "He was probably alarmed at the inspector slamming on the door! He was just protecting us." She patted his head. "Thank you, Mogi."

The large creature nudged her head gently in response while giving the inspector a suspicious glare.

"You're here early," Sarai said, stepping out from behind Halla. "I hadn't unlocked the doors yet."

"Yes, well." Mooran rose and dusted off his uniform. "I received an update this morning. It's urgent. Can we discuss inside?" He eyed Mogi, as if wanting to get as far away from the creature as possible.

"Of course," Sarai said. "Let's discuss over breakfast."

The four of them settled around the table in the back.

"What was so urgent, Inspector?" Halla asked, curious.

"It's bad." Mooran sighed. "My captain called this morning saying a new piece of evidence has been uncovered."

Halla's heart pounded. "What was it?"

The man shook his head. "More like, 'Who was it?' An eyewitness came forward."

"An eyewitness?" Sarai said. "What are they claiming?"

"They're saying they saw Halla bring in the Cru bribe money and prescribe poison to Rex."

"What!?" Halla stood, chair toppling from the force. "I never did such a thing! Who is this?"

"Yeah!" Rex agreed. "I poisoned myself—well, most recently! Halla had nothing to do with this."

"I know." The inspector pinched the bridge of his nose. "They won't release the name to my division. The eyewitness went to the Onyx. Anyway, they're ready to file a warrant for your arrest, Halla—once the witness makes their statement. They hadn't since my division was running the case for you, but the Onyx is looking to take over."

Halla slumped, hands catching herself on the breakfast table as she leaned over it. *How could it get any worse? Who's this witness? Why are they lying?*

"This is clearly a fake witness," Sarai said.

Inspector Mooran nodded. "It's indeed suspicious. Why come forward now? Why didn't this person say anything earlier? It's not like this case has been a secret. It's been quite the talk since the news agencies kept running stories. But it's not looking good for you, Halla."

They sat in silence as they absorbed the news.

"Additionally," Mooran finally said.

"Oh, great. What else could it be?" Halla's words dripped sarcasm, masking the panic of imagining herself in a cell for the next decade and being stripped of her medical license forever. Maybe she could treat the inmates at the facility and trade in goods that way.

"The two Onyx Division officers who were on my trail are close. They'll be here in an hour."

Sarai inhaled sharply. "I was hoping the people in Hanashuku and Chuli could hold them up longer."

"The Onyx is made of the best of the best. They probably figured out that the locals were trying to lead them astray."

"What's the difference between your division and their division?" Rex asked as she attempted to dip her meat sandwich into her bowl of soy milk, which only resulted in the braised slices of meat slipping from the sandwich into the milk abyss.

Inspector Mooran frowned at her mess. "We cover different kinds of cases. This delegation of work allows for the entire department's efficiency in serving our citizens."

Sounds like a recorded and practiced response.

"What does that mean?" Rex asked while she tried to fish the pieces of meat out of the soy milk with chopsticks.

The frown lines between Mooran's brows deepened. "Well, the Onyx takes on high-profile or complicated cases. That's why they consist of the best inspectors."

"What about your division?" Halla prompted.

"The Greens," he hesitated, "work on open-and-shut-cases. Ones that are clear from the get-go."

Halla narrowed her eyes. "So, if you're in the Green, are you saying it was super clear who the perpetrator in my case was? And you questioned me that night at my shop, so clearly, it was assumed to be me?"

"It's more complicated than that," Mooran said. "The Onyx conducted the initial review of your case. They determined that it was clear and handed it to the Green to finish out the paperwork." Halla opened her mouth, but Mooran put up a hand. "However, the details didn't line up to myself nor to my captain, so here I am to investigate further."

"So," Rex said as Halla processed. "Since you're in Green, you're not as good as the inspectors in Onyx?"

Sarai and Halla stifled their laughs while the inspector huffed quietly. "I used to be in the Onyx!" he said.

"Why aren't you in it anymore?" Rex asked innocently.

The inspector made a sound as if about to respond but then paused and took a deep breath.

Well, that's quite a reaction, Halla thought. *I guess everyone's lives are complicated.*

"That's not the point of this conversation. Getting back on topic, the issue is that our window to prove Halla's innocence is closing. A witness has come forward, and given the circumstances, I'm willing to bet—even though I'm not a betting man—that this witness will disappear mysteriously shortly after giving their statement. We need to go back as soon as possible. With the heir." He looked at Halla and Rexford with intensity.

Halla stared at the inspector dumbly as she registered how quickly this had escalated. "But we can't leave yet. Rex isn't fully recovered."

"She's not." Sarai agreed. "But she's on the mend. She is fine to travel as long as you continue to monitor her and provide our herbs. You know how to treat her now."

"But..." Halla found herself unwilling to leave this small, warm cottage surrounded by quiet serenity, a bustling town, geothermal waters, excellent herbs, and a good cup of tea, even if that shop was run by a certain annoying tea brewer who she hadn't gotten much of a chance to speak to.

Why was she thinking of Shyou anyway? Halla shook her head and spared a glance at Rex. She found the girl staring at her plate, unmoving. Already, it felt like the talk of going back had caused Rex to retreat back into the Urquart heir shell.

"You both have to come back," Inspector Mooran pressed. "We don't have much time left." He checked his watch, which did nothing to assuage the growing tightness within Halla's chest. "I'm told the witness will take a stand at court tomorrow."

"It's time," Sarai agreed.

"But Rex—" Halla started.

"It's okay, Halla," Rex said looking up at Halla with her large, glistening eyes. *Brave eyes,* Halla thought. "I started this mess you're in. It's my responsibility to fix it."

"Rex," Halla started.

The little girl shook her head with a gravity that felt unnatural on a child. "I've been running, Halla. I've had a lot of fun living a life I'd always imagined. Running through the wind, feeling how massive the world is compared to me, meeting mythical creatures, smelling all the herbs here, eating whatever I want, tasting flavors." Her gaze went distant before she focused again. "But we always knew I'd have to go back. With this," she waved her arm to encompass the shop and more, "I can go back finally knowing what it's like."

"Wouldn't that make it harder to go back?" Halla asked, for a moment wondering if she was asking Rex or herself.

The young girl gave Halla a small smile. "Sure, but I'd prefer this over ignorance. And I need to go back to clear your name. How can I lead this territory in the future if I can't even face my own fears and do this?"

A lump forming in her throat, Halla took the girl's hands in both of hers.

"Great," Inspector Mooran interrupted. "I hate to ruin the moment, but we need to run. The court hearing is tomorrow. If we're to make it, we need to leave now and travel through the night."

"A court hearing?" Halla asked. How could they hold one if she wasn't present?

"Yes, I mentioned it earlier. That's how they'll have the witness come forward and declare to the jury. Once they declare a ruling, we could contest it, but no one has successfully overturned a ruling in four decades, so I wouldn't count on it. They're able to hold court because you've been missing for more than forty-eight hours. It's a law that allows the branch to continue working even if a criminal may not be present."

"I'm not a criminal," Halla mumbled.

"I know," Mooran said exasperatedly. "But they think you are! Sometimes, they don't care about the truth. It's about closing cases." He said the last line with a quiet bitterness.

"That sounds like a bad way for our government to function." Rex scrunched her nose. "Who made that law? I'll talk to my dad! If he doesn't listen, then when I come into power, that'll be the first thing I change! The truth matters!"

"That's a very nice sentiment," Sarai said, patting the girl's back. "But your father doesn't run everything. As Urquart Head, he gets a big say, yes. But the ruling body is also comprised of a board. We're not a monarchy."

"Oh," Rex said, slumping slightly in disappointment. "Right."

"You'll do great—" Sarai stopped suddenly, eyes widening as she looked out the window facing her.

"What?" Halla turned.

Inspector Mooran, who was sitting with his back facing the window, twisted to look and stood suddenly.

"They're coming," he announced, leaping into action by locking the front doors and pulling down the window curtains. Halla caught sight of two specks within a cloud of dust in the distance. "You two go ahead. I'll tell them that they just missed you."

"Don't we need you to take us to the courtroom? That's happening soon?" Halla asked.

"Oh, right."

Sarai grabbed Halla and Rex, pulling them to the back. "You both need to go out the back. Inspector," she turned to Mooran, "I'm afraid you won't be able to retrieve your car."

"Can your ranyi carry three people?" Inspector Mooran asked.

"He's going to have to," Sarai said as she rushed them through the kitchen and out the screened porch.

The silver-green fish-snake was already outside, clawed talons tilling the dirt as he pawed impatiently. Sarai affixed his simple saddle before lifting Rex onto his back. Halla wondered whether Sarai had her own steed hidden somewhere with how expertly and efficiently she moved, but this was not the time to ask. She turned to Mogi instead.

"Can you carry a third?" she asked.

Mogi turned to face Mooran which caused the man to flinch slightly. The beast immediately stretched out his back to make space for another person. He typically kept his body naturally bent in parts while keeping the part near the front where Halla rode parallel to the ground. Halla knew this was a skill that had to be trained into ranyi.

"Thank you," she said.

"He'll be slower with more weight, but you can lose the inspectors' trail in the forest," Sarai said.

"Speed will be of essence," a voice said from the treeline.

They turned to find Shylou atop his lushu.

"The tiger-horse!" Rex exclaimed.

"Shylou!" Halla's heart skipped a beat. "What're you doing here?"

The man, still in his shop apron, slid off his lushu's back. "The whole town saw the inspectors come in. They didn't look like good news, so I came to warn you." He eyed the inspector. "It seems someone beat me to it."

"I received news of their arrival from my captain, so I had a head start," Mooran said. "If you saw them in town, how did you get here before them?"

"I know a few shortcuts," Shylou said, giving Halla a playful smile.

Why's he looking at me like that? Halla thought frantically while her stomach did a flip.

"They need to go," Sarai said.

"Right," Shylou said, breaking Halla's gaze and dismounting. "I'd also wanted to offer Aarthanon, my lushu. He agreed to it and will take you where you need. He'll be able to find his way back himself."

At that, the tiger-pelted horse seemed to stand a bit taller. Mogi huffed loudly in response.

"Of course," Shylou continued, looking at the fish-snake, "I'm not saying you're unable to carry many, but speed is important. I know you are strong, but in this case, we also need you to be fast. And Aarthanon can keep up with you."

The horse gave an affronted grunt at the implication that Mogi was faster, and Shylou shot his steed an apologetic look. Mogi seemed satisfied, though, and relaxed his stance.

Ranyis and their ego. Halla rolled her eyes.

"Excellent. Aarthanon knows how to get out of Tanheli unseen. Follow his lead," Sarai said.

In a few moments, Halla mounted Mogi right behind Rex, and Inspector Mooran was atop Aarthanon. The horse gave an eerily human-like wail and loped into the forest. Mogi followed. They picked up speed within the forest, both Aarthanon and Mogi somehow running while avoiding hanging branches and protruding roots as if the forest shifted out of their way, urging them forward.

Halla and Rex both looked over their shoulders. Shylou and Sarai were quickly swallowed by the density of the trees. Everything had happened so quickly, Halla didn't get a proper goodbye with Sarai. The woman who patiently taught her over the last week, showed her that relaxing and being serious weren't mutually exclusive, and revealed so much about the core of their art. The woman who helped her reconnect with Grandma. And then there was Shylou and his annoying smirks and shining hair looking all handsome in his crisp shirts... Halla stopped herself in surprise. She noticed Rex was still looking back.

"You can always come back, Rex. Once we resolve everything," she said close to the girl's ear to be heard over the rushing wind.

"I don't know about that," Rexford said, voice barely audible. She stared back as if trying to sear it all into her memory.

CHAPTER 28

Herb had never ridden a mythical creature. He'd maybe ridden a horse twice in his life. Finding himself atop a lushu, he was very uncomfortable, to say the least. Shylou had assured him that Aarthanon wouldn't allow him to fall, but he clung for his life as the creature somehow galloped silently through the forest. The fish-snake that carried Halla and the heir also seemed to have no footsteps as they ran; it was almost as if they were aloft the wind.

Not to mention that creepy sound this lushu made right before we left. So... human.

He thought of his trusty car and promised he'd come back to get her. His priority was to ensure the wrong person wasn't going to jail.

They eventually exited the forest a few li away from Tanheli. Herb assumed it was so that the Onyx inspectors wouldn't see them. *This lushu is pretty smart.*

"Aarthanon," a voice rumbled inside his head.

Herb almost lost his grip on the horse's mane in shock. He looked around as the wind pelted his face, seeing nothing but the girls behind him atop the ranyi, which looked even more intimidating in action. Herb was just about to relax when the voice came again.

"I'm right here, Inspectorrr." The voice drew out the 'r' at the end with emphasis.

Herb started and looked at the galloping steed carrying him. *There's no way the lushu...*

"There is," the voice said. "And need I remind you that I have a naaame?"

Spittlebork. "You can hear my thoughts and speak?" Herb asked. "Are all mythical beasts able to do that?"

A rumble like grating stones sounded in Herb's head that made him wince. It seemed to be a chuckle from the lushu.

"No, no. A few, yesss. But not all. For my kind, it is because we sing human folk songs that we can communicate with your bipedal kind." The lushu turned his white head to glance at Herb with one large eye before turning back.

"You sing folk songs?" Herb didn't know how much more information he could ingest.

"I do not like to repeat myself, Inspectorrr."

"Sorry," Herb said.

"We dooo. We communicate with it. Although I wouldn't call it 'singing,' I know humans think it sounds as such, so I used the term to help you..." Aarthanon paused, "visualize it."

Herb thought it was still hard to believe regardless of whatever word Aarthanon used.

"Hey!" Rex called from beside them.

The ranyi had picked up speed and ran in step next to the tiger-pelted horse.

"Race ya!" the heir called as the ranyi flapped its fins and surged forward.

Halla sat behind grimly but allowed their antics.

"You don't even know the way!" Herb called.

"Ranyisss," Aarthanon growled and sped up.

Herb clung on like his life depended on it while the heir hooted in front of him, and Aarthanon gave a long wail of three notes, like a song.

I miss my car.

At dusk, the beasts stopped at a pond.

"You may get off now, unless you want to get wet," the lushu said.

Herb eagerly slid off the lushu's back, his legs almost buckling when he landed on solid ground. Good, solid, dependable ground. From his academy training, he knew he had to move around to make sure he didn't cramp up. "I thought we were running through the night to make it in time," Herb said aloud.

Aarthanon entered the water to his knees and lowered his head to drink. "The ranyi and myself are the ones running through the night, yes," the lushu corrected. "But we are still living beings. We need to stop to hydrate. We've stopped before nightfall out of respect for your weak human eyes, so that you may be more comfortable. Your kind are always overly dependent on vision."

"I see," Herb said, deciding to ignore the jab. It was not untrue, anyway.

He reached into his pockets for some soybean bars.

"Who're you talking to?" Halla asked.

"What?" Herb said as he handed her a bar.

She nodded in thanks. "Just now. You were talking out loud."

Herb had forgotten that no one else could hear Aarthanon. He glanced at the tiger-pelted horse still drinking from the pond as the ranyi dove in, slithering below the pond's surface. The lushu made no motion, so Herb figured it was fine to tell Halla.

"The lushu," he said.

"Aarthanon," the low voice reminded him.

"What about him?" Halla asked, looking at the horse.

"Does..." Herb lowered his voice. "Does your ranyi speak to you, too?"

"I can still hear you, and no, ranyi do not communicate to humans the same way we can," Aarthanon said within Herb's mind.

Halla furrowed her brows and crossed her arms in thought. "Well, Mogi definitely communicates in body language, but he doesn't talk to me, if that's what you mean."

"Aarthanon talks. Inside my head." Herb pointed to his temple, hoping he didn't sound crazy.

Halla's eyes widened. *Great Doa, she probably thinks I'm crazy. A crazy inspector who's trying to save her case.*

"That's incredible," she exhaled. "I'll have to report this to my father. My family only ever works with ranyi, so we don't know as much about the other mythical creatures. I wonder if lushus can communicate to everyone or just one person."

"I can choooose," Aarthanon rumbled inside Herb's, Halla's, and the heir's heads.

"Whoa!" the heir called out, running toward Herb and Halla. "Did you hear that?"

Herb handed the girl a soybean bar. "It's the lushu."

"That's so cool!" she exclaimed. "Do you talk to Shylou, Aarthanon?"

The lushu seemed pleased with the usage of his name as he shook his mane and stepped out of the water. "All the time, little one," he answered with a snort. He then looked to the sky. Herb looked too but couldn't see whatever Aarthanon was looking at. "We must gooo. Call back your ranyi."

Halla did so, and they alighted their mounts again. Halla and the heir seemed to be swelling with questions about Aarthanon, but the tiger-pelted horse ran ahead, making it difficult for them to call out to him.

"You could talk to them through their minds. They have questions, you know?" Herb thought to Aarthanon.

"And I'm not obligated to answer themmm," he responded. "I'm not great with children," Aarthanon said after a pause.

Herb stifled a laugh. He hadn't imagined he'd hear a horse say he wasn't good with kids.

"It'll be a long night," Aarthanon said. "Strap in."

Herb hoped they'd make it in time. They had to.

The journey to Tanheli had been much more comfortable than this rapid-speed return to the city now. Halla hadn't known Mogi could run so fast and lightly. She barely remembered the evening run as she dozed off multiple times, only to be jolted awake by a lurch. She and Rex had strapped themselves to Mogi in case they fell asleep, and she was grateful for their foresight. Rex's head lulled and flopped around in front of her.

How she sleeps through this, I have no idea. She took a moment to hold Rex's hand to synth her. Almost instantaneously, the form of Rex's small body appeared in her mental map, colored blueberry purple. Overall, Rex was looking good.

As she removed her hand, glancing to the beast below her, another thought occurred. Her hand hovered hesitantly over Mogi's neck, moving with the motion of his run. She lowered it.

Warmth built at her fingertips, and Halla pushed it out, as if pushing past his thick scales. As she did, she saw the light energy flow into Mogi and mapped into his long, moving body. She gasped. The color was an emerald green with an occasional iridescent shimmer running through. The first time his colors shimmered in her mental map, she started, thinking something was acutely wrong with him. But then she realized the shimmer occurred at a regular cadence, like waves.

"Wow," she whispered.

There were a few light pink spots around his legs, and Halla knew his muscles were straining from the run, but he was still in good condition for the hours ahead of them.

That brought her mind back to the case. Who was this witness? She'd heard of false allegations or wrongful convictions, only to be uncovered years later. She hoped she wouldn't be a part of that statistic. Were Rex's poisoning and her being framed connected? Why would someone want to frame her? Was it a competing apothecary? Or was she just the extremely unlucky scapegoat for some larger political ploy?

She shook her head. These ruminations would not help her. She fell into a fitful doze.

The next time she opened her eyes, the world was alight with the dim yellow haze of dawn, the capital's skyline on the horizon. Halla's heart skipped as she shook Rex awake.

"Home stretch," she said to Mogi.

He flapped his pectoral neck fins in response, his speed unchanging. Aarthanon and Inspector Mooran were a few lengths ahead.

They'd made it.

Halla didn't know if they had passed the Nuan estate on the way; it had likely still been dark if they had. She thought of her mother and Grandma Wen and closed her eyes.

"Please," she prayed. "Please give me the time I need to reconcile. I just reconnected with what Grandma Wen always loved. Please."

Ahead of them, Aarthanon stopped.

What were they doing? They hadn't entered the city yet. They were about another hour outside the city limits. As Mogi neared, Halla saw what had caused Herb and Aarthanon to stop.

"What's this tree doing here?" Rex asked.

"I don't know," Mooran responded. "But Aarthanon tells me that it's too high for him to jump."

Halla peered up at the tree, and indeed, it was taller than two people stacked on top of each other, the top shrouded in a haze that was setting in. Where had this tree come from, anyway? Halla looked around, but only saw normal-sized trees. It was as if this massive tree had been placed in their path on purpose.

A cold dread seeped into Halla's stomach. *Someone placed this here.* She whipped toward the inspector. "We have to get out of here."

His hand flew to the baton on his belt at her tone. "Why? Where?"

"This tree doesn't belong here. It didn't fall naturally."

"Spittlebork," Inspector Mooran muttered as he surveyed their surroundings. "We can enter the thick forests, but I don't know how long it will take to get around."

"Maybe Mogi can climb it," Rex suggested.

Halla considered for a moment before shaking her head. "I think he could if he were alone. With us on top, it'll be difficult. He might be able to ferry one person at a time, though."

"Let's do it," Mooran said, dismounting the lushu shakily. The tiger-pelted horse cocked his head, gave the group a slight nod, and then loped back the way they came. "Aarthanon left since he said he couldn't get over this trunk and that we were near the city. He wished us luck."

Halla hopped off Mogi and helped Rex off. If this tree had been placed intentionally, whoever did it might come to check their trap soon. "Who should go first?"

"I hate to leave the two of you alone, but I think it's best if I check the other side," Mooran said. "Take my baton, just in case."

Halla held it awkwardly. "How do I use it?"

"It's a synth-imbued tool. It'll expand with your intention."

What did that even mean? Before Halla could ask, the inspector was already on her ranyi, and Mogi took off, immediately sinking his talons into the tree and climbing, sometimes slipping with falling bark but moving pretty quickly. They were soon out of sight above the mist.

Halla turned to face Rex. "They'll be back soon," she assured the girl, though she knew she was also talking to herself.

She shivered involuntarily as she looked at the emptiness around them and the tree that didn't belong. How did someone get it out here? Was it brought from another forest? Or enlarged somehow with synthing? What if she missed her court hearing? And then what? This fake witness would give a statement and disappear, and Halla would have to work for years to try to contest or overrule the judgement while she slowly rotted in jail.

Footsteps sounded behind them. Halla spun, holding up the baton. *Open up, open up, open up,* she thought at it and to her shock, the baton expanded on both ends. She tried to hold it firmly but found her grip shaking. She was going to tell Rex to stand behind her, but the child was already there, clinging to her *changshan* tunic.

A mist had set in, and a tall, slender man slowly appeared. He was in a dark blue *daopao* made of shimmering brocade. The daopao was a long, loose robe with narrow sleeves, and it was accented with a thick, leather band along his waist. From his clothes, Halla knew this man was of decent economical standing.

She covered her mouth in silent horror as she recognized him. Thrum.

"I'm glad I caught you," he said.

Halla's heart pounded. She and Rex were backed against the tree trunk. Where was Mogi?

"Stay back!" she warned, brandishing her baton-turned-staff.

The tall man frowned in confusion before his eyes widened as he spotted Rex behind her. "Rexford? What're you doing here?" Thrum asked in shock. "And why are you in public in your true form? Quickly change before anyone else sees you!"

"No!" Rex exclaimed. "You already know my true form anyway. What does it matter if anyone else sees me? Where are Mother and Father? Did they send you?"

"Mr. and Mrs. Urquart are at the estate. They've been worried sick, Rexford. Now, activate your pendant. This is unseemly." Thrum's tone grew firm.

Why is that his concern? She was glad he was distracted, though.

"You do not command me, Mr. Thrum," Rex said as she stepped out from behind Halla.

Halla had witnessed Rex's stubbornness multiple times, but she'd never seen nor heard this tone from the little girl: the regal, confident tone of a ruler.

The tall man dipped his head slightly. "Apologies if I came across as commanding. But I do carry your mother's will. It is your duty to obey."

Halla seethed at those words, but if they bothered Rex, the girl did not show it. Instead, she said, "Why are you here, Mr. Thrum? For Halla's case? To stop us from getting to her hearing?"

The man frowned again, stepping forward. "Stop you from getting to the hearing? I was hoping she'd come so that I could bring her in quickly, and I hoped she'd know where you were. I didn't know you'd be together."

Halla furrowed her brows. What did he mean that he was waiting to bring her in quickly? To help her? Or get her arrested?

"While you've been gone," Thrum continued in a low tone, "your mother was so worried that she collapsed."

"Mother collapsed?" Rex said. "Is she okay?"

"She's fine," Thrum snapped, to Halla's surprise.

Thrum always seemed so collected. Was he annoyed at Rex for disappearing and foiling his plans, or was it possible he actually cared for the family and Mrs. Urquart…? Halla shook her head to dispel the thought.

Rex crossed her arms. "I left a note when I ran away. Mother and Father should have seen it. I left it so they wouldn't worry."

"There was no note," Thrum growled. "It was extremely irresponsible of you. Even if there was, how would a piece of paper assuage their worries when the heir, who they thought was in a coma, was suddenly gone?"

Halla couldn't let Rex face this tall man alone. She straightened. "I've been taking care of her. Leave her alone."

Rex clasped Halla's hand tightly. Thrum turned his attention to her as well, and his eyes narrowed in the morning light.

"I definitely left a note," Rex said, her attention bouncing back to Thrum's earlier statement. "What do *you* know of Halla's case anyway? Are you a morph?" She looked at the man expectantly.

Halla's heart leaped. She hadn't expected the girl to ask the man point-blank. Would Thrum tell them truthfully?

Thrum paused and gave them a hard look. "Where did you hear that?" He didn't wait for an answer. Instead, he started pacing, as if thinking. "How are we going to get back?" he muttered. "I wasn't expecting to find the road blocked after I came out here."

Was he not the one who placed the tree here? Was he… worried?

Halla heard another sound in the near distance from behind her. "Mogi," she breathed. Where was the inspector when they needed him!?

A figure hopped down from the fallen tree to their left, about ten feet away. To her dismay, it was not Mogi nor Herb Mooran.

CHAPTER 29

"Dr. Kurand?" Thrum said aloud.

"Thank goodness, you're here, Dr. Kurand!" Rex said as she ran toward him. The doctor was dressed in a teal daopao robe, and he kneeled as Rex met him to give her a hug.

"Rexford, you're alive," he said.

Halla thought she heard a tinge of surprise, but Rex *had* been dying the last he knew.

"Thanks to Halla!" Rex said, pointing to Halla who was still standing near Thrum.

Dr. Kurand looked up and met her gaze. Halla froze at his cold look.

"We finally meet, Halla Nuan." He emphasized her surname almost aggressively as he walked toward her and Thrum.

"I guess it's nice to meet you, too," Halla said as she took a step back before remembering Thrum was nearby as well. She was surrounded.

At Dr. Kurand's tone, Rex ran ahead, placing herself between Halla and the doctor. "Wait. What's going on?"

The doctor glanced at Rex before returning his gaze to Halla. "So, you got the heir to work with you?" He shook his head, laughing shrilly, before focusing on Halla. "You Nuans were always so sly. So slippery. Never doing your own dirty work. Well, this will be faster anyway."

He raised his arm to his chest level over Rex's head, palm facing up and middle finger tucked right under his thumb, as if preparing to flick something at Halla.

"No!" Rex screamed, reaching to grab Dr. Kurand's arm.

Halla's hearing dimmed as her heartbeat echoed in her ears. She had no idea what the motion meant, but Rex's panicked scream pulled out a primal fear.

A large figure blocked her vision, and silence ensued.

Thrum had moved inhumanly fast, splitting Halla from the doctor and Rex. He fell to his knees before slumping to the ground.

"Mr. Thrum?" Rex clung to Dr. Kurand's flicking arm, but she was unsuccessful at moving him.

Halla stared at Thrum's crumpled form. What had just happened? Why did Thrum do that? Why were they all here right outside the city before her hearing? Was Dr. Kurand the one who placed this tree here?

Dr. Kurand looked equally surprised at Thrum's actions but collected himself. "That's unfortunate. But Mrs. Urquart can always find another Chief of Staff. I can say there was a tussle, and you killed him." He looked at Halla.

"What?" she spluttered. This was all too much. "Why would anyone believe that? I don't even know what you did to him!"

Rex stood frozen, staring at Thrum's figure.

"I merely flicked a poisoned needle at his pressure point with my enhancement-ring." He raised his flicking hand to show off a jade ring on his middle finger.

Was that a ring crafted and imbued by Synesthology? "Clearly," she said, stuttering, "I didn't do that!"

Dr. Kurand shrugged, dropping his hand. "Would they believe an almost-convicted criminal or a decorated doctor of the Urquart household?"

Halla's heart sank. Where was Mooran? Could he hear them? Wouldn't he have come back after this long? Was he tricked and led away? Or was he lying on the other side of the tree, knocked unconscious? Did that mean Thrum wasn't involved in her case at all? Had Halla been wrong? She stared down at Dr. Kurand's cold look as he pulled another small needle out of his robes.

"Who do you think they'd believe?" a low voice said. "A doctor gone mad, or three eye-witness accounts, including that of an inspector?"

Herb appeared from the shadows behind Dr. Kurand, leveling the tip of a six-foot long spear at the doctor's back.

Halla's heart swelled with relief. *Thank Doa,* she thought. Then, *Did he carry two batons that could expand?*

"Inspector Mooran!" Rex called out.

"Don't come here, Rex," Herb said. "Go to Halla. I have the doctor under watch."

"Where have you been?" Halla asked Herb as Rex ran into her arms. "How did you know to come back?"

The inspector gave a small smile while remaining focused on Dr. Kurand's back. "I thought someone would come for you, so I pretended to leave with Mogi."

"If we're done with the chit chat here..." Dr. Kurand started.

"Be careful, Inspector," Halla interrupted. "Dr. Kurand can flick poisoned needles. That's what happened to Thrum."

The inspector spared a fleeting glance at the crumpled body on the forest floor.

"You must be that inspector working under Captain Asma. In the Green," Dr. Kurand drawled. "Weren't you just demoted? A man with so much potential, brought down by numbers."

Inspector Mooran frowned. "How did you know that?"

Dr. Kurand shrugged. "I do my research."

Halla glanced behind her. Perhaps she could take Rex and run, wait for Inspector Mooran to deal with Dr. Kurand, and then scale the trunk and get to her hearing in time. She knew the timing was already tight, but it was her best plan so far. She grabbed Rex's hand and gave a small squeeze, but before she could turn, another figure approached Inspector Mooran.

"Behind you!" Halla warned.

Mooran shifted to see the newcomer—spear still focused on Dr. Kurand.

The figure approached slowly, shuffling limply. Halla squinted to better make out who it was through the mist.

"Cerul?" Halla called. What was she doing here?

The small woman squinted her eyes. "Halla? Is that you? And who are these other men? And..." Her eyes rested on Thrum's body and widened. "Oh, my Doa."

"Wait! Cerul, please hear us out! Please!" Halla cried.

She needed to keep Cerul here. Surely, Dr. Kurand wouldn't try to kill anyone with his poison needles if another witness was present.

Cerul pointed at Thrum's body. "Tell me that's not a body on the floor. Is he... dead?" she squeaked.

"Well," Halla hesitated, worried about scaring her employee off again. She shared a glance with Herb. "I haven't been able to confirm," she said. "He might just be unconscious." *From a poisoned needle? Sure.*

Cerul nodded to Herb, likely recognizing him from handing over the keys to The Green Thumb, before turning to Dr. Kurand. "And who's he? Why's the inspector holding a spear to his back?"

"I caught this man attempting to attack them," Herb answered. "I'll need help to secure him. You're closer to me right now. Can you come here? I'd ask for you to call for help, but no one's around anyway. Approach me first, and then fan out so we can surround the doctor."

"What're you doing here, Cerul?" Halla asked.

She spared a glance for the doctor who was strangely quiet. To her surprise, he was grinning, as if he wasn't about to be surrounded and arrested. She narrowed her eyes but turned her attention back to Cerul.

"I'm—I'm here for you," Cerul stuttered. "I wanted to support you. I heard about your hearing and wanted to let you know I'm on your side."

Cerul walked toward Herb. He had his back to her again, facing the doctor with his spear.

"Oh." Halla hadn't known Cerul felt that close to her. It figured Cerul would show and not Brandus. But how did she hear about her hearing and know to be here, of all places? "Thanks, Cerul, that's actually so nice."

"More than you've been to me."

"What?" The statement was so quick, Halla thought she heard incorrectly.

As Cerul moved, her gait changed. The usual shuffle lengthened to confident strides.

"You heard me," Cerul said. "I know you never liked me. You always had little side remarks or took out your anger on me. But I bore the brunt of it. I bore it because you had no idea what I had waiting for you. I bore it knowing each day, you walked closer to your demise."

Halla's fingertips went cold, and Rex gripped her shirt tighter. Herb stared at her, spear still raised to Dr. Kurand's back with an alarmed expression. The doctor's smug smile never wavered.

The inspector pivoted to face Cerul, spear ready to fend her off. But in the moment Herb moved, Dr. Kurand also spun, right hand outstretched.

"No!" Halla yelled, stomach twisting, but it was too late. In a flow of fabric, Dr. Kurand had flicked a needle at Herb at close range.

"Now, why would you turn your attention to me? A harmless, little woman?" Cerul asked as Herb dropped his spear and grabbed his arm.

Upon hitting the floor, the spear contracted in segments, blade and length disappearing until only a plain baton was left.

"I've learned not to underestimate women," Herb managed out of gritted teeth.

Cerul gave a wide smile Halla had never seen before. Cerul had always been shy, unsure—a great practitioner of course, but a small woman in numerous ways. This woman in front of them felt like she was growing with each moment as she expelled that mousy aura.

"Well, you're right about that," she said to Herb as she walked past him.

Halla itched to run to Herb, but Cerul put up a wagging index finger. "Nuh uh. Don't even think about it. He's as good as gone anyway." She turned her attention to Rex still clinging to Halla. "And who is this?"

Cerul must not have recognized Rex's female form. Dr. Kurand hesitated as Cerul stood next to him. Did he want to protect Rex's secret? Rex hugged Halla tighter.

"Well, if you won't answer, then I suppose it's unimportant.Take care of her, Kurand."

Halla shielded Rex with more of her body, but Dr. Kurand said, "We can't do that."

Cerul put her hands to her hips. "And why's that? Since when do you call the shots?"

He looked away. "She's the heir."

Cerul stared at him. "Oh, sorry. I thought you were joking," she said humorlessly.

"It's true, Cerul. She is the Urquart heir," Dr. Kurand said quietly.

Cerul's eyes widened, and she walked closer as if to get a better look at Rex but stopped before Thrum's body. "Fascinating. The son was a disguise. You Urquarts really have all the best imbued synth tools. A disguise tool, strength-enhancing rings, the Judgement Pen. It's no wonder you enjoy working for them, Kurand."

"And I'd like to keep it that way. We have no qualms with the Urquarts. It would be dangerous to. Our only grievance is with the Nuans."

"Why are you doing this?" Rex asked quietly from Halla's arms. "I trusted you, Dr. Kurand."

Cerul laughed, but Halla thought she saw a flash of remorse on Dr. Kurand's face.

Were the two not working together?

"Why don't you tell them, Kurand?" Cerul said. "It doesn't matter if they know or not because," she looked at Halla, "they won't be leaving here. Not of their own volition anyway."

What did that mean? Were they going to kill her? Or ensure she couldn't make it to court and was found guilty? When the courts found her guilty, she would be immediately hauled away. But what about Rex? Halla looked at the little girl.

Cerul noticed. "Oh, her? Well. I suppose she's important. But the public doesn't know her in this female form. And the heir is known to be very sickly—previously comatose. It wouldn't be unreasonable to say he passed due to those reasons."

"That wasn't a part of the plan," Kurand said sharply.

Halla felt fear creep up her throat. *This woman is insane.* "Yeah," she agreed. "You can't do that! The Urquarts will come after you."

"You don't get to tell us what we can or can't do," Dr. Kurand snapped.

Halla jumped at his strong reaction. She didn't understand why he seemed to have a grudge against her specifically and why he had called her sly and slippery. Even if this was some long-held family rift, she'd never met the man before. There was no reason for *him* to hate *her*. Still, could this all be related to Tronjone Kurand and her ancestor?

She slowly moved away.

"Don't you dare move," Cerul warned. "You move another step, and I won't guarantee the heir's safety."

Halla paused in her tracks. "Why are you doing this? What do you have against me when I don't even know you?"

"Why?" Dr. Kurand laughed. "You really don't know?"

Halla fell silent. She suspected it was related to their family history, but she needed them to continue talking. She had to prolong this as much as possible as she tried to figure out what to do next or waited for Mogi to come back. *What was taking them so long?* She'd never seen her family ranyis fight, but they were historically ferocious.

"You *really* don't know," Dr. Kurand said incredulously.

"Of course, she doesn't," Cerul snapped. "That's how trivial our family was to them. They simply moved on."

Our family? Were Cerul and Dr. Kurand related?

"She should know. She should know that they can't look down on us," Dr. Kurand said.

"I've never done that!" Halla said.

"But your great-grandmother did. And your family did by subsequently forgetting about us," Cerul spat.

"Grandma Wen's mother? What happened?" Halla held onto Rex as she tried to gauge how fast they could run for cover in the woods off the path. *Keep talking*. As long as they weren't getting closer.

Cerul started pacing, as if about to give a lecture. "Long ago," she waved a hand, "the Kurand family was a top sense synthing family. We even ran a Synesthology school."

"You're a Kurand?" Halla furrowed her brows. "But your last name is Poral."

"I'm getting there," Cerul said. Halla clamped her mouth shut, inching farther with the distraction while Cerul was feeling more talkative than murderous. "Anyway, my great-grand-uncle was wrongly accused of malpractice. Much like how you are right now. And he was stripped of his license. We were shamed."

"What happened?" Halla prompted.

"Your great-grandmother set him up!" Dr. Kurand burst out.

"I said, I was *getting* there," Cerul snapped, shooting him a sharp look before relaxing as she faced Halla and Rex. "The patient was relentless and pulled in capital officials. My great-grand-uncle Tronjone Kurand had no way of fighting back. We wondered how that village patient had so much pull."

Halla stilled as she remembered Grandma Wen boasting about how many people the Nuans knew and how the Nuans had a finger almost everywhere. Halla hadn't believed it. Who would believe that her family who settled on acres of land with ranyi would be in constant communication with city officials? Small ten-year-old Halla certainly hadn't.

"Your great-grandmother," Dr. Kurand said.

"Yes," Cerul nodded. "Rui Nuan and Tronjone Kurand worked closely at The Yan Academy of Medicinal Synesthology. Our family ran the school for generations. But your great-grandmother wanted more. She set Tronjone up."

"Hold on," Halla said. "That's not what I heard. My great-grandmother stepped in only after your ancestor left."

She couldn't imagine anyone in her family being so nefarious. Her family had always been focused on healing.

"Why would they tell you the true story?" Cerul seethed. "It's a blight on the Nuan's pristine history. With the Nuan connections, Rui Nuan hired a patient and pulled all of her government contacts to bring down Tronjone. At the end, he had to step down, and she took his place to lead the school."

"Tronjone Kurand, my great-grandfather, left the territory. Moved to the Cru territory," Dr. Kurand added. "There, at least we could avoid the shame that followed the Kurand name. We continued practicing under our name in Cru."

Cru. "Did you plant that Cru bribe money at my shop?" Halla asked.

Cerul laughed. "That wasn't actually from the Cru, but I thought it was a nice touch."

Halla looked at her employee with widened eyes. "*You* planted it."

"I did. I tried your office, but you always kept it airtight. It put a wrinkle in my plans, but it was still enough to plant suspicion on you. Anyway, yes, Dr. Kurand's side of the family moved, but mine stayed. Because of that, my family changed our name, and I had to live rejecting the Kurand mantle. Because Tronjone Kurand, our head, left—ran away with his tail tucked—my side of the family was left with nothing. We struggled to shed the shameful name and put food on the table. While you," she looked pointedly at Dr. Kurand, "lived in relative comfort in another country."

"That's unfair," Dr. Kurand said. "We suffered the same as you and had to start over."

"We didn't have to start over," Cerul retorted. "We had to start from *nothing.*"

As Halla watched the cracks growing between Dr. Kurand and Cerul, she considered whether there might be a way to exploit it.

Cerul and Dr. Kurand stared at each other intensely before the man broke the silence. "I'd always wanted to come back. So, I searched for jobs after I completed schooling and residency. When I found employment at the Urquart household, I was ecstatic. Everything was working out. Until I found out you Nuans were still around." He glared at Halla. "I saw an article about Wen Nuan still carrying out work on your estate and vowed to make you suffer the same way Tronjone Kurand suffered. I knew I could somehow use the Urquart influence I had access to. But I wasn't sure how since I solely treated Urquart household members."

"That's where I came in." Cerul smirked. "Although my family hid, I wanted to retain Kurand glory, so I pursued traditional medicine. I went to a guest lecture featuring Dr. Kurand and recognized the name, so I approached him. Long story short, we realized we were related and held the same disdain for you Nuans."

Great. Two angry people colluding to exact revenge for something that didn't even concern any of us.

"Kurand being at the Urquart household was perfect. As my employer, you know I specialize in plant toxicity, don't you, Halla?"

"That's a part of why I hired you. Many medicinal plants could be toxic in some dosages but helpful in others. Sometimes, we fight toxins with other toxins. All this requires expertise." As Halla spoke, a terrifying conclusion dawned on her. Rex being exposed to prolonged poisoning for years? Only someone with a keen expertise on poisons could do that. How had Halla not seen this before?

"Indeed. So, I convinced Kurand to slowly poison the heir. I told him it had to be the long game, so they'd never see it coming." Cerul confirmed Halla's realization. "I had the dosages perfectly calculated. It wouldn't hurt the heir. He—or she," Cerul corrected herself glancing at Rex, "wouldn't have died. Just gotten sick enough that the family would need to consider other doctors."

"We had to make sure a few failed before the Urquarts finally got to you," Dr. Kurand added. "That's where I helped sabotage their prescriptions. It helped that The Green Thumb was popular, and you had a brief press moment when it first opened. Your name was floating around."

Grandma Wen's words of staying humble and keeping a lower profile echoed in the back of Halla's mind.

"After that, it was a matter of planting a few illicit drugs around the shop. The fake bribe money was a small touch," Cerul said. "Then Dr. Kurand would help pressure the Urquarts to pressure the inspectors to close the case as quickly as they could. Now, I didn't expect the heir to actually go comatose and run away."

Dr. Kurand shook his head. "Rexford gave herself the draught and antidote. I didn't realize until I found Rexford's note and saw that a potions book had gone missing from my study."

"So, you found the note!" Rex said.

"I did," he nodded. "And then I burned it."

Rex gasped, looking at Thrum on the floor. "That's why Mr. Thrum didn't know about it either."

"I couldn't let them know you did it yourself," Dr. Kurand said. "This worked perfectly in our plans. 'Celebrity Apothecary Puts Heir into Coma'." He ran his hand across the air as if reading a newspaper headline.

Cerul chuckled. "I have to say, I was delighted to see your shocked face up close when it all happened, Halla."

"You're sick," Halla spat.

"Your great-grandmother started it," Cerul said venomously.

Halla could sense the conversation ending, and she didn't want to know what would happen when they were done talking. "Why would you hold a grudge that isn't even yours? I didn't do this to you."

"But you did!" Cerul shot back. "Your family did this to me. Because of your family, we groveled and dipped our heads, never looking up. I had to till the fields, pick and scrub plants until my hands were raw, watch my grandparents live with shame, see the fear that lived constantly within my mother's eyes. They actually asked me not to go into traditional medicine because they feared our history would come to light. I was tired of living in fear. I wanted to do what I loved."

For a moment, Halla felt a tug of understanding at the want to do what she wanted rather than what her family told her to. But that quickly disappeared when she saw the crazed look in Cerul's eyes. There was no talking sense into her, but maybe she could talk some sense into Dr. Kurand.

She turned her attention to him. "You could have lived in comfort working for the Urquarts. Why are you jeopardizing that now? Rex trusted you. I'm sure the family was kind to you."

Dr. Kurand hesitated; Cerul butted in.

"His family had to move out of the country because of you!"

"Because of my ancestors. But he came back, and he succeeded in finding a good job."

"I, too, saw my grandparents struggle," Dr. Kurand said quietly. "We didn't live with the scrutiny Cerul's family saw. But we were foreigners on politically unfriendly soil. We couldn't tell anyone we came from Urquart territory. My grandparents and parents tried so hard to fit in."

"It's because of the Nuans," Cerul said.

"Yeah," Dr. Kurand said slowly, a fire lighting in his eyes again. "They caused my family to suffer and move away from home."

Even Halla could see Cerul egging on Dr. Kurand. In fact, it seemed Cerul had preyed on their familial connection and his emotions for this plan. "So, you planned all of this just to put me in jail?"

"It would be a hard hit to the Nuans," Cerul said. "The famous Nuan heir put in jail through malpractice, just like my great-grand-uncle would have been if he hadn't left Urquart Territory. How fitting."

"And who's this new witness who supposedly saw everything? Was it you?" Halla asked, realization dawning as she tried to keep them talking. She shuffled back with Rex again and hoped they wouldn't notice.

"Guilty," Cerul smiled. "Dr. Kurand here told me that Mrs. Urquart was getting suspicious of the case. Her Chief of Staff was sniffing around." Halla glanced at Thrum's unmoving form again and felt a pang of guilt for suspecting him. "So, to move things forward, I decided to come forward as a witness. There was no need to hold up appearances with you anymore, especially if you weren't around. You'd never know it was me. And how better to put you away than to be intimately involved on the stand."

The woman's eyes glinted. "But then I got word that you were told about your court hearing, so..." She motioned at the massive fallen tree. "We had to stop you from reaching court somehow. Once I deal with you here, I'll head over to your hearing and give my statement. I was hoping to place you in jail, so we were going to restrain you. But now that you've seen our faces, I'm thinking we can just end you, and then ruin your family reputation at court for good measure."

Halla couldn't believe she'd never seen this insanity within the woman who worked for her for years.

"It's almost time." Dr. Kurand checked his watch. "We need to leave now."

"Right. Well, time to wrap up the story, hmm? Do the deed, Douglas."

Dr. Kurand rolled his eyes. It seemed Cerul was the brains of the operation, and Dr. Kurand didn't quite like taking orders from her.

"I was surprised to find Mr. Thrum and the heir here," Dr. Kurand said honestly. "I'm sorry you had to see all this Rexford. That wasn't my intention. I would have healed you after Halla was put away. And I'd always liked Mr. Thrum's efficiency." He *tsk*ed. "A pity."

"Take care of them quickly so we can frame Halla for good," Cerul said.

Halla's heart pounded.

"Both of them?" Dr. Kurand questioned.

"Yes," Cerul said impatiently. "The heir knows too much. She'll look like a random girl to the authorities for now. Unless you have a memory-wiping imbued synth tool lying around?"

Dr. Kurand shook his head.

"There!" Cerul said as if she solved an easy problem. "Take care of them, and we can deal with the rest."

No, no, no. Halla hugged Rex tighter.

"I'm sorry, Halla," Rex said. "I didn't know I had an evil doctor, and everything I did looked even worse for you."

"It's okay, Rex," Halla comforted the young girl even while her heart filled with dread, realizing this misty road with two dead bodies and two vengeful people would be the last things she saw.

She cradled Rex's head between her hands. She much preferred her last vision to be Rex's face and her synthed blueberry-purple color.

Dr. Kurand's heavy footsteps approached, and she thought she heard a soft, "Sorry."

She stared intently at Rex, wiping the girl's slow tears with her thumbs. "It'll be okay, Rex."

CHAPTER 30

There was a loud hiss and the *thud* of a body hitting the ground. Something heavier than a body, actually. She looked away from Rex and found Mogi pinning the doctor, sharp talons sinking into the man's flesh as he screamed. Mogi looked ferocious, fins fully extended, body writhing, and jaws open wide, baring his long fangs.

"Mogi!" Rex exclaimed.

Multiple bodies clad in emerald uniforms dropped from above. A dozen inspectors fanned out around them. A woman with two gold armbands approached, a device mounted like a giant spider glowing across her chest.

Cerul reached for her pocket.

"Stop right there," the uniformed woman warned. "Don't think you'll get any movement past myself or my inspectors. My Apprehender will fire."

Halla saw the glowing chest mount on all of the inspectors. These spider-like tools were much more terrifying in person than seeing them on television.

Cerul stopped moving but kept her hand in her pocket. The uniformed woman scanned the area, gaze pausing on Inspector Mooran slumped on the forest floor.

"Inspectors Khour, Tran. Check on Inspector Mooran."

Two women left the perimeter and carefully approached Herb, one checking on his pulse while the other kept watch.

"It's over, Cerul Poral," the armband woman said.

Cerul paid her no attention. "Douglas. What're you doing?"

Dr. Kurand grunted. "I'm pinned and impaled by this multi-legged beast, if you couldn't tell already."

His clothes were soaked in his blood, and Mogi didn't let up.

"Douglas Kurand. Cerul Poral. You're under arrest for attempted murder and poisoning. Anything you say can be used against you in court," Armband Lady said.

Cerul frowned at Kurand and eyed the surrounding inspectors. "No," she said quietly.

"What's that?" the lead inspector asked, trying to approach slowly and signaling for her team to close in.

"No," Cerul said more loudly. "No, no, no. It can't end like this. It won't end like this!"

She turned and ran toward Mogi.

"Mogi, watch out!" Halla yelled, but to her surprise, the woman did not attack the ranyi.

Instead, she deftly leaped over Mogi and ran for Halla and Rex at full speed, hands outstretched. Halla instinctively pushed Rex away while bracing, but before Cerul could reach her, ropes enveloped the woman, and she was yanked to the ground. Thick, steel-like ropes trapped Cerul's entire body like a metal sarcophagus. There were a few muffled cries, but Cerul remained still.

Halla exhaled and collapsed to her knees as her adrenaline ran out.

"Halla!" Rex embraced Halla and nuzzled her head into Halla's neck, face wet with tears.

The lead inspector gave instructions to her squad, but Halla couldn't hear any of it over the high-pitched ringing in her ears. Rex's hug grounded her, and she closed her eyes.

Halla had not let go of Rex's hand throughout the entire ordeal, and they were now sitting on a temporary cot while emergency medics checked on them.

They'd cut a section out of the massive tree to create a path for more emergency responders to reach them. Captain Asma, the lead inspector who had captured Cerul and Dr. Kurand, had informed Halla that they got to Inspector Mooran just in time and were giving him the antidote to the poisoned needle. Mr. and Mrs. Urquart were on the way.

Thrum had shocked everyone, becoming animated when the medics checked on him. Turns out, Dr. Kurand shot the poisoned needle at a pressure point that took out Thrum's legs and movement, but because the poison was synth-imbued, it was ineffective on Thrum, proving that he was a morph.

The fact still shocked Halla even though she'd suspected the entire time. The inspectors kept it under wraps, since they didn't know what to do with the knowledge. As morphs were not legally seen as individual entities, it would be something to discuss with the Urquart family. The morph currently hovered near Halla and Rex, likely to keep an eye on the heir before her parents came.

"Thank you," Halla said to Thrum.

He turned to her with a quizzical expression. "Whatever for?"

"For taking the shot for me," she said. "I'll admit that I suspected you had set me up. I'm sorry for that. Thank you for saving me."

The tall man smiled with all his teeth as if he didn't know how. It made Halla cringe. "As a morph, I've had a long life with multiple purposes. I've found this peaceful life of protecting the heir and people very rewarding. You are welcome."

Halla raised her brows, wondering what this morph had seen and done throughout his life. How old was he really?

Captain Asma approached, which drew Halla's attention. "Thank you," Halla said to Captain Asma.

The woman in the tight bun put up a hand. "Just doing my job."

"If you hadn't shown up in time..." Halla started.

"Don't think about that," Captain Asma said.

"How did you know where we were?" Rex asked from next to Halla.

"Inspector Mooran. He sent me a message that he was here with you. I found it strange that you were blocked so close to your court time. When Herb didn't respond to me again, I knew he needed backup right away. I immediately got a team together and set out in the direction. That's when your ranyi showed up, hissing and fins flaring." The captain frowned at the memory. "We were trying to get around him when I saw a note with the Green Division emblem attached to him. Herb had left a note saying to following the beast." She smiled and shook her head. "That's how we found you so quickly."

Inspector Mooran must have sent Mogi ahead for backup while he confirmed who the perpetrators were. Halla raised a hand to pet and praise Mogi for the help, but he was nowhere in sight. Captain Asma continued speaking.

"I was also digging into this new witness and discovered this morning that it was Cerul Poral, your employee. I thought that paired with the timing was strange, so I looked into her further. That's when I found she'd been communicating with Dr. Kurand. I hadn't known she was a part of this entire plan, nor that she was related to Kurand. As for how she knew all these details about your case, I think she had someone inside our division."

So, Cerul and Dr. Kurand weren't working alone? Were there others with grudges against her family? Or was this person simply a hired hand? Halla shuddered.

"Poisoning the heir is of the highest treason," Captain Asma continued. "So, rest assured that we'll take care of this. The Urquarts wouldn't let this go anyway. Now, we have Dr. Kurand and Cerul on attempted murder, too. Needless to say, you don't need to worry about ever seeing them again."

Halla nodded. The sound of rolling wheels caught her attention. She looked up to find Herb being pushed toward them in a wheelchair.

"Inspector Mooran!" Halla and Rex called out. "You're okay!"

They got up to greet him, but he put a hand up weakly.

"You can call me 'Herb'." He smiled weakly. "Fortunately, the poison used is well-known. Once Dr. Kurand told them what it was, the emergency medics had the antidote on hand. I just woke up, but I wanted to make sure you two were okay." He nodded to Captain Asma in greeting.

"Good to see you awake, Inspector," the captain said to Herb.

"It's good to see you too, Captain. Thanks for saving me."

The captain gave Halla and Rex curt nods and patted Herb on the back, making him wince. Then she left to yell instructions at others.

"Well, this saved us the trouble of needing to contest any court decision," Herb said, smiling.

"I suppose so," Halla said with a small smile.

"Your hearing was postponed, and I have a feeling with all of this evidence, you'll be acquitted rather quickly."

"You're free!" Rex exclaimed, jumping up.

"I was never in jail," Halla said.

"You almost were," Rex responded.

"And who's fault was that?" Halla said, shooting the girl a dirty look.

Rex had the good sense to look slightly ashamed but then retorted softly, "I wasn't the one actively framing you."

Halla laughed, relief washing over her as she realized she was indeed free. Free of any suspicion. "That's true."

The last week or so had been strained knowing the allegations against her. Her business could reopen, Rex was healing, and she could synth better. She felt the pressure lift from her shoulders. The story from Dr. Kurand and Cerul nagged at Halla's mind, however. Why had they had a different perspective from what Halla had been told? Did her family really sabotage the Kurands all those years ago?

"Rex!" a woman called.

Mrs. Urquart ran toward them, Mr. Urquart close behind, speaking with an official.

"Mother!" Rex leaped up and ran for her mother. Thrum quietly followed.

Halla looked at his receding back curiously. He was indeed a morph. Morphs existed. And the Urquart family had one. *Why do they have one?* Was it in response to the Cru threats they'd been seeing on the news?

"So, what're you going to do now?" Herb interrupted Halla's thoughts.

Halla considered for a moment and recalled her other employee, Brandus, telling her how she'd never taken time off. She thought of the slower pace of life at Tanheli and smiled. "I'm going to take an extended vacation. I'm going to go back to the Nuan estate to further hone my synthing and reconnect."

She glanced at Rex in the distance being examined by her mother and father and wondered if she'd be able to see the girl again or if she'd be locked away from the world once more.

Halla turned back to Herb. "The Green Thumb can afford to be closed for a few more days. And I'll probably re-run background checks on all of my employees."

She hoped there weren't any other vengeful employees on her staff. Had Cerul applied to The Green Thumb to get closer to her? Halla shook her head to dispel the thoughts. There was no need to question these things at this moment.

Herb laughed. "Sometimes, you have to watch the people closest to you."

Halla did not share that laugh with him. She didn't find it particularly funny at all. "What about you, Herb? What will you do?"

"Well..." Herb looked down at his body. "I suppose I'll have to take a sick day or two to recover. But it'll be back to work for me." He rolled his eyes.

"What is it?"

"My job's day-to-day is usually sitting at a computer, reading and stamping files. It's quite monotonous. But," he looked away thoughtfully, "the person that was giving Cerul information from our department is still out there. And frankly, your case was so strange and rushed, I wonder if anyone in the Onyx Division was compromised."

Halla pursed her lips. "You mean Dr. Kurand and Cerul had someone in the Onyx working with them?"

"It's possible. They could have paid them off. But we need to find them. Anyone who can be paid off isn't fit for the force." He frowned. "Anyway, there's plenty of work to do. But," he looked behind Halla and smiled, "I think your long-overdue vacation is starting soon."

Halla looked over her shoulder and found her mother atop Mogi, running at top speed. He must have gone to fetch her after the inspectors successfully restrained Dr. Kurand and Cerul. Mrs. Nuan deftly leaped from the beast before he came to a full stop and embraced her daughter. Halla inhaled her mother's scent of shampooed hair and sunshine and wrapped her arms tightly around her. Mogi nudged her arms, and she patted his head while still in the embrace.

It was time to go home.

健安堂

EPILOGUE

It had been five months since Halla was acquitted of all charges. Halla had taken a month-long personal break, splitting her time between searching for other mythical beasts with her father and teaching her mother what she'd learned from Sarai.

In the second month, Halla buried herself in work, initiating a project to rebrand The Green Thumb as a synthing apothecary, currently the only one of its kind. She wanted to bring it back, but it would take some convincing with the Board of Investors. She'd sold them on a year-long test run, and today was the start.

There was a skip to her step at The Green Thumb. Sarai had sent a qingniao message that she'd visit.

"Boss!" Brandus waved before he pulled up his sleeves to wash his hands. "How was your vacation?" He grinned.

Halla grinned back. She had thought of firing him, since she thought he was friends with Cerul, but as it turned out, he barely knew Cerul. He stood up for her because they were the most tenured practitioners, and he felt like she needed help speaking up. It really went to show how little Halla knew her employees, and she vowed to do better.

"It was much needed, thanks," Halla replied.

He nodded. "I noticed we have a few new hires? I can help with the training. And I promise I'll keep an eye out." He shook his head as he dried his hands. "I would have never thought. Cerul! I'm usually a good judge of character."

Halla shuddered at Cerul's name, thinking of the small woman's crazed eyes and anger. "Thanks, Brandus. Let's just get through this first day back."

"Aye, aye, Boss," he said and left the room.

Halla checked in with each of her employees before stepping out the front doors. Customers were already queuing for her store, peeking through the glass windows. The street was busy with people walking about or trying to snag a parking spot. It seemed news of her acquittal brought people back in droves.

Halla wiped the sweat from her palms on her flowing top, in the traditional style. She was nervous for opening day, nervous how her employees would do, nervous about Sarai seeing The Green Thumb for the first time. There was a tug at her sleeve. She looked down to find Rex's golden eyes looking back at her.

"Rex!" Halla bent and scooped the girl into a hug. "How are you here?"

The girl hugged her tightly while laughing. "How could I miss your opening day?"

Halla detached herself. "How does it feel being out in your true form?"

Ever since the court incident five months ago, the Urquarts gave a statement about Rexford. Some of the public bashed the family for lying all these years, but many simply didn't care and embraced her as she was.

Rex smiled impishly. "It feels amazing!" She gave a little hop. "But I do need to be chaperoned all the time."

She nodded slightly to her right, and Halla spotted a bodyguard a respectful distance away.

"Ah." She smiled warmly at Rex and took her hand, seeing the blueberry-purple hue of Rex's body. "While you're here, would you like to greet my family and Sarai with me?"

"They're coming?" Rex said excitedly.

At that moment, gasps sounded from the queue, and yelps echoed in the street. Halla caught a glint of gold and smiled. *Did Mom bring Jin this time?* Halla heard Mrs. Nuan before she saw her.

"Excuse me! Ranyi coming through! Excuse me! Please move to the side!" Mrs. Nuan instructed as she rode up the street.

Her hair was now dyed with a golden sheen, and she rode atop Jin, her golden ranyi. The massive fish-snake ran proudly, occasionally snapping at a few onlookers who came too close. The woman and the ranyi were quite the sight.

Closely behind Jin was Mogi, glimmering with his silver-green scales as he pulled the family carriage, her brother at the helm. Harley waved, struggling to hold onto the reins, when Mogi caught sight of Halla and Rex and sped up.

"Mogi!" Rex jumped up and down, waving with fervor.

Mrs. Nuan and Jin arrived first, the woman dismounting smoothly and gathering Halla and Rex into a hug. She wore a cobalt blue flowing top and trousers with lapis lazuli-adorned hair ornaments. "Has it happened yet?" she asked.

"Not yet, Mom. The ribbon cutting is in a few minutes. But I would have waited for you all," Halla said.

The older woman smiled as she greeted Rex in the standard palm-up greeting. Harley pulled to a stop behind them.

"I didn't know you were coming!" Halla yelled up to her brother on the carriage, wrestling to keep Mogi from greeting Halla and Rex.

"I missed your last one. Didn't want to miss this one!" he yelled back. "And can you two please say hi to Mogi before he topples our entire carriage?"

Rex laughed and ran to the beast, wrapping her arms around his thick neck. Mogi flapped his pectoral fins and focused an eye on Halla.

"I'm coming, I'm coming," Halla said and approached, patting his side fondly. She was met with a light headbutt.

Halla's father, Mr. Yong, and Ahming emerged from the carriage to Halla's delight. Ahming gave Halla a hug as Mr. Yong admired the storefront.

"So proud of you, dear Halla," her father said. "And..." He stood back, adjusting his glasses, "I wanted to let you know we've successfully procured a flock of four-eyed birds."

"Dad!" Halla gasped. "That's amazing! Anyone in the legal field—or maybe the inspectors—would be interested in them."

"Indeed." Mr. Yong nodded. "As symbols of wisdom, writing, and decipher-ing truths, I'm sure they'll be popular among test-takers in general, too. Now, there have also been sightings of a *qiongqi*, and the locals are asking me to capture it, but..." his look wavered, "I don't think I want to."

Halla shuddered at the thought of trying to keep a qiongqi, the winged tiger with a human face. "Maybe not." Halla agreed. "Any luck trading for lushus with Shylou's family?"

Mr. Yong shook his head. "Their family is prideful of their lushus. I cannot fault them, though. They're not interested in our ranyis, and even if they were, our family would be hesitant to trade our ranyis, as well. But maybe we can work with them for any lushu hair or hide."

Halla nodded, disappointed that the two families hadn't found a way to work together yet but also unsurprised. She knew Shylou's stubbornness must have come from somewhere. Perhaps if she visited Tanheli again soon, she could try to convince Shylou to talk to his family about this business proposition with the Nuans... She shook her head. Who was she to think she could convince him? But then she thought of him coming to help them at their time of need and those lingering looks and playful smiles...

A screech filled the air that had people covering their ears and ducking for safety.

"Up there!"

A few onlookers pointed to the sky. Halla looked up to find a massive blue bird, wingspan so large it covered the sun momentarily. It flapped its wings once to steady itself as it hovered lower. Everyone gasped and raised their arms to shield themselves as a strong gust of wind nearly took them all out.

"What is that?" Rex yelled over the wind.

"A bird of some sort," Halla said, squinting to see better.

"Clearly," Rex grumbled.

"Wait, it's a fish-bird," Halla corrected herself.

The beast had the long body of a blue fish with a finned tail that swished as if it were still swimming. It had no neck. Instead, a bird's face was at the front of the fish. As it neared the ground, two taloned legs sprouted from the fish's belly to land.

"A *kunpeng*," Halla breathed. Her father stood openmouthed next to her.

"What's a kunpeng? And did it just grow legs?" Rex said with a mixture of awe and horror.

"It's a creature that can change between being a large fish and a bird. They're said to be a symbol of change and growth. Their ability to change is said to inspire people to want to better themselves and to encourage people to achieve their goals," Halla's father responded reverentially as he took off his glasses.

"Wow," Rex said dreamily.

Halla noticed many onlookers had a similar expression as they looked at this new beast.

"Halla! Rex!" a voice called from atop the kunpeng.

Halla squinted before she recognized the tiny figure on the truck-sized kunpeng. "Sarai!?"

The woman grinned back. "I never got to introduce you both to my steed, Shuilian!"

Halla raised her brows in disbelief as Rex gawked, and Mr. Yong fell to his knees in amazement.

"Hey!" Another head peeked out from behind Sarai.

Halla had been so enthralled by the kunpeng that she hadn't noticed the larger frame of a man sitting behind Sarai.

"Shylou?" she said incredulously.

He shot her a wide smile, and her stomach fluttered. "Thought I'd check out where you and Rex hail from," he yelled over the flapping wings. "Maybe bring some good tea, too!"

Halla smiled back and waved both arms. "Welcome to The Green Thumb!"

ACKNOWLEDGEMENTS

I want to start first by thanking you for being here. Thank you for giving this book and these characters a chance. This was my first full novel after several years of not being sure what to write, and the story took off. It was tough making myself write every single day, but I found the research fun. The research didn't only include searching the depths of the internet but also kitchen experimentations. My pantry is now filled with ingredients that I don't quite know how to use, but that's okay. I'd also purchased a nut milk maker to make all sorts of soy milk, black sesame milk, and warm concoctions. It was fun while I was in it, and it brought me great delight getting to share these with friends to try in their coffees.

Amber, thank you for always believing in me. Thank you to my beta readers, Kit Aldridge and R.L. Newt. You read the early version of this book and not only caught a lot of points that I've since edited to make it better, but also gave me the confidence to continue forward.

Thank you to my partner, Andy, for always listening to me ramble about ideas, giving me those wide eyes of excitement, making song jingles for me, and for always doing book events with me — I made a character for you years ago and incorporated him into this story.

Of course, I have to give my token of gratitude toward my incredible editor, E.A. Whyte. Erin immediately understood where I was trying to go with this story, and I had the grandest time reading her comments throughout my manuscript. She transformed it into something much more polished. I couldn't have asked for a better developmental, line, and copy editor for *Synthers & Beasts*. Thank you.

Speaking of people who made this book better, thank you to all the incredible artists who made this book so beautiful. Andy Payne, thank you for this gorgeous, cozy cover. Mario, thank you for painstakingly sketching out each ranyi scale and the details within the shop illustration, making this world come to life. Cindy, thank you for art making the food leap off the page. Yeseo, thank you for imagining Halla and her intrigue for me and also for keeping me sane at work. Vi, thank you for the beautiful recipe page through which readers can bring a bit of this magic home with them.

To Nadège, you made this happen. Thank you and Imaginarium for taking the chance on this wee author many years ago and for your continued support. It was that conversation we had summer 2025 that drove me to gather my wits and commit to making this book happen.

To my Bookstagram community, I would not be here without your support. Thank you all for following my journey. I cherish these online friendships and interactions, and the indie authors and readers there continue to inspire me to keep weaving stories.

As some of you may know, this book was made possible through a Kickstarter. A massive thank you to this community of incredible people who believed in me and this book so strongly that they preordered their special copies (in no particular order):

Kyra Ann Dawkins, Bugalino, Courtney Foradory, Sukejna Kovacevic, E .A. Whyte, Jeffrey Men, Eliza Posada, Sam Blatchford, William D., Shivam Khanna, Avi Kejriwal, Avanika & Eshan Kejriwal, Tia Ledvina, Nick and Brian Nguyen, SeraZ, Vaishali Bhakta, Zohaib Waliany, Ashley Espinoza, Cori Holden-Williams, Benjamin Hong, Megan Kelly, Ampal Kaur, M.H. Elrich, Grace Hoffman, Lucy Xie, Effie Joe Stock, Steph Marchany, Kit Aldridge, Amy Ho, Stephanie Teague Hostetter, Nritya Kamath, San-Pei Lee, Julia Libby, Timothy Lee, Trip Space-Parasite, Kathleen L., Molly Fessel, Irene Te, Brittany Dawn, Kathryn Kundrot, Eddie Joo, Victoria E. Lancaster, Cassie Evans, Corrie Pelc, Lin, Emily Yuyuenyongwatana, Kate (my favorite coworker), Hannah

Dyer-Holzhauer & Patrick Crawford, Florentina, Tommy Tang, Nimish Mittal, Alexandra G., Clint Wu, Thomas Szilard, Lexie C, Andy Lau, Shrina P., Nicha K., Andy Yu, Ted Y., Dr. May Li, Hetali, Anita Kapyur, Sofía, Clark Johnson

RESOURCES

Although this is a work of fiction derived from my fascination with Traditional Chinese Medicine "TCM", I do reference some real Chinese literary pieces and have referred to several TCM sources. This book is not meant to be a guide nor accurate, so if you were interested in some of the referenced works, see below:

Ni, Maoshing, trans. *The Yellow Emperor's Classic of Medicine: A New Translation of the Neijing Suwen*. Boston: Shambhala, 1995.

Wu, Cheng'en. *Journey to the West*. Translated by Anthony C. Yu. Revised edition. Chicago: University of Chicago Press, 2012.

Cao, Xueqin. *The Story of the Stone (or Dream of the Red Chamber)*. Translated by David Hawkes. London: Penguin Books, 1973.

Raise the Red Lantern. Directed by Zhang Yimou. Orion Classics, 1991.

Huwe, Brian. "Tongue Diagnosis Chart: Plus How to Read It." Brian Huwe. https://brianhuwe.com/tongue-diagnosis-chart-plus-how-to-read-it/.

Thomson Medical. "Tongue Diagnosis." Thomson Medical Blog. July 10, 2019. https://www.thomsonmedical.com/blog/tongue-diagnosis.

TCM Healthcare. "Nine Body Constitutions Chinese Medicine." https://tcmhealthcare.com.au/nine-body-constitutions-chinese-medicine/.

Ren, Jian-Li, Ai-Hua Zhang, and Xi-Jun Wang. "Traditional Chinese Medicine for COVID-19: Treatment and Mechanisms." *Pharmacological Research* 155 (May 2020): 104742. https://doi.org/10.1016/j.phrs.2020.104742.

NUAN FAMILY RECIPE
Poached Pear

INGREDIENTS

1 Asian PEAR ...or... Nashi PEAR
PEELED

1 TBSP of Rock Sugar (OR TO TASTE)

1/2 TBSP of Goji Berries

WATER

2-3 ...DRIED... ...Chinese DATES

INSTRUCTIONS

YOU CAN EITHER STEAM OR BOIL THIS DISH.
WE USUALLY STEAM IT, BUT IF YOU DON'T HAVE
A STEAMER, YOU CAN BOIL IT ON THE STOVE

IF BOILING OVER THE STOVE INSTEAD OF STEAMING,
CUT THE PEELED PEARS INTO SLICES OR CUBES

1. Cut off the top of the pear to create a lid
2. Use a spoon to remove the core
~ Fill the hole with rock sugar & half of the goji berries
3. Put the top back on
YOU CAN USE TOOTHPICKS TO KEEP THE LID ON ...BUT YOU DON'T HAVE TO!
4. Cut the dried dates in half & remove any pits
YOU CAN SLICE THE DATES INTO DISKS IF YOU'D LIKE
Sprinkle these & the rest of the berries around the pear
5. Fill the bowl with the pear with water
6. Steam on medium heat for 30-40 MINUTES
Enjoy either HOT OR CHILLED

About the Author

Inspired by her love of sci-fi, old Taiwanese dramas, and ridiculous anime, Judy scribbles mini-stories wherever she can (and subsequently forgets them!). Her debut novel, *The Vending Portal*, is an award-winning cozy, soft-sci-fi, dystopian fantasy. With her writing, Liu hopes to meaningfully add to Asian American literature to further enrich the YA genre. She studied history, Asian studies, and education before spending some time living in rural Japan and returning to Texas.

Outside of work and writing, Judy is a perpetually tired human being who teeters on the paradox of enjoying collecting various hobbies and rotting on the couch. She enjoys dancing with her teammates and friends, exploring unknown spots or cities, smelling incense, and making nonsense sounds to her sister.

judyliuauthor.com
IG & Threads: @judyliu_author

ALSO BY JUDY LIU

The Vending Portal

The Memory Extracts: A Companion Anthology to The Vending Portal

Unconventional Love: Anthology on the Expanse of Love ("It Takes Two", a short

story)

Symador ("The Cultivator", a short story)